CW01510065

BUSINESS IS MURDER

SERIES BY NELLIE H. STEELE

Cate Kensie Mysteries

Shadow Slayers Stories

Lily & Cassie by the Sea Mysteries

Pearl Party Mysteries

Middle Age is Murder Cozy Mysteries

Duchess of Blackmoore Mysteries

Maggie Edwards Adventures

Clif & Ri on the Sea Adventures

Shelving Magic

BUSINESS IS MURDER

A SALEM FALLS B&B PARANORMAL COZY MYSTERY

MIDDLE AGE IS MURDER COZY MYSTERIES
BOOK TWO

NELLIE H. STEELE

CHAPTER 1

"*Y*ou're crazy," Cleo, the black cat, said as she sashayed back and forth on the counter. "Absolutely insane."

Ellie stretched her neck as she sat on the hard wooden kitchen chair, rolling it from side to side, and sucked in a deep breath as the cat continued her pacing.

Lola's head swiveled back and forth to follow her movement. "But why, Cleo?"

"Why? *Why*? Are you serious? You can't possibly be that dumb."

"Hey," Ellie cut in, wagging a finger in the air, "what did I say about calling Lola dumb?"

Cleo settled onto her haunches and narrowed her green eyes. "Well, if the dog collar fits."

Lola flicked her dark brown eyes to Ellie. "What collar?"

Ellie shook her head, dismissing the comment. "She doesn't mean it literally."

"What I do mean literally is that you are crazy. Both of you. I think something went haywire in your brain when that nurse held you at gunpoint."

Lola's part-bulldog face wrinkled more than normal. "She didn't hold me at gunpoint."

"I'm not crazy. Aunt Susie was going to do it, too!"

Cleo wrinkled her nose. "And I told her she was crazy, too."

Ellie grabbed her empty tea mug off the table and shuffled to the sink. "Well, I think it's a good idea."

"Me too, Ellie," Lola agreed. "I'm excited."

"What for? Because you'll have more people to bark at?"

Lola nodded her wrinkled head, her floppy ears bobbing. "Yeah."

"No," Ellie corrected as she swirled the soapy sponge around the mug. "We talked about this. No barking."

"Oh, right. I keep forgetting."

Cleo shook her furry head back and forth. "Opening a B&B. What a horrible idea."

"I think it's great," Ellie answered with a grin. She dumped the washed mug in the drainer and grabbed a dishtowel to wipe her hands. "I've always wanted to own a business."

"Try owning something that doesn't require people traipsing into my home and destroying it."

"Destroying it? They're not going to destroy it. They're guests."

"They're home-wreckers," Cleo shot back, poking a claw in the air. "And if any one of them tries to touch me, I'll pop a claw in their–"

"All right, that's enough. I'll make sure to warn them not to touch the ornery black cat."

"Ornery?" Cleo waved a paw at her, claws extended. "I'll show you ornery."

Ellie shot her a sideways glance. "You already do. Listen, we have a beautiful place here. It's not a surprise that people want to share it. Salem Falls is a beautiful town, the B&B is a beautiful building–"

"Stop calling it a B&B. It's our home!"

"And now it'll be the temporary home for–"

"Hooligans and home-wreckers," Cleo finished.

Ellie settled her arms across her chest and glared at the cat. "That's not what I was going to say and you know it."

"I know," Cleo said with a bob of her head, "which is why I jumped in to correct you."

Ellie stalked from the kitchen into the hall. A floorboard on the porch creaked before a knock sounded on the door.

Lola raced from the kitchen, her claws digging into the hardwood as she rounded the corner and sped toward the door with a high-pitched howl.

"Lola!" Ellie hollered after her. "Stop barking!"

"And this is what we have to look forward to every time some idiot comes to check in," Cleo said as she ran down the hall with her belly scraping the ground before she slinked up the stairs.

Ellie followed her flight with a roll of her eyes before she crossed to the door and pulled it open.

Mac stood on the other side with his hands shoved into the pocket of his khakis. He offered her a broad grin. "Hi, Ellie."

"Hi, Mac," Ellie and Lola answered together. Lola's rear wiggled excitedly as Mac pulled open the screen door and stepped inside.

Mac dropped to a knee to give the dog a pet. "Hiya, big Lol!"

Lola's tail continued to wag. "Mac, we're opening a B&B."

He shot a glance over his shoulder as he rubbed Lola's ears. "Just wanted to drop by and tell you in person that your business application's been approved."

"I'm a business owner!" Ellie pumped a fist in the air.

Mac straightened and poked a finger at her. "That you are."

"And not a moment too soon," Ellie said. "Opening weekend is in a few days. What was I thinking?"

"That you had a stellar application that no one could turn down," Mac answered with a grin. "And that the town's Harvest Festival is this weekend. No better time to capitalize than when everyone is looking for a place to stay."

"And capitalize we did," Ellie said with a nod. "Full house. Mia's website went up and we sold out in minutes."

"That's what we like to hear." Mac gave a fist pump in front of his chest.

Ellie tilted her head. "I think I agree. I'll let you know for sure after the first weekend."

"It was a clever idea doing the murder mystery weekend and involving the town and the festival."

"I was glad they let me do a few of the activities during the scheduled events. I think that'll really make it fun. Can I get you a cup of coffee?"

"I'd love one, but what do you say we head out to the diner for a celebratory meal?"

Ellie tugged her lips back into a wince. "I don't know. Now that I'm clear to proceed, I should cross a few more things off my to-do list."

"Well, one of those things has to be eating, and there's nothing faster than Val's service."

Ellie stared up the staircase past the polished wooden banister. "I do have most things under control already. Just a few last-minute items like printing a welcome note and sticking it in each room, but I can do that tomorrow."

A grin spread across her face, and she waved a hand at him. "Yeah, what the heck. Let's go celebrate."

"That's the spirit! And it's those little touches like the

welcome note that'll keep 'em coming back for more. You're going to make an excellent businesswoman, Ellie."

"Just let me grab my purse."

"Ellie, I'll have a burger, please," Lola said as Ellie crossed to the foyer table and swung her bag over her shoulder.

"And I'll have a milkshake, extra whipped cream," Cleo shouted from upstairs.

Ellie shook her head. "And a burger and milkshake for the pets."

Mac burst into laughter. "Just like Susie used to say."

Ellie patted Lola's head. "I'll bring you something, I promise."

She followed Mac to the porch, pulling the door shut and locking it before descending the steps to Mac's waiting car. She slid inside, pulling her phone from her purse as Mac swung the car around and trundled down the gravel drive.

"Sorry, I just wanted to text Mia, and let her know we were approved."

"Why not invite her?" Mac asked.

A grin turned up the corners of her lips as her thumbs flew across the virtual keyboard. "Okay. Done. I told her we're celebrating at Val's. Then I've got to get home and finish that work. No more procrastinating."

"You couldn't honestly have thought you'd get turned down." Mac aimed the car toward town, accelerating down the tree-lined country road. A few leaves danced their way down to the pavement, painting the gray road with sprays of orange, red, and yellow.

"I had some strong opposition," Ellie said as she stowed her phone in her purse.

"From who?"

She shrugged. "Andy. And Dominic didn't seem too pleased, either."

"Bah, Andy opposes everything. If it doesn't benefit him directly, he won't support it."

"But it does. I'll have to buy extra groceries from him. Direct benefit."

"He doesn't see it that way. Thinks most people will patronize the diner and the other local businesses." Mac rounded the sharp bend in the road, bringing the small town of Salem Falls into view.

"Which is a boon for the town," Ellie said, waving her hand toward the quaint buildings that lined Main Street.

"Like I said, Andy opposes everything."

"What about Dominic?" Ellie asked as Mac turned his car onto the road leading toward the diner.

"Dominic's too busy worrying about getting re-elected. He blows whatever way the wind goes for votes."

"Okay, and then Delilah was weirdly opposed, though far less vocal than Andy. And I'm allowing pets, so her pet store may benefit. People will love the idea of taking their dog to Right Meow for a treat and a toy."

Mac eased his car into a parking space and killed the engine. He waved a hand at her before popping his door open. "You worry too much about what some of these folks think."

"Well," she said as she stood and slammed her door shut, "I do when it comes to their opinion on opening my business since I literally couldn't without their approval."

"Most of them know what's good for them and this town. And that's definitely to have the B&B open again." Mac held the door open as Ellie slipped in past him.

"Hey, Ellie," Val called from behind the counter. "Congratulations. I just came from the council vote."

Ellie's stomach rumbled as she caught a whiff of the fried food. "Thank you. We're here to celebrate."

"Burgers and shakes coming right up," Val said with a grin.

"Make it three!" a new voice said. Ellie turned to find Mia hurrying through the still-open door in front of Mac.

"You got it!" Val waved over her head as she scribbled on her order pad before ripping off a sheet and sticking it on the carousel.

Mac led them to his favorite booth. Ellie and Mia slid in together, leaving Mac across from them.

Mia wrapped her arm around Ellie and squeezed her shoulders, grinning. "Congratulations, Ellie."

"Thank you, and thanks for your help with the website."

She flicked a lock of her long, blonde hair over her shoulder. "Oh, you're welcome."

"How are the other ones coming?"

"Great. I'm almost done with the diner's website, *and* we're adding online ordering."

"That sounds like it'll really send some traffic," Mac said as he traced the outline of the paper placemat.

Mia nodded. "I think it will."

Ellie slid her purse strap from her shoulder and tossed it onto the windowsill. "What others are you working on?"

"Ice cream shop and newspaper."

Mac's eyebrows shot up. "Is Scarlett driving you crazy yet?"

Val bustled over with steaming plates of food. She set a plate down in front of everyone, delivered the milkshakes, and told them to enjoy themselves.

"Scarlett is…interesting to work with. We're only on initial concepts. She's got lots of ideas, some of which are…well, let's just say I'm going to have to do some more research before I know if I can implement everything on her list of demands."

"Are you adding online ordering for ice cream?"

Mia poked a finger at her as she bit into her burger. "Sort of. She and Val are discussing sharing a delivery person. That way you can order ice cream to go."

"Heaven help our waistlines if that happens," Ellie said with a chuckle. "Oh, that reminds me. Mac, would you mind swinging by the ice cream shop before we head back?"

"No problem. Can't forget a treat for Cleo and Lola."

"I'll never hear the end of it if I do," Ellie said with a grin as Mac gave her a hearty laugh.

"Any progress on getting Andy to add online ordering to the grocery store?" Ellie bit into a crisp onion ring as she waited for her answer.

"Nothing yet. He insists it's a 'useless' idea, and that he doesn't need a website beyond one that states his hours and location." Mia rolled her eyes and shook her head.

Mac rearranged the pickles slipping off his burger. "That'd be our Andy. If anyone's going to stand in the way of progress, it's him."

"Guess he didn't win when it came to stopping Ellie's B&B," Mia said after a sip of her shake.

"Nope." Mac lifted his strawberry-pink milkshake glass in the air, waving it toward them. "To new beginnings."

Ellie and Mia lifted their chocolate shakes, clinking glasses before taking a sip of the thick, decadent drink.

The bell above the door chimed as a new patron pushed into the diner. Jake shuffled inside with his hands shoved into the pockets of his khakis. Mac gave him a wave before wiping his hands on a balled-up napkin.

The young reporter grabbed the strap of his messenger bag as he meandered toward them.

"Hey, Jake," Mac said with a grin.

"Hey, guys, how's it going?"

"We should be asking you that," Ellie said with a grin. "What's the latest on the wire?"

Jake crinkled his brow. "What?"

"I think she means with the news," Mia explained. "Us old-timers used to call it the wire."

Jake chuckled. "Oh, right. Uh, slow news day. You know what I did hear though?"

"What's that?" Ellie asked after a bite of her burger.

"Someone in town got approved to open a B&B." He cracked a smile.

Ellie's eyes went wide, and she dropped her jaw open. "No! Really?"

Jake winced, clutching the strap of his messenger bag tighter. "Oh, geez. You didn't know. Oh, I'm sorry, I shouldn't have–"

Mac slapped the table, a loud laugh bursting from his lips. "Of course, she knew. I told her. She got you good, boy."

Val bustled to the table and clapped the young man on the shoulder. "Good to see you, sweetie. You want me to plate your to-go?"

"Ah," Jake began.

"Heck yes, he does," Mac said, sliding over. "He's joining the celebration."

Jake smiled and patted Val's hand. "If you wouldn't mind."

"Coming right up!" She waved a finger in the air as Jake slid into the booth and shed his messenger bag.

"Do you have everything ready for this weekend?" he asked as Val slid a grilled cheese and fries in front of him along with a milkshake.

Ellie took a sip of her chocolate shake and nodded. "For the most part. There are just a few things left to do, but the big stuff is done. You're still coming to the opening, right?"

Jake set down a wedge of his grilled cheese. "You know it. I think everyone in town is planning on coming to the kick-off party."

"Maybe not a few." Ellie arched an eyebrow as she retrieved an onion ring from her plate.

"Andy?" Jake asked as he popped a fry in his mouth.

Ellie rolled her eyes, wiping her fingers on her napkin. "Yep."

"I don't think anyone listened to anything he said after he claimed it would 'break the universe' if you reopened."

Mia choked on her shake, slamming the glass down on the Formica table. "What? He didn't say that."

"Oh, yes, he did," Ellie said with an emphatic nod.

"He was a little overzealous in his appeal to the town council," Jake admitted as the bell over the door chimed again.

"Speaking of overzealous..." Mac began, allowing the words to hang in the air.

High-heeled shoes stomped toward them, and Ellie pressed her lips into a thin line, realizing exactly who he meant.

Scarlett appeared at their table a moment later, flicking her dark locks over her red-clad shoulder. "Well, if it isn't the town's newest business owner."

"Hi Scarlett," Ellie answered with a wave, "thanks."

"For what? I didn't congratulate you."

Ellie puckered her lips, realizing she hadn't. "True."

"I would like to do a photo shoot for the paper. Is tomorrow morning good?" Scarlett arched an eyebrow and fluttered her eyelashes.

"Excellent," she answered before Ellie could. "Be ready for nine. Wear something professional. At least *try* to look the part."

She spun on her heel and stormed toward the counter, her dark curls bouncing.

"Wow," Mia mouthed as she bobbed her straw up and down.

Ellie glanced down at her clothes with a wrinkled nose. "Guess I can't wear this."

Mac shoved the last bite of his burger into his mouth. "At least she didn't ask for a photoshoot while you check in your first guest. That could have been a disaster."

Ellie flicked her eyebrows up and down. "Right. Thank goodness for small miracles."

"I'm sure she'll do a nice feature," Mac said as Scarlett's shrill voice floated across the diner.

"And make sure there are *three* pickles on the burger this time, not two."

Val scrawled on her order pad as she nodded. "At least three pickles, got it."

"No, not at least three. Three. No more, no less."

Val underlined something three times. "Three. Got it."

Ellie snuck a glance over her shoulder. "She really is something."

"Try working for her," Jake answered. "Anyway, I'm sure the feature will be nice. I'm writing it."

"Oh, good. So, if I'm not wearing a business suit you can say something about how hard-working I am or something."

"I think the town will see just how hard-working you are when you make this business a success, Ellie," Mac said, using his glass for another salute.

"From your lips," Ellie answered as the bell chimed again.

"Uh-oh," Mac said, wrinkling his nose.

Mia and Ellie glanced over their shoulders.

"What?" Ellie asked.

Andy stood inside the door, scanning the crowd at the diner.

"Ohhhhh." Ellie spun in her seat to face forward. "Maybe he won't–"

"There you are!" Andy's snippy voice called.

11

Ellie glanced over her shoulder to find him storming toward them.

"Hey, Andy, look, no hard feelings, huh?" Ellie began. "You weren't for my business opening, and everyone has a right to their opinion but–"

"But you got your way, didn't you? Let's just see how well this goes!" He wagged a finger at her in front of his red face.

Ellie fluttered her eyelashes as she let her gaze fall to her empty plate.

"Look, Andy," Mia cut in, "this is really out of line. You have no right–"

"I have every right!" Andy shouted in his nasally voice. "When something is about to destroy my hometown, I not only have the right, I have the duty!"

Ellie rolled her eyes again. "Destroy Salem Falls? Really, Andy? Don't you think you're being just a tad dramatic?"

"I'm not! Your B&B is going to ruin this town. And I won't let it happen. One way or another, Eleanor Byrne, I'm going to stop you! Mark my words! One way or another!"

He waved a fist in the air in a dramatic display before he stomped out of the diner.

Ellie scrunched her features, eyeing the others at her table. "Did he just threaten me?"

CHAPTER 2

*M*ac patted her hand. "Now, Ellie, don't get too riled up over what Andy says. He's just being dramatic."

Ellie sighed, then took a last sip of her chocolate shake. "He's just determined to make sure I fail. What's next? Refusing to sell me groceries so my guests can't eat?"

Mac poked a finger at her. "Now, if he does that, you call me. I'll sue him."

"Let's hope he doesn't," Ellie said.

Mia patted her shoulder. "I'm sure it'll be fine. He's probably just blowing off steam."

"Yeah," Jake agreed. "He's a sore loser, that's all."

Ellie shouldered her purse and passed Mia's to her. "Well, it sounds like everyone else in town is on board. And that's what matters. I think I'm still just stuck on this idea of acceptance after the divorce from Toby."

Mia wrinkled her nose while she fiddled with the strap on her handbag. "I know *exactly* what you mean. This whole debacle with Joe is messing with my head. I don't know which way is up."

"You two girls have been through it," Mac said. "But don't ever let anyone tell you you're not worth it. Susie used to always use that quote from Jane Goodall. It doesn't take much to be considered a difficult woman. That's why there are so many of us."

"Wow, that's pretty profound." Mia slumped back against the booth's bouncy back.

"Yeah," Ellie answered. "I keep going back to Toby's thing about how I didn't pay enough attention to him. Meanwhile, I had a job, a house, he expected me to cook and clean, but I got no help."

"Right!" Mia agreed, slapping the table. "At the end of a long week, if I didn't want to go out to see a movie, I was being difficult."

Ellie poked her finger at Mia. "And let me guess, he was a saint for taking you out to eat so you didn't have to cook."

Mia's eyes went wide as she sucked up the last of her shake, and she nodded. "Yes! He just didn't get that it had nothing to do with him, but I just wanted to sit in sweats, order Chinese, and watch Netflix."

"We married idiots," Ellie said.

"And we divorced them, too. No more idiots!" Mia pumped a fist in the air. "And that includes everyone in this town, including Andy."

"I hope there are some exceptions," a southern voice said from behind.

Ellie twisted to find Sheriff Rick Crawford striding toward them. "How y'all doing? Ellie, congratulations on the business approval."

Ellie grinned at him, lifting her chin. "Thank you."

He twirled his hat in his hands, letting his gaze settle on Mia with a tentative grin. "Still waiting for an answer to that question."

Color rose in her cheeks, and she offered him a demure smile. "Oh, there are some exceptions."

"I'm afraid we've gone and empowered these ladies too much," Mac said with a chuckle. "Next thing you know, they'll have some hare-brained ideas about voting and driving."

"Whoa, that's when we need to put our foot down, right, men?" Rick said with a coy smile.

"Darn right. Can you imagine women drivers?" Mac clapped Jake on the shoulder.

Jake waved a hand in the air. "Don't get me involved in this. I'm not saying a word."

Ellie pointed a finger in Jake's direction. "There's the smart one in the group."

"All right, then, come on, smart one. Let's go get some ice cream for the pets," Mac said.

Mia bounded out of the booth. "And me. I didn't have dessert."

"Neither did I," Ellie said with a shake of her head as she slid across the red pleather.

"Mind if I join you?" Rick asked.

"Not at all," Mac answered. "The more the merrier. Besides, we need to keep our numbers up."

"Right," Rick said with an amused smile.

They paid their bills and, after a quick conversation about pies with Val for her opening weekend, left the diner and walked the short distance to Main Street. They meandered toward Salem Scoops. The ice cream shop bustled in the early evening hour with patrons coming and going with their treats, and the tables on the patio almost filled.

They pushed inside the shop, making their selections before they settled at a round table outside, shielded from the setting sun by a red and white umbrella.

"Oh, hi, everyone," Hazel's bubbly voice said from behind Ellie.

She twisted to wave at the police secretary who sat with the town's deputy, Nathan Hawk, as she licked her cotton candy cone. "Hi, Hazel."

"Congratulations on the business, Ellie," Hazel said. She offered a broad grin as Nathan reached toward her with a napkin.

"You've got some cotton candy ice cream on your nose."

"Oh," she said with a giggle, "oops." She snatched the napkin and wiped the tip of her nose. "Are you all ready for the weekend?"

"Mostly, yes. Thanks for your support."

"Of course," she said, her blonde curls bobbing up and down as she nodded. "I thought it was a great idea. Just Andy and Delilah didn't. Oh, and that one anonymous person."

"Anonymous person?" Ellie questioned.

"Yeah," Hazel answered. "Someone lodged an anonymous complaint against the business plan."

"Can they do that?" Mia asked, cutting her gaze to Mac.

"Oh, yeah," Mac said. "Council decided a while back that anonymous complaints should be allowed. There was a big battle over it. Businesses felt they should have the right to know who lodged a protest so they could adequately prepare a rebuttal, but the council felt different. Thought in a small town like this, it could lead to trouble and people should have the ability to complain without fear of retaliation."

"Hmm," Ellie said with a furrowed brow. "Wonder who else wanted the B&B to remain closed."

"You'll never know," Mac said. "Not unless the person identifies themselves."

"Oh, well, I guess it doesn't much matter," Ellie answered with a shrug.

She took a few more licks of her ice cream before she

spun to face Hazel again. "Can I at least know what the criticism was on the anonymous note?"

Hazel bobbed her head up and down. "Oh, yeah. It said the house is cursed and everyone would die if it became a B&B again."

Ellie crinkled her brow, scoffing. "What?"

Hazel shrugged. "That's what it said."

"Oh, that's a bunch of baloney," Mac said with a wave of his hand. "That story's been going around the town for as long as I can remember. Bunch of bunk."

"There's a story about it?" Ellie questioned.

Mac nodded as he scooped another spoonful of strawberry ice cream from his waffle bowl.

Mia leaned closer to him. "Ohhh, a legend. Do tell."

"It's silly," Mac answered with a wave of his spoon.

"I want to hear it," Mia said with a pout.

Jake poked at the sprinkles on his chocolate ice cream. "Me too. Maybe this would make a cool story for the paper."

"Don't go printing this nonsense. That's all it is."

"Come on, Mac," Rick said, wiping the vanilla ice cream from his lips and grinning. "We want to hear the story."

Mac grumbled as he licked another spoonful of ice cream from the plastic spoon.

"It's cursed, sheriff. Everyone knows that," Hazel answered.

Nathan crinkled his dark brows. "Really?"

"Uh-huh," Hazel said with a bob of her head. "Since not long after it was built in 1875."

"Cursed?" Ellie asked. "By what?"

"Or who?" Mia added.

"Unhappy B&B guest?" Ellie guessed after a lick of ice cream.

Jake jabbed his spoon toward Mac. "Disgruntled maid."

"Angry owner," Nathan yelled from the other table.

"Oh, disinherited family member," Rick tried.

"Ehhh, you're getting warmer," Mac said with a tilt of his head.

Mia narrowed her eyes. "Wait, don't give it away yet, I didn't guess."

She chewed her lower lip as she considered the culprit further. Mac pointed his spoon at Hazel. "And don't you give it away. I know you know."

"Come on, Mia, take your guess. I want to hear the story," Ellie prompted.

"Don't rush me," she answered, holding a finger up. She took another bite of her butterscotch ice cream, sloshing the cold treat around in her mouth. "Mmm, I got it. Fighting siblings."

A grin spread across Mac's lips. "Hey, you're pretty good, girl."

Mia lifted a shoulder before she bowed her head. "Please, no applause."

"So, wait," Jake asked as he scooped more sprinkle-covered ice cream from his bowl, "both siblings cursed it or one cursed the other?"

"Neither of the siblings actually did the cursing. Here's what happened," Mac said, tossing his plastic spoon in the nearby trash can before he broke off a piece of his waffle bowl and popped it into his mouth.

"The property was purchased in 1860 by the Portsmith family. John Portsmith was a farmer at the time he bought the land."

"Did he plan to farm here in Pennsylvania?" Rick asked.

Mac turned the corners of his mouth down and shook his head. "Heck no. He took his life savings and sank it into that property to woo a woman."

"Ooooh," Mia said as Hazel tugged her chair over to their table. "Lucky gal."

"Well," Mac said with a tilt of his head, "hold your assessment of that until you hear the rest of the story."

Ellie slid closer to Mia, allowing Hazel to pull her chair up to the table. "Come on over, Nathan, we've got room."

Nathan tossed away his napkin and dusted off his hands before the metal legs scraped against the patio as he dragged his chair toward them and settled in to listen.

"John brought his intended bride-to-be to the property. He told her they'd build a home here if she'd have him."

"Did she say yes?" Mia asked before biting her lower lip as she awaited the response.

"She said maybe," Mac answered.

"Maybe?" Ellie questioned. "What kind of an answer is that?"

Sam pushed out of the ice cream shop's door, her dark ponytail swaying with each step. "What's going on here? A party and I wasn't invited?"

"Of course, you're invited, Sam," Mac said with a wave. "Sit down. We're telling the new folks all about the Curse of Salem Falls Manor."

"Woo, now there's a good ghost story."

"Ghost story?" Ellie asked, wiping at the corners of her mouth. "I thought this was a curse?"

Mac wagged a finger. "Well, you didn't let me finish."

"Oh, boy," Ellie said with a shake of her head as she drew her sweater tighter around her, "am I going to be afraid to go home tonight?"

"Maybe," Hazel said with a nod of her head.

"Now, where was I?" Mac asked, clapping a hand on the table.

"The girl said maybe to John," Mia answered. "We didn't know what that meant."

Mac wagged a finger in the air. "Oh, right, old Loretta

said maybe. Now, Loretta was a looker. Prettiest girl in Hogback Hollow."

"Hogback Hollow?" Ellie questioned with a wrinkled nose.

"Yep. They came from Virginia. John and his father had traveled north and stayed in the town of Salem Falls. That's when John got to thinking. He hated being a farmer. And he loved Loretta. He figured if he loved Salem Falls, so would she."

"But she didn't," Mia said. "That's why she only said maybe."

"No. Like I said, Loretta was a pretty girl. She knew she could have her pick. And while John gave her the chance to get out of Hogback Hollow, she wanted more. So she told him if he could build her the grandest house in town, she'd marry him."

"Did he agree?" Mia asked.

Mac settled his clasped hands over his belly as he leaned back in the chair. "Yep. He promised her. And she said the day they started building, she'd walk down the aisle."

Ellie's jaw dropped open as a cool fall breeze rustled her hair and sent the umbrella flapping. "Wow, demanding! That'd be the day I'd tell a man that and he would agree."

"Right? I could barely get Joe to take me on a weekend getaway, let alone build me the grandest house in town."

"Okay, okay, just hold on here," Rick said, waving a hand in the air. "How did a farmer from Hogback Hollow afford to build the grandest house in town?"

"Especially after he poured all his money into the property?" Nathan added.

"He got clever," Sam said with a grin and a flick of her long ponytail.

Ellie furrowed her brow, leaning forward and lowering her voice. "Is that code for illegal stuff?"

Mac crossed his arms and leaned back in the chair with a loud belly laugh. "No. Well, not yet."

"Not yet?" Mia questioned.

"Old John took a position with the railroad. Started out running errands for the bigwigs."

"And then he stole from them?" Nathan asked.

"No," Mac said with a shake of his head. "He learned from them."

"Learned from 'em?" Rick asked, sliding his head forward.

"Yep. And he became invaluable to them. Got to a point where they couldn't run unless old John was there. He knew the ins and outs of everything. He advised them on some major moves that grew their holdings even more."

Mia rested her forearms against the table. "And then what?"

"They rewarded him. Gave him stock in their companies." Mac offered a coy grin. "He managed to get stock from every one of them, too. Making him the majority shareholder."

"So, he swindled them?" Ellie popped the last of her cone into her mouth and shimmied her sweater tighter around her as the air grew chillier.

"He was slick, you can say that," Mac answered.

Jake zipped up his hoodie as a chilly burst of air rustled the foliage, sending a few colorful leaves crashing down to the pavement. "Okay, so how does this lead to the curse?"

Mac waved a finger in the air in a silent plea for more patience. "Old John made his fortune and built his bride a house."

Mia propped her chin in her hands. "So, Loretta married him and moved to Salem Falls?"

"Yep," Mac answered.

"So romantic," she said with a raise of her shoulder.

Mac shook his head. "I wouldn't go that far. Loretta was money-hungry. She wanted more and more. New furnishings constantly. New dresses. Travel. And John had to figure out a way to keep the coffers full."

"So, he turned to a life of crime," Hazel said with a nod.

"What did he do?" Jake questioned.

Mac leaned forward, and let his gaze slide around the group. "Well, as majority owner of the railroad, he had access to all the information about the trains."

"Oh my gosh, he robbed them," Ellie said, letting her head fall back between her shoulders.

Mac poked a finger at her. "You're a smart cookie, Ellie."

"Oh, wow," Ellie said with a shake of her head. "Robbed his own trains."

"And he made out good. He had the stolen items–"

"And the insurance money," Rick finished for him.

Mac winked at him. "Bingo."

Ellie scoffed and shook her head. "Some people."

Hazel shrugged and shot a glance at Ellie. "At least you got a nice house because of it, Ellie."

"So, how does this correspond to the curse?" Mia asked. "Was one of the stolen items cursed?"

"No, he said it was sparring siblings," Jake answered. "Unless John had a sibling we don't know about who cursed him, we haven't gotten that far yet."

"Very good, Jake. No wonder you're Salem Falls' star reporter." Mac rubbed his hands together and blew into them as the sun disappeared below the horizon.

"A few years after they moved into the house, Loretta got pregnant with twins."

Ellie winced. "Ouch, I bet that shut down her spending sprees."

"It did more than that. It killed her. She died in childbirth, but not before she had a boy and a girl. John grieved her death, but–"

"Was secretly glad?" Nathan questioned. All eyes turned

to him and he shrugged. "What? She seemed like a real…you know what."

Mac chuckled at his statement. "No, the thing was, he couldn't stop himself from robbing his own trains. And some of what he stole never resurfaced. It's supposedly somewhere on his estate."

"In my B&B?" Ellie asked.

"In your B&B," Mac confirmed with a nod. "Now, his daughter, a little spitfire by the name of Clara, helped him hide the stash. She assumed she'd inherit the place because her brother had gone to New York to practice law."

"And did she?" Mia asked.

Mac pushed out his lower lip and shook his head. "Old John died and Clara's brother, Charles, took her to court."

"He sued her?" Ellie asked, her eyebrows shooting high.

"Yep. Won, too. Left her destitute and threw her out of the house."

"OMG!" Mia said with a wrinkled nose. "What? His own sister?"

"His own sister," Mac said with an emphatic nod. "So, his own sister brought a gypsy woman around who cursed the house and the owners."

"What was the curse?" Nathan questioned.

Hazel lifted a shoulder, offering the group an ominous stare. "That anyone who tried to profit from the property or its contents would die."

CHAPTER 3

"Oh, what? Are you joking? This is a joke, right?" Ellie wadded up her napkin and tossed it on the table.

"No," Hazel answered with a shake of her head. "That's what it was. Ask Mac."

Mac cocked his head. "She's right."

Ellie narrowed her eyes as she studied the twinkling lights strung above them that worked to beat back the darkness. "I mean, this is a self-fulling prophecy, right? Everyone dies. So, technically anyone who owns the property will die."

Mac wagged a finger at her. "Well, the curse was a bit more specific. They'd die a horrible death."

"And has anyone died a horrible death?" Nathan questioned.

Mac ticked each one off on his fingers. "Let me list them. Charles was trampled to death by a horse in a freak accident six months after he won the case. His son took ownership of the property next. He opened it as a hotel for those stopping over when the railroad still ran through here."

"And did he die a horrible death?"

"Crashed his Model T into the ravine two years after opening."

Mia wrinkled her brow. "Then who got it?"

"It went out of the family. Charles's son was only twenty-two when he died. He had no heirs."

"And the next poor person got caught in the crossfire?" Ellie asked.

"You could say that. Every person who has opened it has died in a strange way. Odd accidents, strange circumstances, bizarre manners of death…even murder."

"Like Aunt Susie," Ellie said with a shiver.

Mia rubbed her shoulders. "Aww, Ellie."

Mac winced. "I'm sorry, I didn't mean to–"

"No, it's okay. She was murdered. It's a fact."

"She wasn't the only one," Hazel answered. The owner in the 60s shot his entire family then killed himself."

Ellie wrinkled her nose and grimaced. "In the house?"

"Oh, no. In a rental cabin in New York."

"So, has every single owner of that property died under mysterious circumstances?" Mia asked.

"Every one of them for over a hundred years. Some of them lasted longer than others. But most of them died very shortly after they profited from the property."

Ellie lowered her gaze to the wrought iron table, the frown still etched into her features. "Suddenly, the B&B doesn't seem like a great idea."

"Oh, now, curses aren't real," Mac said. "Susie didn't believe in it. She wanted to reopen the B&B. And she had run it successfully for years before that and nothing happened to her."

"Until she was murdered," Ellie answered.

"But she technically wasn't profiting off the place at the time of her murder," Rick pointed out.

"No, but she had, right?" Ellie asked.

Mac bobbed his head up and down. "Oh, yeah. Had quite a successful business going before that."

"And it sounds like she lasted the longest against the curse. She lived there for years before anything happened to her," Nathan added.

Mac poked a finger at him. "He's got a point. Your Aunt Susie could have broken the curse if she wouldn't have met that greedy nurse."

"Why did she close the place anyway? If she had a good business, why not keep it open?"

"Oh, uh," Mac said, avoiding her gaze, "she wanted a break. It was a lot of work."

"Also, the trouble there wore on her," Hazel added.

Mac scrunched up his face and wrinkled his nose at the statement.

"The trouble?" Ellie questioned.

"Yeah. She had some trouble right before she closed. Break-ins and things like that," Hazel answered. "I remember because I worked for the sheriff then. Not Sheriff Rick, the other sheriff."

"Right," Ellie said with a nod, her brow crinkled as she processed all the information.

Silence fell over the group until Rick's radio crackled to life, startling everyone. "Hey, Sheriff, it's Deputy Wilkins."

Rick grabbed the device from his shoulder and spoke into it. "Yeah?"

"Mrs. Hammons lost her cat again."

"All right, I'm on it. Well, duty calls," he said as he rose from the table. "Interesting story, Mac."

Mac nodded at him. "You find that cat now."

"Oh, I will."

"I should be heading out too," Nathan said, rising to stand. "Hazel, would you like me to drop you off at home?"

"Oh, sure, thanks. Take care, Ellie, good luck with the opening."

Ellie smiled and nodded, unable to form any words as she continued to ponder whether or not the opening was a good idea.

Jake shoved his hands into his pockets as he stood. "I'm going to take off, too. I've still got an article to finish for the paper tomorrow."

"Good night, Jake," Mia said with a wave. Sam passed along her good nights as well before she ducked back into the shop to help a few newcomers with their orders.

"Well, I guess we should get going too. Back to my haunted house." Ellie heaved a sigh as the train of deaths hit her. She wondered if she'd become the next victim of the curse.

"Don't forget the doggy bag," Mac said.

"Oh, right," Ellie answered, smacking her palm against her forehead. "Let me grab it from Sam."

Mac reached out to grab her hand before she could stand. "Ellie, don't get too upset over those stories. They're just stories. Anything has a pattern if you look hard enough. Most people in the town know the tale, and they don't pay it any mind."

She offered him a weak smile as she shouldered her purse. "Right. Let me just grab the doggy bag."

She ducked into the shop and returned a moment later with the treats in hand. "Got 'em. Thanks for reminding me."

"Okay, let's head out."

"Actually," Mia said as they strode toward the diner, "would you mind some company tonight?"

"Not at all," Ellie answered, cracking a genuine smile for the first time since the terrifying tale.

"Great," Mia said with a grin. "Looks like you're off the

hook, Mac. I can drive her back with me. As long as you don't mind stopping by my place first."

"Not at all." Ellie shook her head.

"I won't be long. I promise the ice cream won't melt."

"I'm sure it'll be fine," Ellie answered as they arrived at the cars.

"You sure? I can take you," Mac said.

"I'm sure. Thanks, Mac."

Mac nodded as he pulled his door open. He hesitated his hand on the corner. "Hey, Ellie, I'm sorry if I upset you–"

"Don't give it a second thought," Ellie said with a wave of her hand. "It's okay."

"You sure? I didn't mean to make you uncomfortable. It's just a story."

Ellie offered him a tight-lipped smile and a nod. "There are no such things as curses."

"That's right," Mac said with a grin and a nod. He poked a finger at her. "And don't you start believing in them now."

"I won't," Ellie called over the roof of Mia's car before she slid inside.

Mac gave her a final wave and hopped into his own car. He waited until Mia fired her engine and backed from her space before he headed for his own home.

"Nothing like scaring you half to death, then telling you not to be scared," Mia murmured as she rolled to a stop at the sign across from her apartment building.

"I don't think he meant any harm," Ellie said with a chuckle.

"Your face says different."

Ellie laughed again. "Yeah, I know. I'll admit it was unnerving, but you know these town legends. Half of it is made up and the other half is so distorted from the original story that it's not even close to being true."

Mia slid the car into a parking space and slipped out of her seat belt. "Give me two minutes to grab my jammies."

"Take your time," Ellie called as Mia hopped from the car. She hurried up the wooden steps leading to the second-story apartment and pushed inside.

As she disappeared, Ellie pursed her lips, studying her hands. The words shared around the table echoed in her mind. Would she become a victim of the curse?

An owl hooted in the distance, setting her nerves further on edge as she waited. Finally, Mia popped out of her apartment and locked the door behind her before hurrying down the stairs and cutting off any more of her dwelling on the curse.

"Okay, ready," she said as she slid behind the wheel and tossed her weekend bag into the backseat. "I bet your ice cream is still intact."

"I'm sure it is. You didn't even give me long enough to wonder how the curse will kill me."

Mia tugged the shifter into reverse and backed onto the street. "You're kidding, right?"

Ellie shrugged as Mia pulled away from her apartment building. "We could take bets. Make it fun."

"Ugh, there is nothing fun about betting on how you'll die." She swung onto the winding road leading to the B&B. "You can't seriously believe in the curse?"

"I don't. Not really," Ellie answered. "Although I'll probably spend some time on Google learning about the people who owned the property before Aunt Susie and I did."

"Oh, Ellie," Mia said with a shake of her head as leaves cascaded down onto the windshield as a gust of wind whipped through the trees. She flicked on the windshield wipers to clear them. "This is exactly why I'm staying with you tonight. I knew that story bothered you."

"It's not *that* surprising. My aunt was just murdered."

"But a curse? Come on. Your aunt was murdered out of greed. Not because of some gypsy's curse."

"Still, it may be an interesting project to look into the house's history. And, hey, how about the stuff he stole? I wonder if it's anything important or valuable. That could be fun to look into."

"Okay, now you're talking. A treasure hunt is way better than dwelling on a curse."

"All right, then we'll settle on the couch with a hot chocolate and search the internet for treasure," Ellie answered as they trundled down the gravel driveway.

"That sounds like a plan."

Ellie popped her door open. "And I now have a new idea for another mystery weekend. Treasure hunt."

"Ooooh, that sounds like fun," Mia answered as she grabbed her bag from the back.

"Great, you can help me plan it."

"Not before I change into my jammies!" Mia said as Ellie shoved her key into the lock and twisted it. She pushed into the foyer to the sounds of the ticking grandfather clock punctuated by Lola's barks.

"Hey, pretty girl!" Mia said as the dog raced toward them.

"Oh, hey, Mia," Lola answered.

Ellie set the doggy bag down on the foyer table along with her purse. "Why are you barking? It's just us."

"How would I know that? I just heard someone on the porch."

"I guess that trip to the vet didn't teach you anything about attacking people on the porch, huh?"

"I didn't attack her," Lola answered as Mia squatted down to rub her ears.

Cleo stalked down the stairs, stopping halfway down them to sniff the air. "Ugh, what's she doing here?"

"Mia's going to stay overnight and help with the B&B. What do you think, girls?"

"I don't like her," Cleo said, settling onto a step to lick her foot. "Did you get my milkshake?"

"I got you both ice cream from Sam's. Just let me change, and you can eat it."

Mia rose to stand and winced. "Oh, do you think that's a good idea so late?"

"Do you eat ice cream late?" Cleo asked her. "Step off, Mia."

Ellie shrugged as she mounted the first step. "It should be fine."

"Idiot," Cleo murmured, speeding past them to join Lola on the lower level.

"I don't think I have a choice. Cleo will bug me until I give it to her."

"It's amazing how they know you have something for them," Mia said as she trailed behind Ellie up the steps. "They catch on so quick."

"Unlike you," Cleo shouted after her. "Idiot."

Ellie fluttered her eyelashes as the cat insulted her friend who remained completely unaware of the talking animals.

"Mind if I take my same room?" Mia asked as they reached the top.

"It's all yours. I don't rent that one out in case you want to stay any time. You know, you don't need to pay for that apartment, you could have stayed here."

"I know. But it's important that I have my own space and feel like I control my own life. I spent so much time with Joe, I just…never had anything that's my own."

"I understand completely. But like I said, that room's always here for you."

"Meet in the kitchen for the HC?"

"HC?" Ellie asked as she hovered in the doorway to her room.

"Hot chocolate."

"Oh, right. Sorry, I can't keep up with all this slang anymore."

Mia chuckled as she headed down the hall toward her room at the back.

"Yeah, yeah, yeah," Ellie shouted back as she disappeared into her bedroom. She tugged off her shirt, replaced it with a pajama top, and switched her pants. As she tossed her clothes into the hamper, a bang sounded.

Ellie froze with the lid still open. She eased it down as another bang reverberated. Her heart skipped a beat. Maybe the curse was real.

CHAPTER 4

*E*llie slid into her slippers and tiptoed from her room. She shot a glance at Mia's door which remained closed. It wasn't Mia down there. Ellie craned her neck to peer over the railing as another thud sounded.

She inched down the steps, staring down at the foyer. Lola stood on her hind legs, sniffing at the take-out bag while Cleo paraded across the top of the table.

"Hit it with your foot again," Lola said. "I still can't reach."

"What are you two doing?" Ellie said as she came down the stairs.

Cleo glanced at her with wide eyes. "Nothing."

Lola sank onto her haunches, wagging her stubby tail. "Trying to get the ice cream down."

Ellie paused at the bottom of the stairs, sliding her eyes closed and shaking her head. "At least you're honest."

"I was not doing anything of the sort. Lola was trying to get the ice cream down. And I was guarding it."

"Sure, you were," Ellie said, grabbing the bag and shuffling to the kitchen.

"I was!" Cleo shouted, leaping from the table and stalking after her. "You gotta watch with Lola. She'll steal anything."

"Oh, sort of like you, huh?"

"Me?" Cleo asked as she leapt onto her spot on the counter and waited for her treat. "I have no idea what you're talking about."

"Oh, don't you?" Ellie asked as she pulled two Styrofoam containers from the brown bag. "You have no idea what happened to the bread I left on the counter last week?"

"Uh-uh," Cleo said with a shake of her head.

"Or the English muffins?"

"Nope," the black cat answered.

"And what about that bag of cotton candy I brought home a week ago?"

"No idea."

Ellie pulled the lids off each container. "Mmm-hmm. It's funny because there were teeth marks on all of them. Little Cleo-sized teeth marks."

"That's some accusation you're making, lady. I don't care for your tone."

"I don't care for a bite taken out of my loaf of bread if I forget to tuck it away in a safe spot, but here we are." She placed the container with extra whipped cream in front of the cat before bending to give Lola the larger bowl.

"Mmmm, Sam's ice cream is my favorite," Lola said as she licked around the bone stuck inside before chomping on it.

Cleo lapped at the whipped cream before she licked the ice cream, shaking a foot in the air as the coldness hit her tongue.

"Awww, kitty likes that," Mia cooed from the doorway.

"Why does she talk to me like that?" Cleo asked.

"Yes, she does," Ellie said, rubbing the cat's head.

"Stop it," Cleo answered.

"You can rub my head, Ellie," Lola said before she chased

the bowl around to lick every drop of ice cream from the surface.

"And looks like this big girl does, too," Mia said, smooshing Lola's face in her hands.

"She's right," Lola answered.

Ellie yanked open the fridge, rattling the bottles in the door, and grabbed the gallon of milk. She set it on the counter and slid a machine out next to the coffee pot. "Check this baby out."

"What is it?" Mia asked, craning her neck.

Ellie filled the metal pitcher on top with milk, emptied two deluxe hot chocolate packets inside and gave it a quick stir. She popped the lid onto it and pressed a button. "This heats the milk *and* froths it."

"What?" Mia asked, feigning shock. "Frothy hot chocolate at the touch of a button?"

"Yep. No more stove top warming or microwaving milk. This is one-stop shop and froths it too." She grabbed a canister of whipped cream from the refrigerator and a bag of marshmallows from the cupboard. "Whipped cream or marshmallows?"

"Both," Mia answered.

"Oh, the widdle wady wikes the whipped cream," Cleo said as she stared at her.

"Kitty knows what I'm talking about. As soon as I said both, she stared at me," Mia said with a nod, oblivious to Cleo's commentary.

"Kitty has a name, as–"

"Oh, she knows," Ellie interrupted before she could finish.

"I'll bet you'd love a frothy hot chocolate, huh, kitty?"

"Are you crazy? Cats can't eat chocolate." Cleo shifted her gaze to Ellie who drummed her fingers on the counter as she waited for the milk warmer to finish whirring. "Ellie, she's trying to kill me."

"Can I eat chocolate?" Lola asked.

"Neither cats nor dogs can eat chocolate, so it looks like you two are out of luck." She poured the steaming, frothy chocolate milk into two mugs, poured a handful of marshmallows in each, and topped it off with a generous helping of whipped cream.

She stuffed the marshmallow bag back into the cupboard and spun to return the whipped cream to the refrigerator. Mia swiped it from her hand before she could, spraying her fingers with it and holding them out to the cat. "You can't have chocolate, Kitty, but you can have more of this."

Cleo's nose crinkled as she sniffed it before lapping at the melting confection. "I'm starting to like you, Mia."

Ellie rolled her eyes at the cat. Mia sprayed more onto her fingers, letting Lola lick it off before she rinsed her hands. "Okay, now I'm ready."

"You're determined to make friends, huh?" Ellie said, handing her a mug.

"I am. And I think it's working," Mia answered with a wink as she sniffed the fragrant aroma of the hot chocolate.

"Now," Ellie said as she led her to the living room, "where do you want to start with our treasure hunt?"

"Treasure hunt?" Cleo asked as she followed.

"What's a treasure hunt?" Lola asked.

"We can start with writing up a weekend party plan or dive into researching the treasure supposedly hidden in the house," Ellie said, filling in her pets on their plans as they settled on the couch. She fluffed a pillow and stuck it behind her before she took a sip of her hot chocolate.

Mia slumped onto the couch, pulling her feet up under her. "Hmm. I think we go for the real story and see what we can capitalize on."

"Good idea," Ellie said, setting the hot chocolate aside and tugging her laptop onto her lap.

"What treasure?" Cleo asked.

Ellie opened her laptop and pulled up her browser. "Okay, let's see what we can find out about the treasure stolen from the trains owned by the original owner."

"Oh, that," Cleo said. "I thought you meant real treasure." She opened her mouth in a wide yawn before she crawled under the wing-backed chair near the fireplace.

"There's a treasure here?" Lola questioned.

Mia scooped some whipped cream from the top of her drink with her pinky finger and licked it off. "Look up the legend of the curse. Maybe there's some information on that."

"Curse?" Lola asked, her eyes going wide.

Ellie grabbed the remote control from the coffee table and turned on the fireplace. "Why don't you take a nap by the fire, Lola?"

Lola wandered closer to the warm fireplace. "Okay, Ellie, that sounds nice."

"You dummy, you're supposed to find out about the curse. And she distracted you with a nap," Cleo hissed from under the chair.

Lola picked her head up and glanced over her shoulder at the chair. "What? What curse? I am pretty tired after that ice cream."

"Go to sleep, Lola, we'll work on the curse over here."

Lola let her head sink onto the fireplace rug, and her eyes slid closed.

"They are so sweet, Ellie," Mia said after a sip of her hot chocolate.

"Mmmm," Ellie murmured, tapping on her keyboard. "They're a real pair, those two. Okay, let's see what we've got in terms of Salem Falls lore."

Mia set her mug down and craned her neck to stare at the list of websites populated by the internet search.

"Oh, maybe at the historical society website," Ellie said, sliding her pointer toward the link and clicking it.

The page loaded, showing a picture of the town's library.

"Information for visitors, try that," Mia said, pointing to the link.

"Really? Come visit our town where people die all the time from a curse?" Ellie gave her a dubious glance.

Mia shrugged. "I don't know. This website isn't very intuitive, they really need a new one."

"I wonder if they'd let you redesign one for them. This is truly awful. There is barely any information on here."

"Go to another page."

Ellie clicked the back button and scanned the list. She wrinkled her nose as she spotted an article on her aunt's murder.

Mia side-eyed her, retrieving her mug again. "We don't have to look if you don't want to."

"It's fine. Like I said, my aunt was murdered. It's a fact."

"We may need to troll the library's old newspaper articles to find more information," Mia said.

Ellie wagged a finger in the air. "Wait, wait, wait." She slid her arrow over to another link and clicked it.

Mia narrowed her eyes as she leaned toward the screen. "Salem Falls Secrets?"

Ellie shrugged, wrapping her fingers around the handle of her mug and lifting it to take a sip. "It might be an interesting read."

The website loaded, and Mia wrinkled her nose. "Ew!"

Ellie smacked her friend's shoulder with a chuckle. "Snob."

"What? When was this website made? 1993?"

"Not everyone's a web designer extraordinaire like you."

Mia wrapped her hands around her mug and stared at the

front page. "This looks like a child designed it a decade ago. I'm surprised there's not a link to MySpace."

"Hey, I liked MySpace."

Mia chuckled at her friend's statement as Ellie scrolled down past the picture of the "Welcome to Salem Falls" sign.

"Let's see what we have here." Ellie studied the list of bright yellow links on the starry background.

"Oh my gosh, look!" Mia pointed at the bottom of the screen.

Ellie squinted to read it. "I can't see that stupid small print."

"It says 'Created in 2012.'" She slapped her hand against her thigh. "Told you!"

"You were two decades too early. Okay, here are our choices. Secrets of the townsfolk. Hauntings. Legends and Lore."

"Legends and Lore is our most likely bet, but I'd really like to know the secrets of the townsfolk," Mia said.

Ellie clicked on the townsfolk link. "A quick peek before we move on. Although to be honest, I'd love to read Hauntings, too."

"What are you going to do if this place is listed as haunted?"

Ellie shrugged as she scrolled down the page. "I mean, it's already cursed, how much worse can it be?"

"Haunted and cursed," Mia said. "That's how much worse."

"Okay, let's see what we have here. Ohhh, this is recent stuff."

"Well," Mia said with a tilt of her head, "recent-ish. This is still like a decade old."

"But I mean I recognize some of these names."

"Ohhhh, like who?" Mia asked as she directed her attention to the screen.

"Like Val, distinguished diner owner and descendent of famed mobster Tommy Two-Toes."

"What?" Mia asked. "Who is Tommy Two-Toes?"

Ellie held back a laugh as she opened a new tab and typed it in. She scanned the list of results before she clicked on a Smartpedia article. "Tommy Two-Toes was a racketeer in the 1920s. He is best known for bank robberies in which he'd pay each hostage one hundred dollars for their help in allowing him to escape as one of them."

"OMG, you're kidding me."

Ellie pursed her lips and shook her head. "Nope. Says he owned a speakeasy on the site of the current diner."

"Does it say why he's named Tommy Two-Toes?"

"Uh…yes. He had only two toes on his left foot. Three of them were shot off accidentally by his own gun."

"Wow. Okay, so Val's from a mob family. Good to know."

Ellie switched back to the Salem Falls Secrets page and scanned the other information.

"Anybody else we know?" Mia asked after a sip of her hot chocolate.

"Andy. Ohhhhh, what?"

"What is it? What? Was his grandfather also a mobster?"

"No," Ellie said with a shake of her head as her lips formed an O. "He came from New York. Well, his family did. His ancestor was a disgraced senator. He used inside information to profit just before the market crash in the 30s then got out of the market before it fell. Oh, wow."

"No wonder he's tightly wound. He made his fortune off the backs of other people who lost everything. Did he go to jail?"

"No, fled the state and by the time they found him here in Salem Falls, he'd already passed away."

Mia sipped more of her hot chocolate. "Anybody else good?"

"The mayor's grandfather was also the mayor. During the time of…whoa! The time of the mine crisis. A mine shaft collapsed and trapped thirteen miners. It says he owned shares in the mine and swept under the rug how little was done to rescue them. He was later charged with reckless endangerment and obstruction but the charges didn't stick."

"I'm surprised they voted in another member of his family."

"Really. He must have dug pretty deep to get himself out of that," Ellie said, savoring a long drink of the sweet liquid. "Okay, enough of that, let's move on."

"Oh, do the haunting one before the legends. Please?"

Ellie rolled her eyes as she clicked on it. "Fine."

Mia leaned closer to study the screen as it loaded. "Ghosts of Salem Falls," she read from the top.

Ellie scrolled further down the page. "Okay, let's see. The falls are haunted by the spirit of a…what? This isn't serious."

"What does it say? I can't read it."

"The falls are haunted by the spirit of a Nixie."

"A what now?" Mia asked, screwing up her face.

"The article says it's a humanoid water spirit. This is ridiculous. And suddenly I'm not sure anything on this site is real," Ellie said.

"Go to the next haunting. That one feels like it's more legend and lore. Maybe he put it on the wrong page."

"Okay," Ellie said, scrolling further down. "Here's the next one. Oh, this is more intriguing. One of the houses on Main Street is haunted."

"Which one?"

"The big Victorian right on the corner of First and Main."

"Ohhh, haunted by what? A Trixie?"

Ellie scanned the screen. "Very funny. This says haunted by multiple spirits, some nefarious."

Mia puckered her lips, sliding her gaze sideways. "That sounds bad."

"Oh my gosh, it says in addition to minor annoyances like all kitchen cupboards being opened, and random items being moved, there are larger problems."

"All the cupboards open was enough for me. That's a large enough problem. That's creepy." Mia shivered and pulled a blanket over her legs.

"It gets worse."

"Oh, no. Really?"

"Do you not want me to tell you?" Ellie asked, flicking a glance at Mia over the rim of her mug.

Mia chewed her lower lip. "I feel like I have to know now."

Ellie flicked her eyebrows up. "Okay, you asked for it. On several occasions, the family has been awoken by banging in the middle of the night. It always occurs at one eleven in the morning. The source of the banging can never be found as it sounds like it's coming from everywhere and nowhere.

"In some instances, the banging is accompanied by other odd occurrences such as bleeding walls and an incredible coldness."

"No," Mia whispered, her eyes wide.

"Oh, yes. So cold, they can see their breath. At times, the family has camped out in their living room because the instances are so terrifying they can't stand to sleep alone."

Mia winced and tucked the blanket closer around her. "I'm never going into that house."

"Just don't go there at one in the morning," Ellie said with a laugh as she scrolled further down the page.

"I'm not kidding, El," Mia said. "These things are real."

Ellie chuckled, shooting a sideways glance at her friend. She stopped laughing and tilted her head. "Mia, you can't honestly tell me you believe in ghosts."

"I can and I will. Because I do. There are disturbances. I'm never going into that house."

"It's not real. I mean, come on, bleeding walls? Where's the evidence? I bet they just missed getting it on camera."

Mia wagged a finger at her. "You better watch before they come to haunt you."

Ellie sucked in a breath. "They're not going to haunt me. Because there are no such things as ghosts."

"I wouldn't be so cavalier about that living in a house that's as old as this one."

Ellie scrolled to the bottom of the page. "Look, we're safe. It's not listed on the site. No ghosts here."

"Yeah, right. Just curses and stolen property and bad vibes here."

"Better than ghosts, right?"

"Maybe no one documented the ghosts here."

Ellie rolled her eyes. "Because there are none. I've been here for over a month now and I haven't had my kitchen cupboards open, or anything moved, or any bang–"

A loud bang interrupted her words. She froze, and the two women exchanged a glance. Her heart beat hard in her chest and she wondered if her new home should be on the town's haunted list.

CHAPTER 5

*E*llie winced and snapped her gaze toward the foyer.

Mia's jaw dropped open, and she shot a glance at Ellie. "You want to say that again about this place not being haunted?"

"It's probably just–"

Another bang sounded. Cleo slinked from under the chair and ran, belly low to the ground, into the foyer and up the stairs. Lola leapt to her feet, letting out a loud bark.

Her nose poked in the air as she sniffed for some source of the noise.

"Shh, Lola!" Ellie chided.

"But something is banging."

Ellie waved a hand at her. "I hear the banging, too, but we don't need to bark."

Another bang startled everyone. Lola raced from her spot near the fireplace to the front door with a raucous string of barks.

"Lola, stop it," Ellie said, rising to her feet. She glanced out the window onto the porch, unable to make anything out in the dark.

A knock sounded on the door, sending Lola into another barking fit. "Lola, stop it!"

"Someone's at the door," Lola said.

"I know someone's at the door. I don't need you to tell me by barking your head off."

Mia approached the foyer, her hands wrapped around her mug. "You need a peephole."

"A peephole? Mia, in two days people will be coming and going through this door all the time."

"Maybe someone came early," Mia said with a shrug.

Ellie slid the chain on the door and tugged it open. "Can I–"

She froze as she stared through the crack in the door at the person on her front porch. "What are you doing here?"

The statement elicited a few more sharp barks from Lola. "Lola, stop that. Stop barking."

The dog's face wrinkled. "Who is it, Ellie?"

"Can I come in?" the figure asked.

Ellie shifted her gaze from the dog to the man outside. "Absolutely not."

"We need to talk," the man answered.

"I think we've said everything we have to say to each other. Get off my porch."

Ellie swung the door closed, but the man slid his hand into the opening, stopping the door from closing.

"Toby, I will call the police if I have to."

"Sheriff Rick's a personal friend," Mia called.

"Ellie, that's ridiculous, I just want to talk."

"Well, I don't, Toby," Ellie said with a sigh. "When I wanted to talk, you were too busy with your new girlfriend. Go talk to her."

"We broke up," he said.

"Aww," Ellie said in a monotone voice, "what a terrible shame."

"Come on, El. I messed up. Big time."

Ellie slapped her thigh with a scoff. Lola gave another bark, wagging her tail at Ellie. Ellie shook her head at the dog. "Yeah, you did. And then you continued to mess up when you sued me for a divorce and asked me to pay for the house. Do you really think after what happened I'd want to even see you again, let alone speak to you?"

"I told you. I messed up big, El. I'm sorry. I just need–"

"Oh-ho-ho. Let me stop you right there. You need? You *need*? I don't give a hoot what you need. You left me. With a mountain of debt, I might add after you cleared our bank account."

Toby sighed, hanging his head. "I get it, El. I get it. I don't know what to say here. I'm here with my hat in hand willing to do anything it takes to fix this."

"You can't fix this. I don't want you to fix this. It's over, Toby. I've moved on. I'm happy. I'm not willing to go back to what we had. I'm sorry if that's not what you want to hear, but it's all I have to give. Now, get off my porch."

She slapped at his fingers as she tried to push the door closed again.

"Wait, El…"

Ellie huffed again. "Toby, you can't–"

"I don't have anywhere to go."

"Go back to your love nest with your girlfriend," Mia shouted.

"I told you we broke up," Toby answered.

Ellie shook her head. "Not my problem. Go to a hotel."

He eyed her through the crack in the door. "Isn't this technically a B&B?"

"Not until Friday. Now go." She pushed at the door again.

"El, wait. I can't go to a hotel. I don't…She took every-thing. My accounts are drained, she ran up my cards. And then she took off to Vegas to marry another guy. I literally don't have any money to go to a hotel with. I'm on the streets."

"What about your job?"

His forehead wrinkled. "I got fired."

Mia burst into laughter, slapping her thigh. "Oh, that's too good. Oh my gosh, she did to you what you did to Ellie. How does it feel, a–"

Ellie held up a hand. "Okay, okay, there's no need for language."

"I would have said it, too," Cleo answered from her perch high on the steps. "Call a spade a spade."

Ellie slid her eyes closed and shook her head, pressing a palm to her forehead. She heaved a sigh as she slid the chain off the door. "You can stay for a few days until you can sort yourself out."

"Ellie!" Mia and Cleo exclaimed simultaneously.

Ellie held her hand up. "I know it's stupid, but I wish someone had offered me a little grace when this happened to me. I'm no better than the people I complained about if I turn him away."

"That's *not* true," Mia answered. "You have no obligation here."

"I know that," Ellie answered while Toby shouldered his bag and stepped across the threshold. Lola backed up a few steps, letting out a piercing howl followed by several loud barks.

"Lola, no barking. It's okay."

"It's not," Cleo said.

"No," Lola answered. "He should leave."

"You can sleep in the attic bedroom. It's the only one I haven't rented out. And I expect you to be gone in a week. Find a job, call your credit card companies, figure it out, and leave."

"Or leave now," Cleo suggested from her perch.

Lola offered a few more barks as he took another step into the foyer.

"Lola, stop. This is Toby. He's a jerk, but he's going to be here for a few days. You'll have to get used to him."

"Hey, girl," Toby said, holding a hand out to her as he squatted down. Lola backed away, raising her hackles.

Toby winced as he rose.

"I feel the same way about you," Mia said.

"I get that," Toby answered, running his hands through his salt and pepper hair.

Cleo slinked down the stairs and stared at him.

"Oh, you have a cat, too," he said, shoving his hands into his jeans pocket.

Cleo wrinkled her nose and hissed at him. "Don't come near me. I hate you more than Mia and Lola combined."

Ellie shook her head and set her hands on her hips. "We're not doing this. We're not making small talk. I'll show you to the room upstairs, give you your bedding and that's it."

"Got it," Toby said with a nod as she mounted the stairs in front of him.

"Come on," she said with a sigh. Lola hurried to follow her, and Cleo darted back up the steps, racing into Ellie's bedroom and diving under the bed.

He shifted the bag onto his back as he climbed up behind her.

"Beautiful place," he said as they reached the upstairs hall.

"I said no talking."

"Sorry," he answered as she led him down the hall, rounding a corner near Mia's room and continuing toward a closed door. "You know if you need anything fixed–"

"Nope," Ellie said, swinging the door open and mounting the narrow stairs to the third floor.

Toby followed behind her. "Okay."

Ellie stopped at a linen closet and pulled out a sheet set and a blanket. She continued down the hall to the lone bedroom on this floor and pushed the door open. "Here it is."

She plopped the sheets down on the mattress and crossed her arms. "One week. No more. Kitchen is stocked, you can use most of it, just don't use the berries, they're for a dessert this weekend. And if you use something up, replace it or at least tell me."

He dropped his duffel bag on the floor. "Right."

Ellie dropped her arms to her sides, her hands curling into fists as she stalked to the door. "Good night."

Toby thrust an arm out, stopping her. She refused to make eye contact with him, biting into her lower lip.

"Hey, Ellie, thanks for this. I know I haven't earned any favors from you, but I think it speaks to what an amazing woman you are."

Ellie slid her eyes closed as tears stung them. She opened them, flexing her jaw, and sliding her gaze to his face. "Don't ever comment on what I am again."

She pushed past him, knocking into his arm before striding out the door and slamming it shut behind her. She hesitated outside, her fingertips lingering on the doorknob as she fought back a sob. She pressed a hand against her quivering stomach, blowing out a long breath.

Lola leapt to her hind legs, stretching her paws onto Ellie's torso. "Ellie, I love you."

The comment brought the flood of tears she'd been holding back. She rubbed the dog's soft ears as she sniffled and wiped at her cheeks. "I love you, too, Lola."

With a deep breath in, she lifted her chin and dried her tears. "Now, let's go finish enjoying our evening."

"Okay," Lola answered, dropping to all fours and wagging her tail.

Ellie strode away from the door, leaving her ex-husband

and his drama behind her. She stomped down the steep stairs and spilled out into the upstairs hall.

Mia waited at the doorway to her room with Cleo sitting next to her. "What happened?" Cleo asked.

"Want to talk about it?" Mia questioned.

"There's nothing to talk about. I offered him a room, probably stupidly, but I did it. He has a week to get his act together."

"El," Mia said with a tilt of her head.

Ellie slid her eyes closed and shook her head. "No, don't. Don't give me that disappointed tone."

"It's not disappointment, it's worry. Ellie…"

Ellie grabbed Mia's hands in hers. "I'm *not* taking him back. I don't want him back. But I can't throw him out on the street."

"That's what he did to you."

"I know that," Ellie answered with a nod. "And I was mad about it, too. But I need to know that I'm not what he was. Is. What he is. Don't for a second think I believe he's changed."

"That's what he wants you to believe."

"Oh, I know that," Ellie said with raised eyebrows. "He's not pulling any fast ones on me."

She glanced over her shoulder before she turned back to face Mia. "Let's go downstairs. What do you say about some popcorn and another hot chocolate?"

"Uh, yes, please. And feel free to put some booze in mine after what just happened."

"No alcohol. We need our wits about us with Toby in the house."

Mia wrinkled her nose as she trailed behind Ellie. Lola and Cleo wandered down the stairs with them. Ellie collected the mugs while Mia tapped around on her phone.

They shuffled to the kitchen, and Ellie started more milk

heating and frothing while she rinsed the residue off of the mugs.

Mia tossed a bag of popcorn in the microwave and pressed the popcorn button. "Leave it to Toby to ruin a perfectly fun night. Talk about a haunting."

"Really," Ellie groaned with a glance over her shoulder. "We can now officially be listed on the Secrets site as haunted."

"Is Toby a ghost?" Lola asked.

"He's my personal ghost."

Lola's eyes went wide. "Really? He's dead?"

Cleo slapped Lola on the head with a paw. "No, you dummy, it's just a figure of speech. He's alive. I can smell him from here. He smells dirty. Like a cheat and a liar."

"Cleo, that's enough. Stop smacking your sister."

"She isn't my sister, *obviously*."

The hot chocolate machine clicked off, and Ellie refilled their mugs while Mia emptied the popcorn into a bowl.

They shuffled into the living room with the pets in tow and plopped on the couch. Lola reclaimed her spot by the fireplace while Cleo opted for a place on the back of the couch. She stared down into the popcorn bowl on the cushion below her.

Mia grabbed a handful as she balanced her mug on one knee. "What a jerk to show up like that."

"Can we please stop talking about Toby? He's ruined enough of our night."

"Well, I'm staying here for the week. That's it. I'm not leaving you here with Idiot of the Year. And I'm making sure he leaves at the end of the week." Mia jabbed a finger at Ellie before grabbing more popcorn.

Cleo narrowed her eyes at the woman. "Oh, look, Mia has a brain."

The cat stared down at the bowl of popcorn before she slowly slid a paw toward it.

"I don't think so," Ellie said, batting it away.

"Hey! I deserve a snack. I'm stressed, too!"

"Are we getting snacks?" Lola asked, picking up her head and wagging her tail.

"Awww," Mia said with a tousle of Cleo's fur.

The cat batted at her. "Get off me."

"Kitty's hungry. Here, Kitty." Mia grabbed a few kernels of popcorn and placed them in front of Cleo.

The cat stared down at the puffy snack. "I'm starting to like you, Mia."

"Remember who gave you those," Ellie said with an arched eyebrow as she tossed a few pieces to Lola before she settled her gaze back to Mia. "And like I said, you're welcome here anytime."

"Good, because I'm staying. That ought to make him squirm, the rat." She tapped around on her phone again before putting it to the side. "Let's check out that legend page now."

"Rat?" Cleo asked. "Oh, he's no rat. That's too good for him. I know rats better than him."

Ellie nodded as she wiped whipped cream from her upper lip. "Yep."

She flipped open the laptop again and clicked back to the main page, this time selecting Legends and Lore. "Okay, here we go. Town legends."

Mia leaned toward the laptop and studied the first one. "Headless horseman. Seriously?"

"I think that's a legend everywhere," Ellie said, scrolling past.

"No, wait, go back up. It says Salem Falls was the inspiration for the story."

"What? Everyone knows Sleepy Hollow was set in Tarry-town, New York." Ellie shook her head.

"Wait, wait," Mia said. "It says that's where it's set, but it says here Washington Irving stayed one night in Salem Falls and came up with the tale. He swears he couldn't sleep, went out for a walk, and encountered a headless rider which inspired the story. The headless rider guarded the path to the falls."

"Right, where the water fairy is."

"Nixie," Mia corrected.

"Whatever," Ellie answered, scrolling further down. "Salem Falls is also known for being the home to an entrance of the underworld. Sources say a cave hidden behind the waterfall leads deep into the earth and then provides a portal to Hell. That's kind of frightening."

"Right," Mia said with a sip of her hot chocolate. "Don't go spelunking in Salem Falls."

"No kidding." Ellie scrolled further down. "Oh, here we go. The house on the edge of town, Salem Falls Manor, is also rumored to be cursed. Following the supposed assemblage of a fortune of stolen goods, the house and its supposed hidden fortune were presumed to go to Clara, the owner's daughter, however, the final will passed it to her brother, Charles. Clara brought a gypsy woman to the property who cursed Charles and any subsequent owner who would seek to profit off her loss.

"The curse killed Charles a mere six months later. Subsequent owners suffered mysterious deaths through the years. The most recent owner closed the B&B after a string of trouble. Not wishing to tempt fate, Susan Byrne converted the home to a private dwelling. When contacted for comment, Susan declined, saying she closed the business for other reasons."

"So, was your aunt superstitious or not?" Mia asked.

Ellie shrugged. Lola glanced at them from beside the fireplace. "Susie wasn't superstitious, but she was a little stitious."

"That's not right, dummy," Cleo snapped. "Susie wasn't superstitious, but she always said this house is filled with treasure."

Ellie stared at the screen for a moment before she glanced at Mia. "So, do you think there's a treasure hidden in these walls?"

"A cursed one," Mia answered with an evil laugh.

"Mia, there are no such things as curses. But look at the list of things supposedly stolen from the railroad and still unaccounted for." Ellie slid the laptop toward Mia.

She leaned forward, squinting at the screen. "Gold, money, jewelry, and..." Mia's jaw dropped open. "Seriously?"

Ellie arched an eyebrow, settling back into the pillows with her hands wrapped around her mug. "Interesting, right?"

"Umm, yes!" Mia said, slapping her thigh.

"What is it?" Cleo asked. "We can't read."

"Pizarro's Pendant. Ellie, do you know how huge of a find that would be? It's a legend. It's...priceless."

Ellie flicked her eyebrows up. "And it's hidden somewhere in this house, I think."

CHAPTER 6

"I'm not so sure about that. I mean, come on. I think this page is a bunch of bunk," Mia said.

"Really? A second ago you believed the mothman lived here."

"I didn't say that. I said Nixie. And I didn't believe it, I just said it was interesting."

"But yet this has some truth to it and you want to write it off," Ellie said, throwing a piece of popcorn at her friend.

"I don't think Pizzaro's Pendant is here. Like I said, it's a legend. A pendant made from solid gold so thick that it's too heavy to be worn around the neck. And don't forget the supposed magical restorative powers from laying it on someone's chest."

"Okay, now who's talking crazy? Restorative powers, I don't believe, but the cross being here? That I can believe."

Mia grabbed a handful of popcorn and popped a few kernels into her mouth. "Okay, say it's here. Why hasn't anyone else found it?"

Ellie shrugged and sipped her hot chocolate. "No one is as smart as us."

"Oh-ho-ho-ho-ha-ha-ha," Mia answered. "That's rich."

"Well, maybe it was forgotten over the years. Or people wrote it off. I don't know, but I'm game to find it if it's here."

"I guess a treasure hunt can pass all that time we have between starting up our businesses and reinventing ourselves."

Ellie drained her mug and raised her eyebrows. "I think it'll be a fun project. We'll tackle it right after we get through this murder mystery weekend, which I also think will be a fun project."

"And don't forget writing our new treasure hunt game," Mia said as she rose from the couch with her empty mug in hand.

"Oh, yeah, that'll be fun. We can base it off our own experiences searching for the treasure." Ellie led her to the kitchen, dumping her mug and the popcorn bowl in the sink.

"Want me to wash these?"

"No," Ellie said with a wave. "Leave them for tomorrow."

"You sure?"

Ellie shuffled out of the kitchen toward the stairs. "Definitely. It's been a long enough night. Let's just head to bed. See you in the morning."

"I hope you sleep. If you can't, knock on my door and we'll do something fun like search for treasure."

Ellie chuckled at her as they parted at the top of the stairs. Lola clicked her way across the hardwood and into the bedroom ahead of Ellie. She leapt onto the bed, sprawling out at the bottom near Cleo who had already claimed the center of the bed.

"I don't think so," Ellie said with a finger wag as she passed the bed, heading for the bathroom. "You're not taking the center of the bed again and shoving me to the side."

"Watch me!" Cleo shouted as Ellie grabbed her toothbrush.

She shook her head as she squeezed toothpaste onto the bristles and swiped them against her teeth. She spun and leaned against the sink as she brushed, pondering the hidden treasure. Was it real? Would they find it?

She chuckled before she rinsed her mouth and tossed her toothbrush into the holder. "Yeah, right," she said as she brushed her hair. "Mia's right."

She set the brush on the counter and meandered back into the bedroom. With her slippers off, she pulled back the sheets and shoved the cat to the side as she tried to slide into bed.

"Watch it!" Cleo shouted, leaping up and glaring at her.

"I have no room here."

"And that's my problem how?" Cleo shook a paw and stalked up the bed, curling up on the other pillow. "Lucky I like you."

Ellie clicked off the light and settled into the pillow, listening to Lola's snoring from the bottom of the bed. She stared at the red lights on the clock before she squeezed her eyes closed.

After a second, she rolled onto her back, studied the ceiling. She puckered her lips before rolling onto her other side.

Cleo's eyes slid open to slits. "Stop jumping around."

"Sorry, I can't sleep."

"Why? Because you want to find a treasure?"

"No," Ellie said, squashing her pillow. "I'd rather be finding a treasure than thinking about what I'm dwelling on."

"How you ate too much junk food?"

Ellie rolled her eyes. "No. Stupid Toby."

"Oh, him. I hate him and think he should leave."

Ellie sighed as she let a hand slap against the comforter. "I'm not far behind you. Why did I let him stay? That was really stupid."

"Yep, it was," Cleo answered.

Ellie flopped onto her back. "Thanks. I appreciate the support."

"Support, my paw. If you had bothered to ask anybody before you jumped in to play Mother Teresa, we could have told you not to do it and avoid this moment of sheer and utter stupidity and regret on your part."

Ellie wrinkled her nose and snapped her head to the side to stare at the cat. "Well, thank you very much, Einstein. I'm so glad you've never made a mistake in your life."

"Sometimes it's hard to relate to people like you. Imperfect people."

Ellie flicked her gaze back to the ceiling. "I'll bet."

"What I can't understand is why you did it. Why would you let him stay here? He's a loser and a jerk. You should have thrown him out on his ear and laughed. That's what I would have done."

"I don't know. I guess because..." Ellie sighed, stretching her arms overhead. "I guess because when I was down and out, no one did anything for me."

"Exactly. Pass the luck right on down the line."

Ellie shook her head. "No, that's the worst thing you can do. I needed a break. I would have been so happy if someone had given me one."

"Yet they didn't."

Ellie rolled onto her side again and tapped the cat's nose. "Not true."

"Ow, stop that." Cleo smacked her hand with a paw.

"Aunt Susie gave me a break. She left me this place. And you. And Lola. And that's exactly what I needed. And I'm so happy for what my life has become and is becoming that I just..." Ellie laughed, throwing a hand in the air. "I guess I feel like I should pass the luck along because I've gotten a pretty nice deal here."

Cleo flicked her emerald eyes to Ellie, her paw curling to grasp the pillow. "You're an idiot."

Ellie clicked her tongue and flopped onto her other side. "Oh, never mind. I don't know what I expected talking to a dang cat."

She closed her eyes and drifted off to sleep.

* * *

"Ellie!" Lola's voice whispered. "Ellie, wake up."

Ellie snapped her eyes open. The first streaks of light painted the sky in the east. "Huh? What?"

"Wake up, dummy," Cleo said. "Something's wrong."

"What? What's wrong? What is it? Are you sick?"

"Someone's in the house," Lola hissed.

Ellie's heart skipped a beat. "What?" She shoved the covers back and swung her legs over the bed. She slid into her slippers and stood, grabbing her robe and pulling it around her. "I can't believe you're not barking."

Lola wagged her tail at Ellie. "Should I?"

"No!" Ellie breathed, waving her hands at the dog. "No, don't give us away."

"Hurry, Ellie," Cleo said.

"Okay, okay." Ellie crept toward the door. Low voices whispered from the lower level. Her pulse quickened, and she inched to the railing and peered over it. The whispers continued. Ellie winced and eased down a few stairs, slicking a lock of hair behind her ear.

She rounded the corner on the landing, tiptoeing farther down as she strained to make out words. Her heart thudded against her ribs by the time she reached the landing. She darted to the closet near the front door and eased it open, wincing as it creaked on its hinges.

She reached inside and withdrew the unloaded rifle,

suddenly wishing she kept shells closer. With the weapon in her hands, she crept toward the kitchen where hushed voices continued to whisper.

A muffled scream sounded, and her heart skipped a beat. Ellie raced forward into the room, raising the weapon to shoulder height. "Don't move!"

"Whoa," Mia said, raising her hands above her head from her seat on the counter. "We surrender."

Her partner in crime spun to face Ellie, taking a step away from the counter.

Sheriff Rick Crawford put his hands in the air with a grin. "Whoa, there, Ellie."

Ellie lowered the gun, her shoulders slumping. "You two scared me half to death."

"Sorry," Mia answered, sliding off the counter and grabbing a mug. She filled it with coffee and handed it off to Ellie who propped the weapon in the corner and accepted the proffered drink. She took a deep inhale of it while shuffling to the refrigerator for cream.

"Thanks. I think I need this, though the adrenaline coursing through my veins is doing a good job at waking me up."

A knock sounded at the door as she poured the light liquid into the dark coffee.

"That'd be Mac," Rick said, sliding past her and heading for the hall. "Hope he brought the donuts."

"Donuts?" Ellie questioned, shooting a glance toward Mia. "What's going on?"

"Well–" Mia said with a crinkled nose and a raise of one shoulder as she spun to fiddle with the dirty dishes in the sink.

"He came prepared," Rick interrupted as he carried a large brown box into the kitchen and set it down on the table.

Mac appeared in the doorway with Cleo and Lola following him. "That I did. Exactly as I was asked."

"Asked?" Ellie inquired after a sip of her coffee.

Another knock sounded at the door, and Lola raced toward it barking. "I can't believe you got in here without Lola screaming at you," Ellie shouted over the noise as she shuffled to the door.

"I knew it was Sheriff Rick," Lola answered. "I don't know who this is."

Ellie rolled her eyes. "You couldn't have told me that before I crept down the stairs and confronted the sheriff with a rifle?"

Lola wagged her tail, her lower teeth showing between her lips in an awkward smile. Ellie shook her head at the dog as she pulled the door open and eyed the visitor.

"Morning," Nathan said with a nod of his head. "Donuts here yet?"

"Yeah, just got here. Come on in," Ellie said, standing back and waving him in with a furrowed brow.

She paraded down the hall behind him with Lola in tow and pushed into the crowded kitchen.

"Hey, I'm hungry," Cleo said from the counter as Nathan grabbed a chocolate frosted donut from the box.

Mia poured him a cup of coffee, handing it off. Another knock sounded at the door.

Ellie blew out an exasperated breath. "I'll get your food as soon as I answer the door. What is going on here?"

She marched down the hall and pulled the door open again. Jake stood on the porch, hands shoved into his khakis and rocking on his heels next to Hazel.

The blonde grinned at her and waved a takeout bag. "Oh, hi, Ellie. I got the breakfast sandwiches."

"Breakfast sandwiches?" Ellie asked as Hazel darted past her into the foyer, followed by Jake.

They proceeded down to the kitchen where Mia handed out filled bowls to both animals and Rick distributed coffees.

"Those the sandwiches?" he asked.

"Yep," Hazel answered with a nod. "Oh, did you get me a jelly donut?"

"I did, Hazel," Mac said from his seat at the table. "On the left."

Jake dove into the bag of sandwiches. "Okay, who had the one with sausage?"

"That's me," Nathan answered, raising his hand. Jake passed it off to him, pulling out another and handing it to Rick.

"Bacon with scrambled egg and cheese for Ellie," he said, passing the wrapped sandwich to her.

She accepted it, her gaze flitting around the room at everyone standing in her kitchen. Her brows knit, and she waved her hands in the air. "Okay, wait. Will someone tell me what's going on here?"

All eyes turned to Mia. The blonde swallowed hard, flipping her braid over her shoulder. "I may have texted Rick last night when Toby showed up."

Ellie's eyes darted from side to side. "Okay?"

Mac slapped a hand on the table. "We're here to support you, Ellie. He can't just walk back in here and take advantage of you. We love you too much to let that happen. We want him to know you've got friends." He jabbed a finger at her. "A lot of 'em. And in high places too."

Ellie eased into a kitchen chair and blinked hard. She let her gaze scan the crowd again. "You all came here because Toby showed up last night?"

Nods met her question.

Rick wagged a finger at her, the wrapper on his open, half-eaten sandwich flapping in the air. "And to let him know that no one walks into Salem Falls without the law knowing. If he so much as sneezes the wrong way, we're all over it."

Tears formed in her eyes, and she glanced down at the coffee in her mug as she let her emotions settle.

"Ellie, why are you crying?" Lola asked.

"Yeah, Ellie," Cleo said. "They did something nice for you. Even the dumb, old sheriff is trying."

"This is just…" Ellie licked her lips and sniffled. "Really nice."

Mia offered her a tight-lipped smile and wrapped an arm around her shoulders. "We just wanted you to know we are here for you. And if he tries anything, we won't let him get away with it."

"Yeah," Rick said with a bob of his head. "All of us. He even so much as takes an extra napkin at dinner, you tell us and we'll lock him up. Nobody takes advantage of one of my residents."

"Thanks, everyone. I really appreciate this. Toby showing up was jarring. This makes it better." Ellie grabbed one of the donuts and bit into it. "So does this."

They shared a chuckle before the conversation turned to general topics about the B&B's upcoming opening.

"So, Mac," Mia said as she poured another cup of coffee, "we did a little poking around last night and stumbled across a pretty interesting website called Salem Falls' Secrets."

A collective groan went up around the room.

"Well, that got a reaction," Ellie said with a chuckle.

Nathan grabbed another donut and settled against the counter. "Some of us don't like that website."

"Don't like it is an understatement," Hazel said. "Some of us sued the person over it. But we lost."

"Oh really?" Ellie asked. "Sued to have it taken down?"

Hazel nodded and shifted her gaze to Mac. "Yeah, but…

someone defended the author, and he was allowed to keep it up."

Mac held a hand up in the air. "Now, now, everyone has the right to freedom of speech."

"Well, I'm glad Mac won," Mia answered as she settled into a chair at the table. "I found it extremely interesting. I will never go into the house on Main Street, and I would like to find the treasure."

"Wait, I thought you didn't believe there was anything here?" Ellie interjected.

Mia shrugged as she sipped her coffee. "I changed my mind. After a good night's sleep, I agree with you. It's somewhere. Someone stole it and put it somewhere and it's never been found."

Jake tapped around on his phone and scrolled. "Whoa, Pizzaro's Pendant is one of the items?"

Ellie poked a finger at him. "And that's the exact one that made Mia think it was a bunch of bunk."

"Pizzaro's Pendant was the biggest item in that stash, but there are a number of things that he stole that never turned up," Mac said, leaning back in his chair with his arms crossed.

"Pizzaro's Pendant is a legend. It's a myth," Ellie answered. "Like the fountain of youth or...whatever else those conquistador guys searched for."

"City of Gold," Jake answered.

"Right," Ellie said with a nod, "and none of those existed."

"That we know of," Jake answered. "But wasn't Pizzaro's Pendant given to him by the Incas? It's less legendary and more factual."

"It's a story, probably based on something real, but embellished to the point of being ridiculous. Come on, gold so thick you can't wear it?" Ellie scoffed.

"Wait, wait, wait," Mia said, waving a half-eaten donut in

the air, "you wanted to find this last night, and now you're all against it!"

"I had a good…well, no, I had a terrible night's sleep, but during my tossing and turning, I gave your argument some thought and agreed."

Mac waved his hand in the air between them. "Ladies, ladies, please. There's no need to argue. I can settle this bet. The treasure is real. And it's hidden somewhere in Salem Falls, possibly right in this very house."

"If it's really hidden here, what are the chances no one has found it?" Ellie asked. "And even better, what are the chances *we* find it?"

Mac shrugged, settling his arms against his chest again. "That I can't tell you. But what I can say is you may want to try."

Ellie flicked her eyebrows up as Hazel jumped into the conversation. "If you read through that page last night, you know that everyone who hasn't found the treasure here has died. So, if you don't find it, you'll be next."

CHAPTER 7

Silence filled the room as the indirect threat hung heavy in the air.

"Whoa," Mia finally breathed out.

Hazel shook her head, her curls bouncing. "Oh, I didn't mean that to sound so bad. I was just saying, it may be a good idea to search for it."

"I think this curse thing is a bunch of bunk," Ellie replied. "I don't mind looking for it, but I'm not going to stress out over it.

Mac wagged a finger at her. "That's the way to be, Ellie. There's no reason to think anything bad's going to happen to you."

"Sure. I mean, so what if all the last owners died in really mysterious ways," Hazel said. "Doesn't mean you will."

Ellie crinkled her nose at the statement as her mind went through the various, odd, life-ending scenarios of the previous owners.

"You're dead meat," Cleo said before licking a paw and raking it over her face.

Lola leapt onto her hind legs and planted her front paws on Ellie's leg. "No, Ellie, you can't die. I'd miss you."

"Well, I'm certainly not planning on dying anytime soon. Treasure or no treasure," Ellie answered with a curt nod. "Curses be darned."

The conversation drew to an abrupt close as Toby wandered, yawning and raking his hands through his unruly hair.

"Oh, hey, everyone." He slid his eyes sideways to Ellie, offering a nervous chuckle. "Did the B&B open already?"

"Everyone, this is Toby Larson, my ex-husband." Ellie cleared her throat and licked her lips. "Toby, these are a few of Salem Falls' finest residents."

"And you all go to other people's houses at six in the morning?"

The group went silent, all eyes on the newcomer. Rick stepped forward, his coffee in one hand and adjusting his belt with the other. "Just friends stopping over for some breakfast."

"Oh, okay," Toby answered, wandering to the coffee pot and grabbing a mug. "Interesting accent you got there. Not from around here, huh?"

"Nope," Rick answered with narrowed eyes.

"Rick's our transplant from Georgia," Mac answered.

Toby took a sip of the black coffee and nodded. "That explains the accent then."

"Yep," Rick said.

Cleo sat straighter, peering at Rick. "This is the first time I have ever liked the sheriff."

"So, what brought you up north?"

Rick sucked in a breath. "Needed a change. Had a nightmare about my town being overrun by zombies. Just figured it was a sign to get out. I found this little gem and have been here ever since. I run a real tight town, too. No trouble. You understand?"

Toby sipped at his coffee again, side-eying the sheriff. "Yeah. I understand. I think." He eyed the donuts. "These look good."

"Why don't you grab one and take it up to your room?" Mia suggested.

"Uh, sure. Actually, El, could I speak with you?" He shot a glance over his shoulder at the full kitchen. "Alone?"

"Do you need something, Toby?"

"Yeah, to speak with you alone."

"Whatever you have to say, you can say it here."

Toby chewed his lower lip as he scanned the crowd again. "Okay, uh, just wanted to make sure it's okay that I stay the week. I, uh, I'm getting the impression that may not be okay."

Ellie stared into her coffee, her fingers tapping the side of the mug. "I said until the end of the week." She flicked her gaze up to him. "And I meant that."

"Great." He scanned the other occupants in the room. "Say, uh, anyone know of anybody in town looking for a worker? I'm a go-getter."

"Certainly seems like you are the way you got that other woman," Hazel said.

Toby pressed his lips together as Nathan smacked her on the shoulder with the back of his hand. "Hazel," he hissed.

"What? He did!"

Rick laid his hand on his weapon. "Why don't you stop by the sheriff's office later today? We can get some information from you and pass it along to any interested residents."

"Ah, sure, I can do that," Toby said with a bob of his head. He ran his fingers through his hair before he snagged a donut. "And if anyone's hiring, just let me know. I'll do anything. Beggars can't be choosers, right?"

"You got that right," Hazel said with a nod.

"Right," Toby murmured as he eyed them again. "Great group. Real fun."

He disappeared from the room, and Ellie let her head fall back between her shoulders with a heavy sigh. "I'm sorry."

"There's nothing to apologize for, Ellie," Mac said with a shake of his head.

"No, just because your ex is a loser, doesn't mean we'd lower our opinion of you," Hazel said, patting her hand. "We all make mistakes."

"He was a huge, long, painful mistake," Ellie said.

Nathan patted her shoulder. "I think what you're doing for him is really nice. I wouldn't do it if he was my ex."

"Thanks, Nathan." Ellie let her gaze roam around the group. "I'm sorry for him putting you on the spot like that with the job."

"Nothing to worry about," Rick answered. "I can handle him."

"You know," Mac said, pointing a finger at Rick, "Val's hiring a cook. If he keeps pestering you, send him there. She knows how to keep someone in line."

"I'll consider it. I'd just as soon want him out of Salem Falls. For all our sakes. I don't trust him."

"Neither do I," Mia answered. "So, I'll be keeping my eye on him, too. But I appreciate you all helping us."

"Of course," Rick answered with a smile. "Well, we better be getting along. If he gives you any trouble, just give us a holler."

"Will do," Ellie said as Hazel rose from her seat at the table and followed the two officers toward the door.

The front door banged shut, and Jake slid into the seat left by Hazel. "Can we go back to talking about the treasure?"

"Wow," Ellie said with a grin, "you're really into this."

"Sounds cool. And I remember reading about Pizzaro's Pendant in school."

"Like yesterday?" Mia said with a coy grin.

"It wasn't quite that recent," Jake answered with a chuckle. "But I'm down to help if you want to look into it. I can do some research on it. I'll use it for a story in the town's paper."

Ellie sipped her coffee. "You don't have to do that."

"I'm actually short a story this week, so I need something to work on. If you don't mind, that is."

"I don't mind," Ellie said, spinning her coffee mug around on the table. "Let us know what you find."

Jake drained his coffee. "Will do. I'm heading to the library to do some research now. I'll email you anything I find."

"Thanks, Jake," Ellie said as he set his mug in the sink and flipped on the faucet. "Oh, just leave that. I'll get it."

"You sure?"

"Yeah. I'm sure I'll have to wash Toby's anyway. What's one more?"

"Okay, thanks. Talk to you later." He waved before he disappeared into the hall.

"Well, time for me to take a nap," Cleo said with a yawn. She leapt off the counter and slinked toward the sunroom. "Wake me if you find anything interesting. Doubt it, though."

"If you don't mind," Lola said as Ellie closed the donut box and rose with her empty mug in her hand, "I'm heading to the sunroom for a nap, too."

"Looks like it's time for us to do some work," Mia said, collecting Mac's mug and her own.

"I should get out of your hair," Mac answered. "Let me know if you need any help, though. I can run anything out from town that you need."

"Thanks, Mac. I'll let you know. I think it's just a few odds and ends, though. Then we should be ready for tomorrow."

"Good luck, Ellie," Mac said with a grin. "See you later."

Ellie rinsed off her mug and set it in the drainer where Mia scooped it to dry.

"Are you excited?"

"About what?" Ellie murmured with a sigh.

"About your colonoscopy. What do you think?"

"Oh, you mean the opening. Yeah, I guess so."

Mia shoved the mug onto its spot on the shelf and returned to collect another one. "You don't sound excited."

Ellie slapped the handle on the faucet and grabbed a dish towel to wipe her hands. "I am. I just…I don't know. I have a bad feeling."

"About the opening?" Mia asked as she shoved the last mug into the cupboard and swung it shut.

Ellie tossed the towel on the counter and nodded with a wrinkled nose.

"Why? It'll be great. You've put so much work into the plan and the party. Everyone who's read it thinks it's fantastic!"

Ellie sucked in a breath. "We'll see. But I just have this niggling feeling in the pit of my stomach that something is off."

Mia waved a hand in the air as she draped her wet towel over the oven handle. "You're just freaked out by all the weird tales we've heard in the past twenty-four hours, *and* Toby's sudden reappearance probably threw you off."

"Ugh, don't remind me. I spent half the night wondering why I'd been so stupid as to let him stay here."

"Me too," Mia said before she stuck her tongue out at her friend.

"Very funny." Ellie shuffled down the hall to the foyer. "I'm going to change, and then put the finishing touches on everything for tomorrow."

"I'll help," Mia said as they reached the top of the stairs.

"Thanks, Mia. There's not too much left, but I appreciate the help."

"Of course." Mia squeezed her hand before she disappeared into her room. "And hey, don't beat yourself up. You did a nice thing for Toby, even though he didn't deserve it. That just means you're a fantastic, fabulous person."

Ellie smiled at her and squeezed her hand. "Thanks. Okay, see you in a jiffy."

She darted into her bedroom and peeled off her robe, tossing it on the bed before she gathered clothes for the day from the dresser.

"I don't care what Mia says, I still think you're stupid," Cleo's voice said from under the bed.

Ellie whipped around, leaning to scan the dark space. "I thought you were in the sunroom."

"I came up here. Lola's snoring again."

"I see. Well, thanks for your input. What's done is done."

Cleo crawled up from under the bed and sat on the edge of the area rug, curling her tail around her legs. "That's where I disagree. Get rid of him. He's trouble."

"Wow, don't hold back, Cleo. Tell me what you really think."

"I just did. Can't you hear?"

"It's a figure of speech," Ellie said as she slipped into her pants.

"The way he showed up out of the blue. I'm starting to think this place really is cursed. And you're about to be the next victim."

Ellie arched an eyebrow before buttoning her flannel. "That's dire."

"It is. But it's because I care. I don't want to see you dead. Lying in a pool of your own blood with wide eyes and a shocked expression on your face."

"Ew, Cleo!" Ellie huffed as she dropped onto the edge of the bed to pull her shoes on.

"I'm just trying to prepare you." Cleo opened her mouth in a wide yawn. "Oh, this conversation has taken it all out of me. I'm going back to sleep. Try not to get yourself killed."

She slid back under the bed and disappeared. Ellie shook her head at the cat, though the words stung her in the wake of her unsettled feeling. She squeezed her eyes closed and sucked in a deep breath, trying to shove the uneasiness aside.

A knock pulled her away from her thoughts. She snapped her eyes open and focused on the figure in the door. "Hey, El," Toby said, leaning against the jam.

"Here we go. Don't let him kill you," Cleo called from under her.

Ellie raised her gaze to the ceiling in a silent plea for strength. "Look, Toby, I'm pretty busy, so if you don't mind…"

"Actually, I do," he answered. "It won't take long."

Ellie heaved a sigh and rose to her feet. "Fine. What is it?"

"I think we need to talk. I feel like we left things unfinished. The divorce was so messy, and that was my fault. I listened to that lawyer that Gloria hired who pushed me to do things I shouldn't have done."

"That's on you."

"Yeah, I get that. And I'm trying to take ownership for that but…El, you gotta understand, my head wasn't right."

"You got that right, loser," Cleo chimed in from under the bed.

"You got that right," Ellie said.

"That's what I just said," Cleo added.

"I feel so stupid now. And I'm trying to apologize."

Ellie flicked her gaze to the floor as she crossed her arms. "I'm not sure I can honestly say apology accepted, but I'd really just like to move on."

"I'm trying to make it up to you."

She snapped her gaze up to him. "Don't bother. I'm counting our divorce as one of the best things that's happened to me. Without it, I wouldn't have the opportunity I have right now. So, I guess let's just call it even."

Toby ran his hands through his hair before sticking them on his hips. "Yeah, that's the thing though. I'm not so sure this is an opportunity. El, I think this is the worst thing you could possibly do. I think it's going to kill you."

CHAPTER 8

"*W*hat?" Ellie asked, fluttering her eyelashes at him. "Are you serious?"

Toby bobbed his head up and down. "Yes, I am. I think this is a terrible idea. I think your aunt closed the business for a reason. And then she ended up dead."

Ellie slid her eyes closed and shook her head. "Get out, Toby."

"Ellie, you don't have a business mind. You're not made that way. You take everything personally. Look at our divorce."

"Oh, I'm sorry I took our divorce personally. It felt oddly personal when you left me for another woman."

"That's not what I meant, and you know it. This is exactly why our marriage fell apart. You insist on being difficult."

Ellie scowled as she slid her eyes closed. "Look, Toby, you can stay until the end of the week, but your opinion on my life is no longer wanted or welcomed. Stay out of my way, leave me alone, get back on your feet, and get out."

"You tell him, Ellie!" Cleo cheered from under the bed as Ellie pushed past him into the hall.

Mia waited for her outside. "I didn't want to interrupt, although I was ready to charge in there until you told him what's what."

Ellie sucked in a breath as Toby pushed past them, hurrying down the hall toward the stairs leading up to his third-floor bedroom. "He's really making me regret being a nice person."

"Kick him out. Oh, wait, let me do it," Mia answered, clasping her hands together under her chin and grinning.

Ellie chuckled in spite of herself. "I told him he can stay, so he can stay. But I want no parts of him. I'm done. Let's just work on what we need to do."

They spent the afternoon putting the finishing touches on the place to welcome the guests the following day. When they collapsed on the couch with take-out containers in the early evening, Ellie heaved a sigh. "Well, that's it. Now just one more sleepless night before we officially open our doors."

"Sleepless night? With all that work? I think I'll be out like a light in seconds."

"I'm sure I'll lay awake worrying about something," Ellie answered as she popped the lid on her linguini.

"You still have a bad feeling?"

Ellie spiraled her fork, twirling noodles around the tines. "Yeah. But maybe it's just nerves. You know, what if someone complains? What if my first rating is a one-star that trashes the place? What if–"

"And what if everything goes right because you're a hell of a businesswoman and really good at this stuff? Stop looking for problems that aren't there yet."

"You're right."

"And if you're having a sleepless night. Come get me, and we'll search for this treasure."

Ellie poked a fork at her friend. "Deal."

"I don't understand this treasure thing," Cleo said from her perch on the back of the couch. "I crawl into all the dark places, and I never saw it."

"So, do you think there's a hidden room in here some-where?" Ellie questioned.

Cleo lifted her chin. "Oh, I get it. A hidden room. I bet it's a great place for naps."

Lola wagged her tail from her spot near the fireplace. "A hidden room? Really?"

"That would be something. I wonder if there is. We should poke around after the party this weekend."

"Or when I can't sleep tonight."

Cleo began to purr. "Yeah, find the hidden room, Ellie. I'd like to try it out for a nap. All my regular spots are getting old."

They finished their meal, discussing various potential locations for the hidden treasure. After they pitched the take-out containers and enjoyed a warm cup of tea, they headed for bed.

Ellie blew out a sigh as she stared up at the ceiling. "I'm never going to sleep. Who was I kidding?"

Cleo's eyes glowed in the dark as she opened them to slits. "Least you could do is keep it down. The rest of us *can* sleep."

"Sorry," Ellie grumbled. She rolled onto her side and stared out at the moonless night. Where would they have put the treasure? Did they get it from nearby? The train station ran through town. Maybe the robbery locations would form a clue.

With a deep sigh, Ellie shoved the covers back and tugged her robe around her shoulders as she rose. She hurried bare-foot across the cold floor and down the stairs, retrieving her laptop from the coffee table in the living room.

She froze in the darkened space when noise sounded

on the porch. Ellie tightened the tie of her robe and tiptoed to the doorway, remaining hidden behind the wall. Something scraped against the door before the knob started to turn.

Her heart skipped a beat. The scratching noise sounded again before the door burst open. Ellie squinted into the darkness as a figure stalked across the threshold.

She caught a whiff of Toby's aftershave. Her shoulders slumped with both relief and irritation. At least it was only Toby, but could the man be any more inconsiderate?

He blew out a long breath while he fiddled with his jacket before he hung it in the coat closet near the door. As he crossed to the stairs, something fluttered to the floor below him. The sound of it smacking off the hardwood was covered by a belch from Toby.

Ellie puckered her lips and shook her head at him, suddenly glad they were divorced.

She waited until his footsteps started up the steps to the third floor before she ducked out of the living room and snatched the paper from the floor.

Writing filled it but she couldn't read it in the dim light. She pocketed it and hurried up the steps to her bedroom. After easing the doors shut behind her, she flicked on the overhead light.

"Hey!" Cleo complained with squinted eyes. "What are you doing?"

"Toby just came in and dropped something. I want to see what it is."

Cleo raised her nose in the air. "Yeah, I smelled him. He stinks. Like fried food and onions."

"Eww," Ellie said with a grimace.

"It's true," Lola agreed, lifting her head from the bed and wagging her tail. "The note smells like more than Toby, though."

"Oh, yeah? What's it smell like?" Ellie held the paper out to the dog's nose.

Her nose wiggled as she sniffed at it. "Another person. I don't know who. I've never smelled them before."

"Male or female?"

"What?" Lola asked.

"Idiot," Cleo murmured before she stretched her paw out and gave a wide yawn.

"Boy or girl?" Ellie tried as she tossed the laptop onto the bed.

"Oh…ummm, I'd have better luck smelling their butt to know that."

"I don't know why you talk to her," Cleo said, rolling onto her other side.

Ellie climbed onto the bed and tugged the laptop onto her lap. She flicked on her bedside lamp and picked up the paper. Writing pressed through from inside. She unfolded the page and stared at the scrawled writing, squinting.

"Put your glasses on, Grandma," Cleo said.

Ellie glared at her. "It's not that. It's all smeared. Like it got wet and the ink ran."

"Let me see," Cleo said, opening her eyes wider.

Ellie flashed the paper toward her.

"Oh, yeah. It looks like nothing."

Ellie spun the paper back toward her and studied it. "Told you."

"Of course, all writing looks like nothing to me."

Ellie shot her an irritated glance and shook her head before she returned to staring at the page. She shoved the laptop off her lap and hopped off the bed.

"What are you doing, Ellie?" Lola asked, her tail wagging.

"I have an idea."

"What is it? Throw the paper away because it's useless?" Cleo asked.

"No," Ellie answered as she tugged the dresser drawer open and rooted around inside. She pulled a notepad and pencil from it before she returned to the bed and plopped on it. She lifted a sheet and shoved Toby's note underneath. She flattened the top sheet down and rubbed it with a pencil.

Charcoal gray strokes filled the sheet but she couldn't make out any words. She lifted the page, pulled the note from under it, and stared at the sheet below. She rubbed the pencil against it before she tossed them aside with a sigh. "Well, that was a bust."

"That was the dumbest idea I've ever seen," Cleo said.

"It works on TV."

"When someone rips the top sheet off and there are indentations on the one below, duh," Cleo said before she licked a paw and rubbed her face.

Ellie puckered her lips as she glared at the cat. She snatched the paper back and erased away the pencil marks before she studied it again. She grabbed the pencil and traced a few of the indentations.

Her forehead crinkled as she went over one particular word again.

"You're going to give yourself wrinkles," Cleo said. "Then you're going to look like Lola."

Ellie gave her a sideways glance. "Lola's cute."

"Yeah, but you won't be."

"I'm working on something. It helps me concentrate."

"What? Did you figure something out?"

"I think so. I'm not sure, though. I'm going to run it past Mia tomorrow."

"Tell us now. I'll never sleep tonight if you don't let us in on the know," Cleo said.

Ellie bit her lower lip and stared down at the sheet. "I think this word is 'pendant.'"

Cleo's eyes went wide. "Like Pizzaro's Pendant."

Ellie raised a shoulder. "Maybe. It would seem like it. Which begs the question, what is Toby doing with that on a list?"

"Do you think he's here to steal it?" Lola asked.

"We don't even know it's here to steal," Cleo shot back.

Ellie set the list on her nightstand and shook her head. "I'm not sure, but I wouldn't put anything past him."

She tugged open her laptop and settled in for some research.

Lola rose to her feet. "What are you doing, Ellie?"

"I'm going to research where the robberies were and see if I can figure out a pattern."

Lola's tail wagged as she stood staring at her.

"What?" Ellie asked, glancing up from the search engine's website.

"I have to go potty."

"Now?" Ellie asked. "You're normally asleep now."

"If I was asleep, I wouldn't have to go, but you woke me up, and now I feel like I have to go."

Ellie heaved a sigh and slammed the laptop shut before shifting it off her lap. "Fine. I won't get any research done with you two around."

"Sorry, Ellie," Lola said, her face wrinkling more.

"It's okay. How can I say no to that face?"

"You could, but then you'd probably be washing the sheets," Cleo answered.

Ellie wrinkled her nose at the comment. "Come on, Lola. It's okay."

The dog leapt off the bed and clopped her way across the floor and down the stairs. Ellie followed behind her and crossed the foyer to the front door. "Idiot didn't even lock it," she muttered as she tugged open the front door.

Lola hurried outside into the cool, fall air with her nose pressed into the ground. Ellie nestled tighter into her robe as she stepped onto the porch. Lola sniffed around on the ground before her head shot up. She sniffed in the air before letting out a sharp bark.

"Lola!" Ellie called from the porch. "Stop that barking. There is *nothing* there to bark at."

"There is," Lola said.

"What? An owl?"

Lola's nose wiggled. "No, it's not an owl. I smell a person."

Ellie's heart skipped a beat, and she peered into the darkness. "Come up here."

Lola gave another fierce string of barks into the night air.

"Lola! Stop that! Get up here."

Lola wagged her tail as she glanced over her shoulder at Ellie. "Someone's out there."

"Okay," Ellie said as she hurried down off the porch and shoved Lola back toward it. "Someone's there. I believe you. Didn't you learn anything from the last time you went after someone in the woods?"

"Of course, I did. I learned–"

A loud pop cut off the rest of the comment, followed by a crack. Ellie instinctively ducked, shielding Lola with her body as she glanced back at the woods.

She spotted no one. Lola struggled against her, offering a few more yips.

"What was that, Ellie?" Lola asked.

Ellie glanced at the railing on the porch, narrowing her eyes in the dim moonlight at a splintered piece. "I think someone just shot at us."

CHAPTER 9

*E*llie's eyes remained affixed to the bullet hole piercing the wood of the railing.

"Like with a gun?" Lola asked.

"Yes, exactly like that. Go back inside." She shooed the dog closer to the house, still bent over after ducking.

"No way," Lola answered. "I'm not leaving you out here alone."

"Lola, I don't want you hurt!"

"I don't want you hurt, either. Maybe you should go back inside."

Ellie glanced back toward the woods with a grimace. "Maybe we should both go back inside."

"Wait, I still have to go potty."

"Well, hurry up. You should have gone when you first came out instead of sniffing around and barking."

"I can't help it," Lola answered, "I smelled someone."

Ellie stood on the first stair to the porch with her arms wrapped around her. "Yeah, a person with a gun, too."

Lola finished her business, and Ellie waved her onto the porch. "Come on, come on."

The dog trundled her way up the steps, stopping to sniff at the splintered railing. Ellie shoved at her. "Go, go. I don't want to be out here any longer than we have to."

"Sorry, Ellie," Lola said as she ran onto the porch and spun to face her.

Ellie pulled the door open and ushered the dog inside before she slipped in and slammed it shut behind her. With a flick of the lock, she breathed out a sigh of relief. "I'm calling Sheriff Rick. This is the last thing we need right before the opening tomorrow."

Lola wagged her tail. "I like Sheriff Rick."

"I like him, too," Ellie said as she started up the stairs, "but I don't like that I have to call him because someone shot at us."

"Cleo doesn't like him at all," Lola said, trailing behind her.

"I know. But I think she's coming around. You know who else likes him?"

"Who?" Lola asked, her forehead wrinkling as they walked into the room.

Ellie offered the dog a coy grin. "Mia. I think there is something going on between them."

"Oooh, gossip," Cleo said, her green eyes popping open. "Mia and Sheriff Rick sitting in a tree?"

"Maybe," Ellie answered, snatching her phone off her charging pad. She tapped the screen to find the number for the police station and pressed the call button.

"Salem Falls Sheriff's Department, how can I help you?"

"Nathan?" Ellie asked. "It's Ellie."

"Hey, Ellie, what's up?"

"I didn't know you were on the night shift tonight. I could have texted you."

"Got trouble? Is it your ex?"

"No," Ellie said with a shake of her head. "Not Toby, but I think someone just shot at me."

"What?" Nathan questioned, his voice sharp. "Are you hurt?"

"I'm not hurt. I think the bullet's lodged in my railing, though. I just want to report it."

"I'm coming right over. Stay inside, keep your doors locked."

"Okay, thanks," Ellie said before ending the call.

Lola stood on the bed, her tail wagging. "Is Sheriff Rick coming?"

"No, Deputy Nathan," Ellie answered, setting her phone on the charging pad again and drumming her fingers on the dresser. "So much for my research."

"You got shot at, and I had to hear it in a conversation with the police?" Cleo asked.

"I'm sorry I didn't tell you, but I figured calling the police was more important than informing my cat."

Cleo narrowed her eyes at Ellie. "That was your first mistake. Although, I don't mind." She stood and stretched before settling onto her haunches and licking a paw. She dragged it over her face a few times before shaking her head. "How do I look?"

"Fine," Ellie answered.

Lola nosed at her. "You smell like you always do."

"Stop it." Cleo batted at the dog with her paw. "Did she mess up my fur?"

Ellie shook her head. "No, it's fine."

"Better not have."

"Why are you being so fussy?" Ellie questioned, checking the time on her phone as sirens sounded in the distance.

"She likes Nathan," Lola answered, her tail wagging faster.

"Shut up."

Ellie's lips curled into an amused grin. "No. Really? You like Nathan."

Cleo wrapped her tail around her legs and narrowed her eyes. "I will admit he is easy on the eyes."

Ellie doubled over, covering her mouth to hold in a chuckle. "Oh my gosh, my cat thinks the deputy is hot."

"I didn't say hot," Cleo said. "He's passable. I don't mind him."

"Oh, right. Of course," Ellie said with a nod. "Passable. You have good taste, Cleo. He's a very handsome man."

"And he's nice, too," Lola said. "He always pets me."

The sirens approached closer and red and blue lights lit the trees outside. "Come on, girls," Ellie said, shuffling from the room, "time to ogle the Deputy."

Cleo sailed off the bed and stalked down the stairs next to Lola. A knock sounded at the door, and Lola let out a bark. "Sheriff."

Ellie heaved a sigh, letting her hand slap against her thigh as she unlocked the door. "You know who it is!"

"Oh, yeah," Lola said, her lower teeth poking out in an upside-down smile.

Ellie pulled the door open, finding Nathan and another deputy outside. "Hey, Ellie. You sure you're okay?"

"Yeah, yeah, I'm fine, come in."

"Hi, Nathan," Lola said with a wag of her tail.

Nathan and the other deputy stalked through the door. He leaned down to pat Lola's head. Cleo leapt to her feet and rubbed against his leg. "Oh, hi, kitty. You're friendly tonight."

Cleo shook a paw at the statement and stalked into the living room.

Nathan shrugged and tugged a notebook from his pocket. "What can you tell me about the incident?"

"Well," Ellie answered, wrapping her arms around herself, "I couldn't sleep. I was going to do a little research on our treasure project, but Lola had to go out. I took her outside, and she started barking at something."

Nathan glanced down at the dog who wagged her tail again. "Smelled something, huh, girl?"

"Yes, a human," Lola answered.

He turned his attention back to Ellie, his pen at the ready. "And then someone shot at you?"

"Basically, yes. I just finished telling Lola there was nothing to bark at when we heard a crack. I think the bullet got lodged in the railing."

"Do you remember what time it was?" Nathan questioned.

"Uh, it was about quarter to twelve."

Nathan jotted down the time. "Anything else? Any other details you can remember?"

"No. I didn't see anyone or anything."

Nathan stared down at his notes for a moment before he flicked his gaze to Ellie. "Are you normally out at that time of the night?"

"No. I was having trouble sleeping probably due to the opening tomorrow. I got up to poke around on the web and that woke Lola."

"Got it."

Ellie wiggled a finger in the air. "Oh, one other thing that may or may not be related. Toby came in shortly before this happened."

"Okay, so we know it wasn't him."

"Right," Ellie said, wrapping her arms around herself. "Well, unless he sneaked out, but I didn't hear him. But when he came in, he dropped a note not in his handwriting, so he was meeting with someone."

Nathan nodded. "What did the note say?"

"I couldn't read it. It had gotten wet, and the ink smeared. I tried to figure it out but couldn't."

"Okay. Do you still have the note?"

"Yeah, let me grab it."

"Thanks," Nathan said with a nod as she hurried up the stairs to grab it.

She returned, waving it in the air. "Sorry, I wrote on it when I was trying to figure out what it said."

Nathan smoothed it out on his notepad and studied it. "The pencil marks are yours, then?"

Ellie nodded.

Nathan waved it in the air. "Can I keep this?"

"Uhh, mind if I make a copy first? Sorry, I just know I'll want to look at it later."

"Sure. It's your property. Well, technically, I guess it was Toby's but...sure." Nathan offered her a broad smile as he handed it back. "We'll go take a look at the railing while you're doing that."

"Okay, meet you out there." Ellie grabbed the paper and hurried back up the stairs and down the hall.

"Ellie, do you think they'll catch the person?" Lola asked as she trailed behind her on the stairs leading to the third floor.

"I'm not sure. I hope so."

"Who do you think it could be?"

Ellie pushed into the office and lifted the copier's lid, pressing the paper onto the glass before she pushed the button to copy. "I don't know. Andy?"

"The grocery man?" Lola asked, her forehead wrinkled.

"Yeah, him. He threatened me. Maybe he's trying to scare me into not opening."

"That's mean."

"Yeah, well," Ellie said as the paper slid out onto the tray, "the world's not a nice place. Come on."

She grabbed the original from the machine and shuffled

from the room with Lola in tow. She came to an abrupt stop as she pulled the door to the office closed.

"Hey, El," Toby said as he stood in just his jeans. "Hey, did you see a little piece of paper with some notes on it? I think I dropped it coming in."

Ellie slid the note into the paper and folded it around the sheet, stuffing both in her pocket. "No."

Toby puckered his lips, glancing down the hall. "I could have sworn I dropped it in here. What are you doing up?"

"Lola had to go outside, and then someone shot at us. The police are downstairs. I was just making a copy of something for Nathan."

Toby's brow furrowed. "What? Are you kidding me?"

"Nope, I'm not. Now, if you'll excuse me…" She tried to step past him when he darted in front of her.

"Whoa, wait a minute, El. Are you okay?"

Fury burned through her at his supposed concern. She set her jaw and shook her head. "I'm fine. Now, get out of my way."

She skirted around him and continued to the stairs. Before descending them, she shot a glance over her shoulder. "Hey, Toby?"

"Yeah?" he asked, spinning to face her.

"Put a shirt on. This is about to be a B&B. No one wants to see your beer gut."

She took a step onto the first stair when Cleo's voice echoed up from the bottom of the steps. "Oh, snap!"

Lola clopped down the stairs after her, meeting Cleo at the bottom.

The cat arched her back and shook her tail as they continued past her down the hall. "Dang, Ellie, you finally got a backbone and told him good."

"It's true, and I'm sick of him with his fake concern. Where was he when I nearly went bankrupt and lost my home? Suing me to make sure that happened. Well, he can stuff it." She thundered down the stairs, tightening her robe's tie before she headed out the door. Lola and Cleo followed onto the porch, squinting at the bright light shining toward the house from the police cruiser.

Nathan's assistant knelt on the ground near the railing, prying at it with a pocketknife.

"Here's the note," Ellie said, pulling it from her pocket. "Sorry it's a little crumpled, but Toby caught me in the hall, and I didn't want him to know I was passing this along to you."

"Did he say anything to you?"

"Yeah, he actually asked for this note. I told him I hadn't seen it," she said as she handed the paper over.

Nathan flicked his eyebrows up. "Oh, really? Sounds important to him."

"Seems to be. But it's hard to tell with him. You can't trust Toby as far as you can throw him. He's a proven liar."

Nathan pressed his lips together into a tight-lipped smile and shoved the note into an evidence bag.

Ellie glanced down at the railing. "Did you find anything?"

"Yep, there's something in here all right."

"Is it a bullet?" she questioned, pushing her hair behind her ear as she squinted at it.

A brass nugget worked its way from the wood, urged by the tip of the deputy's knife. "That it is," he said as he grabbed it with gloved hands and held it up.

Ellie's stomach turned over as she realized she had, in fact, been shot at.

"Looks like it's from a rifle," the deputy said.

Nathan bobbed his head up and down. "Yeah."

"Who has a gun like that?" Ellie asked.

"Lots of people. Rifles are popular," Nathan said. "We can

run a ballistics report and see if we can match it to the type of rifle used. That may help us narrow it down."

Ellie ran her fingers through her hair. "Then you can track it, right? You can look up who has a gun like that in town?"

"Depends. Some people have guns that are generations old. They weren't registered back in the day. It also could come from someone out of town. There's no way of knowing."

Ellie smacked a hand against her forehead. "Right. Okay, well keep me updated."

Nathan narrowed his eyes at her. "Anybody you want us to keep an eye out for?"

Ellie chewed her lower lip as the deputy bagged the bullet and rose. "Andy just threatened me. And then there's Toby. I don't think it was him, but maybe he's involved with someone else."

Nathan tugged his notebook from his pocket and jotted down the names. "Andy is usually more bark than bite, but I've got his name here. If this bullet matches any weapons on file under his name, we may need to have a conversation with him."

"Thanks, Nathan," Ellie said.

"Until then, keep your doors locked, try to keep an eye out when you come outside. We'll keep a patrol car here–"

"No," Ellie said with a shake of her head.

Nathan screwed up his face.

"Nathan, I'm opening a B&B tomorrow. There's nothing worse for business than a police cruiser in the driveway as guests pull up. No one will ever want to stay here."

"Okay," Nathan said with a nod. "As long as you're sure, we'll stay back. But if there's any more trouble–"

"I will be the first to call you," Ellie assured him. "Let's hope not once the guests are here."

"Right," Nathan answered. "All right, well, you take care, and if you have anything else, we're a phone call away."

"Thanks." Ellie shooed Lola back inside and closed and locked the door behind them.

"What the hell is going on here, Ellie?" Toby's voice asked from the stairs.

Ellie swiped her hand across her forehead before she shook it in the air. "Nothing, go to bed."

"Someone just shot at you, and you want me to go to bed?"

"It has nothing to do with you."

He thudded down the last step to the hardwood. "Are you sure you didn't just hear a branch snapping in the woods and *think* someone shot at you?"

"The bullet they just dug out of the railing confirmed it. Now, if you wouldn't mind, I'd like to try to get some sleep before we open the B&B tomorrow. The last thing I'd like my guests to see at check-in is a haggard hostess."

"El," Toby said, his forehead pinching as he reached for her, "wait. This is serious."

"No kidding, Toby," she said, batting his hands away.

"Don't just walk away. Let me help you."

She stepped onto the first stair and shook her head. "I'm going to do exactly that." She twisted to face him. "I know this is going to be a blow, but I no longer want or need your help. And don't paint me as the bad guy in this. Your behavior over the last year has done that to me."

With a bite of her lower lip, she trudged up the stairs with the dog following behind her.

"Good going, Ellie," Cleo said as she walked through her bedroom door and eased it shut. "You tell him what's what."

Ellie shuffled to the bed without a word and collapsed onto it. Emotions bubbled over, and she buried her face in her palms as sobs shook her shoulders.

"Aww, Ellie, are you okay?" Lola questioned, nosing at her hand.

She lifted her chin and wiped at her cheeks. "Yeah," she said with a sniffle. "Just a little overwhelmed."

She dug a tissue from her pocket and blew her nose.

"Don't feel overwhelmed, Ellie," Cleo said. "We're here with you."

Ellie offered a teary-eyed smile at the cat as she stroked her fur. She patted Lola's head as the dog nestled close to her.

"Yeah, you're right. I have the best end of the deal. And if the B&B doesn't work out, it doesn't work out. It's no big deal. I don't need it to live."

"That's right," Cleo said. "In fact, why go through with this opening to begin with? Let's throw in the towel, and–"

"No," Ellie said. "We're not closing before we open. I'll have at least one successful weekend if it kills me."

Cleo shook her paw in the air. "I'm a little worried it just might kill you."

CHAPTER 10

*E*llie wrinkled her nose at the cat's statement. "Okay, that's enough talking for the night. I'm heading to bed."

"I'm not kidding," Cleo said as Ellie shimmied out of her robe. "You were just shot at. Probably because someone has a grudge about the B&B opening. Ellie, you need to be careful."

"The police are looking into it, and I'm not going to be scared into closing before I even open my doors. I'm not that kind of lady."

"Lady is debatable. You're more of a—"

Ellie wagged a finger at the cat as she settled under the covers. "Don't say anything you'll regret."

"I was going to say a real class-act woman, but fine."

"You were not," Ellie answered, tugging the covers up and flicking off the light.

"I was, too. And listen, I've got a bad feeling about this weekend."

"It's just jitters. We'll be fine. It'll all be fine," she said as she settled into the pillows and closed her eyes.

When she opened her eyes again the next morning, the

room remained dim. She glanced at the clock, surprised to find no sun shining inside despite the hour.

She pushed herself up, regretting every moment of the time she spent awake the night before. While pulling her robe around her, she wandered to the window and glanced out.

A gloomy day met her. Dark clouds raced across the sky, threatening to bring strong winds and heavy rains. "Perfect."

"Why would you say that?" Cleo asked as she cleaned herself on the bed.

"What?" Ellie asked.

"Perfect. It's not perfect," Cleo answered.

"Right," Lola answered. "The weather is terrible."

"I understand that," Ellie said with a shake of her head. "I was being sarcastic. I hope this weather moves out of here before the guests come. It'll be miserable bringing in the luggage."

"Knock, knock," Mia called from the hall. "You up?"

"Yep, come on in."

The door creaked open, and Mia poked her head in. With her hair tied up in a messy bun and her robe still around her, she looked fresh out of bed. "Did you sleep?"

Ellie rolled her eyes as she shuffled across the room. "A little. Nerves got me and I ended up trying to do some research on the treasure."

"Trying?" Mia asked as they started down the stairs.

"I'd better tell you before you hear this from Rick. By the way, are you two dating?"

"Unofficially," Mia said with a raise of her shoulder as Ellie unlocked the door and peered warily through the crack before letting Lola out.

"I thought you didn't like him."

Mia stepped onto the porch with her. "I didn't like his investigating. I do like his dating."

"Are you even divorced yet?"

Mia wagged a finger at her as Lola climbed back onto the porch, ducking as a rumble of thunder rolled through the sky. "Don't judge."

"I'm not judging. I'm just…surprised. Listen, I don't want any parts of anyone for a long, long time."

Mia patted Ellie's shoulder as they stepped back through the door. "And I'm not soured on dating quite yet. Now, what were you going to say that Rick would spill the beans about?"

"The cops were here last night." She shuffled her way to the kitchen and grabbed the dog and cat food bowl.

Mia glanced over her shoulder while spooning scoops of coffee grounds into the machine. "Toby?"

"No. At least, I don't think so. Someone shot at me."

The coffee container clattered to the counter. "What? Wait! Okay, back up. Someone shot at you? What were you doing outside? Did you get hurt? Ellie! Why didn't you wake me up?"

"I was up. Lola had to go out. I took her and while we were out there someone shot at me. No, I'm not hurt. The bullet went into the railing. I called Nathan. He came right out. They're trying to match the bullet to a weapon now."

Mia dug her phone from her pocket and tapped around on it. "That's it. I'm texting Rick. He *has* to do something."

Ellie plopped the food bowls down in front of the pets. "They're doing everything they can."

"Well, now they're going to do more. Unless Rick doesn't want to see me at the festival tomorrow."

Ellie rolled her eyes at her friend. "Oh, Mia."

"I think the first place they should look is−"

"Morning, ladies," Toby said as he wandered into the kitchen with bleary eyes. He ran his hands through his bed hair before he shuffled across the room and grabbed the coffeepot.

Cleo hissed at him and darted from the space. Lola offered a bark. Ellie waved a hand at her.

"What?" she asked.

"Stop barking."

Toby arched an eyebrow at the animal. "Does she always bark like that?"

"Usually," Ellie said, avoiding making eye contact with him.

"Probably can be trained out. You might want to look into a school–"

"No!" Lola gasped. "Not school!"

Ellie sliced a hand through the air. "I'm perfectly fine with how things are, thanks."

Toby puckered his lips, holding his hand up in defeat. "Just trying to help."

Mia cocked her hip and stuck a hand on it. "Go just try to help somewhere else."

He rolled his eyes and meandered to the door. He turned back before he left, eyeing Mia. "Hey, Mia, did you happen to find a paper with a few things listed on it laying around here?"

"No," she said, crossing her arms.

"Thanks." He knocked his knuckles against the doorjamb, eliciting another bark from Lola before he moved on.

Mia shot the dog a glance. "You're right, Lola. He's a jerk."

Ellie waved a finger at the coffeepot. "Grab us both a coffee and meet me in the sunroom."

"Ohhh," Mia said with a grin as she spun to fill two mugs, "this sounds ominous, and I'm loving it."

Ellie settled in a rocking chair and stared out as rain began to pelt the windows.

Mia delivered a steaming mug to her before she eased into her own seat. "So, what's the scoop?"

Ellie dug the copy she'd made the night before from her pocket and slid it to Mia.

"What's this?" she asked, squinting down at it.

"*That* is what Toby's been looking for."

Mia's eyes went wide and she snapped her gaze up to Ellie. "Really? OMG, and you didn't say anything? Ellie! Go you!"

"I gave a copy to the police."

"Do you think he's involved with the shooting?" Mia's eyes went wider. "Do you think he did it?"

"No, he was in the house. But what is that? And why is he so interested in getting it back?"

"I can't see anything. The ink's all smeared."

"I know, but I swear this one part says 'pendant.'"

"Where?" Mia asked, scanning the list again.

Ellie poked her finger at the unintelligible scrawl. Mia squinted down at it, tilting her head. "Mmm, maybe. The case could be made."

Ellie arched an eyebrow. "I think so."

Mia studied the paper at a closer distance. "Do you think he found out about the treasure, and he's after it?"

"I don't know. But I find it odd that he's sooooo interested in that paper."

"He probably doesn't know it's unreadable."

"Probably not," Ellie said, tugging the paper back and sliding it into her pocket, "but it's obviously important to him."

Mia leaned back in her chair, sipping her coffee. "I guess we'll keep an eye on him."

"Yeah. Until then, time to get moving here. Guests should be arriving in a few short hours."

Mia grinned at her before taking the last sip of her coffee. "Exciting! I can't *wait* for the party to start tonight. It's going to be *so* fun!"

She squealed as she rose to her feet.

"I'm excited and nervous. I hope it comes off. I keep going over everything in my head constantly. I'm starting to think I should have just done the B&B opening and *not* the murder mystery at the same time."

"Nah, that's not your style. You go big or go home."

Ellie chuckled as she rose to her feet. "That's me. Go big or go home."

"Give me that. I'll wash them."

She handed her mug off to Mia along with her thanks before she shuffled up to her bedroom with Lola in tow. After a shower, she dressed for the day, put the final touches on the opening plans, double-checked all the rooms, put Lola and Cleo in her bedroom, and settled in the front porch's rocker to await the first guests.

Within fifteen minutes, a cloud of dust chased a car down the drive. The vehicle slowed to a stop in the designated parking area, and the doors popped open.

Ellie rose to her feet and waved, greeting the newlywed couple. "Are you Danny and Rose?"

"That's us," the redheaded woman called with a wave. "Oh, my gosh, this looks so great."

They climbed the stairs with their luggage in tow and shook Ellie's hand as she showed them into the house. "You're upstairs, third door on the left. All the rooms have private baths. If you need anything, just let me know. My name's Ellie."

"Thank you, Ellie. What time we going to the diner for the start of the murder mystery?"

"We leave at five," Ellie answered.

After a final goodbye, the couple slipped into the room, and Ellie returned downstairs, finding Mia already leading an older couple through the door.

"Here's our intrepid owner, Ellie, now," Mia said. "Ellie,

this is Carol and Ed Porter. They're here with their poodle, Max."

Ellie squatted down with a smile. "Well, hi, Max. Nice to meet you."

The poodle offered her a black paw, and she shook it.

"Is there a specific pet area we should keep to?" Carol asked.

"If you go off the porch and to the right, that's fine. But you can walk him anywhere as long as you clean up. We've got trash cans and bag stations at various locations."

"This is a lovely B&B. How old is it?"

Ellie rose and slid her pant legs down her thighs. "We were just discussing that a few days ago. It was built in 1875."

"Wow, over a century old. Fantastic!" Ed answered, tapping on the large newel post.

"I think so," Ellie said with a grin. "Let me show you to your room."

After the usual conversation about the en-suite bathroom and a reminder about dinner, she left them to enjoy their space.

"Two down, three to go," Mia said as they returned to the porch. "Who's left?"

"Two couples and a pair of sisters."

The next car rumbled down the driveway fifteen minutes later, and two women emerged.

"Must be the sisters," Ellie said as she stood and waved at them.

"Hi!" the honey-blonde-haired driver said as she slid her massive sunglasses down her nose and stared up at the house. "I'm Anna."

She flicked the polka-dotted scarf that was wrapped around her head over her shoulder as she tugged her suitcase from the backseat.

"This is my sister, Ava," she said as she slammed the door

and the pig-tailed brunette joined her with a backpack in hand.

"This place looks great," Ava said as she tugged her round, hipster sunglasses from her face and studied it.

"I'm so glad you think so," Ellie said. "I have to agree. Let me show you up to your room."

She settled them and returned to find both remaining parties waiting with Mia in the foyer.

Mia pointed to a couple in their thirties on her left. "This is Zane and Lana Cartwright."

The blonde, with her sunglasses still on, puckered her lips as she scanned the space before she shoved her hand out to Ellie. "Hi. Can you show us to our room? This trip took *way* longer than I expected."

"Sure. " Ellie turned to the other couple. "And you must–"

"Zane, grab the bags," Lana said with a wave of her manicured hand before she stalked to the stairs.

"I'll take them," Mia said, scurrying after the couple as they trudged up the stairs.

"Thanks," Ellie said, flicking a lock of hair behind her shoulder. "Sorry, you two must be Jim and Kylie."

Kylie tightened her fingers around her husband's hand and lifted a shoulder. "That's us," she said with a nervous chuckle.

Jim ran a hand through his close-cropped hair with a grin. "Hi. Nice to meet you."

"Nice to meet you, and I'm very glad you're here. Let me show you upstairs."

"Thank you. It was a long drive for us, too, but we're not quite ready to collapse just yet," Kylie said with a smile as she followed Ellie up the steps while Jim hefted the bags behind them.

"This place is great," he said with a strained voice as he hauled the bags up a few more steps.

"Thank you," Ellie said with a grin.

Kylie returned the expression. "And we're so excited about the murder mystery. Can you tell me more about how it works?"

Ellie led them down the hall to the door marked "Green Room." "Sure. Inside your room, you'll find a packet with information about your characters and their background. There's also a list of other characters inside there who will be playing with you. Some of them are your fellow guests and some of them are our intrepid townspeople. At tonight's dinner, someone will be murdered, and you'll have to figure out who did it!"

She pushed their door open and waved them inside. "There are some prompts to help you along the way and a few activities that you'll participate in where you can gather clues."

"Wow, sounds really fun. I can't wait to get started. Will we search for clues here for the most part?"

"Here and in town. There's a festival where you'll work in groups to solve a few puzzles and find more information. That's also a great time to ask others about their potential motives and background."

"Good idea," Kylie said with a smile. "This room is great. Thank you so much. We'll see you later."

Ellie smiled and nodded as she left them behind, bumping into Mia when she pulled their door closed.

"Whew, I got the worse end of that deal."

"*Lana* seems like a bit much," Ellie whispered.

Mia rolled her eyes and grabbed Ellie's hand, tugging her toward her bedroom. "You have *no* idea. Come on, I want to rake everyone over the coals and talk about finding the treasure."

The women spent the next hour in Ellie's room

discussing the new arrivals and planning a treasure hunt for their first free moments.

After letting Lola outside for a quick jaunt, they met the guests on the front porch. The town's Explorer bus pulled down the driveway in a cloud of dust as the last two guests joined them.

"Oh, good, a bus," Lana said, still securing a dangly earring.

"You're welcome to drive if you'd like," Mia said.

"But there's plenty of room on the bus," Ellie finished with a smile.

"It's fine," the woman said with a sneer. She waved a paper in the air. "Do we *have* to wear these?"

Ellie studied the name tag with her character's name on it. "Uh, yes, those will be very helpful for identifying who you are so people can find you and talk to you after the murder."

"I'm…" She huffed out a breath as she spun the name tag around and squinted at it. "Sally Salade. I run the salad shop in town. Can we all just agree to remember that?"

"I'd like to use the name tags," Kylie said, raising her hand. "I think it'll help."

"Yeah, come on, princess, it's not going to ruin your cashmere sweater. They peel right off." Ava demonstrated it by tugging hers off before she reapplied it.

Lana rolled her eyes and stuck the name tag to the bottom of her shirt with a grumbled, "Fine."

"This is going real well," Ellie said to Mia with a forced smile as the others climbed aboard the now-stopped bus.

"Don't let one snob ruin it. Seems like everyone else is excited about the game."

"Let's hope so," Ellie said as she hurried up the few steps and took a seat with Mia in the front. The bus delivered them to the diner a few minutes later and they disembarked and sauntered inside.

A buffet of steaming food along the back wall filled the air with mouth-watering smells. "Hi, everyone!" Val said with a smile. "Grab any seats you'd like and help yourselves. We'll be around to get your drink orders in just a minute, and then Ellie will get the party started."

"Thanks, Val. This smells great."

"No problem. Got a new cook, so we'll see how he works out."

"Oh?" Ellie asked as her guests milled over to the buffet to peruse and add to their plates.

"Yeah. Didn't you know? He said he knew you. Used you as a reference."

A wave of prickly heat washed over Ellie, and she lowered her chin to stare into the kitchen. Toby pressed a few hamburgers into the sizzling grill. She shook her head. "I know him all right."

"So far, so good. Well, go enjoy something to eat. I've got your chocolate shake ready back there. I'll grab it."

"Thanks." Ellie meandered to the buffet, waving to a few of her neighbors who had already arrived for the festivities.

Jake sidled next to her, refilling his plate with a few fries. "Everything ready?"

"I think so. We have a diva among us, so it'll be interesting to see how this goes."

"Oh?" He scanned the guests, focusing on the overly made-up Lana. "Sally Salade?"

Ellie waved a finger in the air. "That's the one."

"Bet she can't top Scarlett. Great casting, by the way, that she finds the body. I'll bet she puts on quite the show."

"Thanks. Call it type-casting, but I think it'll work well."

"You know it. Twenty minutes until showtime."

"Let the games begin," she said as they slid into a booth with Mia and Mac.

"Well, Ellie, you pulled it off. Guests look like they're having a fantastic time, and they're in for a real treat with this game."

Ellie wiggled a fry in her ketchup. "My stomach is so jittery. I'm nervous something won't come off."

"Nah, it'll be fine," Mac said with a wave of his hand.

Ellie sucked in a breath as Val slid a shake in front of her. "I hope so." She took a few sips, letting the cold liquid soothe the hot flash that swept over her.

The clock on the wall ticked the time away. She shot nervous glances at it every few seconds as she counted down the minutes until the murder victim would be found near the restrooms.

As the time approached, Ellie scanned the group, several of the guests were missing. She twisted to eye the alcove leading to the restrooms.

Several of them should be around for the big reveal. Her stomach fluttered as the clock struck 5:45.

A scream ripped through the din of chatter. One corner of Ellie's lips turned up.

"Right on time," Mac said with a chuckle. "And what a scream."

"Told you," Jake said with a wiggle of his eyebrows.

"There's a dead body! Someone call the police!" Scarlett screamed.

A few other shouts rose up. Ellie tried not to laugh.

"I'm serious. I'm not joking. This is not part of the game." A terrified-looking Scarlett raced from the alcove, her features ashen. "Someone is actually dead."

CHAPTER 11

"*W*ow, she's really over the top," Ellie murmured as Scarlett's shaky hand scrambled into her purse for her phone.

"I'm calling the police!" she shouted in a shrill voice.

Ellie turned to Mia, her brow furrowed. "Did you set this up?"

"Peach? Get to the diner right away. There has been a murder." Scarlett proceeded to kick off her pointy heels and climb onto one of the shiny red booths. "Attention patrons! The restrooms are off-limits! No one can enter the area. It is now a crime scene. The police have been notified."

Ellie wrinkled her nose, shooting a glance at Mia. "That's not what's supposed to happen. People are allowed to look at the body, right? Did you get Rick in on this?"

Mia shook her head. "No. I didn't arrange this."

Ellie rolled her eyes as she pushed herself up from the low seat. "I'll bet Scarlett did it thinking it lent some sort of drama to the whole thing. Let me go talk to her."

She strode across the tiled floor as Mia scurried from the booth behind her. "Wait for me."

Jake followed as they approached Scarlett. She hopped down from the booth and slid into her pumps, waving a finger in the air. "No, no. I just said it's a crime scene."

"Yeah, I know," Ellie said with a bob of her head. "One that I set up. We're supposed to let the people view it to add to the ambiance of the event."

"Didn't you hear me?" Scarlett said, flicking a lock of dark hair over her shoulder before crossing her arms. "There is a dead body back there."

"Yeah, I heard you. Like I said, we all expected this. It's right on time. But the calling of the police and the barring of the crime scene wasn't part of it. And quite frankly, Scarlett, I'm a little annoyed—"

"Annoyed? Oh, I'm sorry that an actual dead body kinked your murder mystery weekend plans, Eleanor. But I hardly think it's appropriate to continue the investigation now that an actual crime has been committed."

"Can we back up a second?" Jake said, running his hand through his hair. "Are you trying to say it's not a fake body?"

Scarlett bobbed her pointed chin up and down. "That's exactly what I'm saying. And I do not want this crime scene contaminated. Also, I hope you brought your notebook because I want this scoop."

"Wait, wait, wait," Ellie said, her brow furrowing as she lowered her voice to a whisper and leaned closer to the red-clad woman, "are you saying someone is actually dead?"

Scarlett closed the gap between them. "Yes."

Red and blue lights flashed on the white walls of the diner as two police cars raced into the parking lot. Rick and Nathan leapt from them and raced inside.

With an amused smile plastered across his features, Rick scanned the crowd. "Folks, I'm Sheriff Rick Crawford and this is my deputy, Nathan Hawk. We're the law in this here town and we heard there's been a murder."

He arched an eyebrow, placing his hands on his belt. "Now, no one should panic, but I'm going to ask you all to stay in your seats and not leave the diner until we can question everyone. Until then, continue to enjoy the buffet."

He smacked Nathan against the chest before they crossed the diner to Ellie, Mia, Jake, and Scarlett. "Hey, guys, this is a nice touch. I wasn't expecting this, but I like it. And I'm really excited to be involved."

Scarlett cocked a hip, arching an eyebrow. "Unfortunately, Sheriff, you have been involved because there has been an actual murder."

"Right, I know," he said with a grin before he covered his mouth. "Oops, sorry. Got to stay in character."

Scarlett sucked in a breath, her face flushing. "I am not joking. I went to find the fake body set up for Ellie's game, but I stumbled upon a real body instead. Imagine my shock upon seeing that."

"Wait, are you serious?" Nathan asked.

"Yes, I am!" Scarlett exclaimed. "There is a man with a knife in his chest."

Any signs of amusement slid from Rick's face, replaced with confusion and concern. "What?"

He shoved past Scarlett toward the alcove with Nathan following him. Ellie hurried behind them, pushing between the two men. A pair of brown dress shoes lay sprawled on the black and white tile.

Her lips parted, and her heart skipped a beat. She lifted her eyes from the shoes to the knife poking from his chest. A splotch of red blood stained his tan button-down.

"Oh, no," Ellie said with a shake of her head. She pressed a hand to her lips as she let her gaze rise to his face. Her features scrunched as she recognized him. She spun away, a lump forming in her throat.

Mia hurried forward and wrapped an arm around Ellie.

"Aw, honey, you shouldn't have looked."

"It's not that," Ellie said with a shake of her head. "It's who it is."

"Who?" Mia asked.

"It's Zane," Ellie said, sucking in a shaky breath. "One of our guests is dead."

"Oh, no," Mia said. "Who would have done this?"

Ellie pressed a hand to her forehead. "I don't know."

Rick twisted to face her. "You can identify him?"

Ellie bobbed her head up and down, running a hand through her hair. "Yeah. Yes. Zane Cartwright. One of our guests."

Scarlett's jaw dropped open. "Oh my word, someone needs to tell his wife."

"Wife?" Rick said, shooting a look at Nathan.

Ellie smashed a hand against her chest. "Yeah, he came with his wife, Lana."

"I can tell her," Mia offered.

Rick held up a hand. "Just hold off on that, Cookie. There's a procedure for this."

Ellie screwed up her face, shooting a look at Mia. "Cookie?" she mouthed.

Mia squashed her lips together and shook her head as Carol shuffled toward them with a loaded plate. "Hi, ladies, Ed and I were wondering when we'd get a look-see at the crime scene. We'd like to get a few photos for the scrapbook."

"Oh, uh…" Ellie began, shooting a nervous glance at Mia and shoving her hands into the back pockets of her jeans.

A shrill scream interrupted any further statement on her part.

"Ma'am," Rick said, reaching a hand toward an unknown figure inside the alcove, "I need you to step carefully around the body and come toward me."

Another groan sounded before a shocked Anna, her face

devoid of any color, inched around Zane's feet and collapsed against Nathan with a horrified expression etched into her delicate features.

Nathan winced and wiggled his eyebrows at Ellie who hurried over to pull the grief-stricken woman from his arms.

"Oh, wait," she said, clinging to him. "I feel…faint."

She stared up into his eyes with a wanting expression.

Ellie tightened her grip on the woman. "I'll help you get to a seat."

"Maybe Officer…oh, I didn't catch your name."

Nathan rubbed the back of his neck and shot an uncomfortable glance at Ellie. "Nathan."

"Maybe Officer Nathan can help me. I'm afraid I'll faint."

"No, Officer Nathan can't," a new voice said. Ellie's eyebrows shot up as she twisted to find a sour-faced Hazel with her hands on her hips. "He's busy with an important investigation."

She strode forward, her curls bouncing with every step, and wrangled the blonde away from Nathan before she dragged her toward a booth and plopped her in it. "I'll get you some water."

"Whoa," Mia whispered. "Looks like Hazel's jealous."

"No kidding," Ellie answered. She spun to find Carol jotting something down in a notebook. "About the body–"

"Say no more," Carol said, waving her pen in the air with a grin, "I've got all the notes I need. One suspect in the vicinity who clearly has the hots for the handsome officer. A jealous girlfriend. This is really all very interesting. I'm going back to share this with Ed."

"Oh, but–" Ellie began when Carol spun on her white-sneakered heel and hurried across the diner.

Ellie planted a palm against her forehead. "These people still think this is part of the game."

"We'd better make an announcement."

"Leave it to me," Rick said before pressing his cell phone to his ear. He spoke a few words to Maddie, the town's coroner before he hung up and shoved the phone into his pocket.

He crossed to the doors of the diner and waved his hands. "Folks, folks! Can I have your attention?"

A hush fell over the crowd as all eyes turned to him. "We've got ourselves a little situation here, folks. I'm going to ask that everyone stays calm and remains in your seats."

"When can we see the body? We need to collect clues!" Ed shouted.

"Now, that's not going to be possible," Rick said with a shake of his head.

Carol poked her pen at him. "Ohhh, a cover-up. I see." She scribbled something onto her notepad.

Rick shook his head, setting his hands on his hips. "No, that's not it. The thing is there has been a real murder. This is not part of the game. The game is over, folks. We've got a real case on our hands."

"Wait," Kylie said, leaping from her seat, "someone's actually dead?"

"Yep," Rick answered with a nod, "afraid so."

Gasps went up from the group along with whispers among them.

"We're going to speak to each of you before you leave. So, please, remain in your seats and try to relax while we get this sorted out. We'll get everyone's statement as quickly as possible."

Ellie grabbed Rick's elbow as he backed away toward Nathan. "I hate to be a bother, but the woman in the teal dress with all the jewelry…"

"Yeah?"

"It's her husband that was murdered. Someone needs to…"

"It was one of us that was murdered!" Anna said, her voice shrill as she rose on wobbly knees.

More expressions of shock filled the air as she stumbled forward. Hazel dropped the glass of water. The plastic cup bounced around on the floor before it rolled under one of the booths.

Anna's high-heeled boot splashed through the puddle as she set her wide eyes on Lana and pointed a finger. "Her husband."

Lana rose from her seat, her burgundy-lipsticked lips forming a wide O. "What? Zane?"

Anna's head bobbed up and down. "Yep. He's dead! And someone here killed him!"

Screams arose as Lana pitched headfirst toward the table in front of her, smacking her head off the corner and collapsing to the floor below.

With a huff, Rick grabbed his radio from his shoulder and spoke into it. "Yeah, this is Sheriff Rick Crawford in Salem Falls. I'm going to need a bus. We have got a woman down, repeat a woman down. Possible head injury."

He jabbed a finger at Nathan. "Get these people under control."

"What can I do to help?" Ellie asked.

Rick waved a hand toward the B&B guests. "Try to keep them calm. The townspeople already involved in this will be enough to handle, but those folks are going to panic real fast."

Val, with the assistance of one of her servers, rolled Lana onto her back. She pressed a towel against the cut on her head after placing another one under her.

Whispers rose from the group, and they exchanged panicked glances.

"Okay, everyone," Ellie said, waving her hands in the air. "I know this is not what we expected, but Sheriff Rick is working hard to get to the bottom of this. In the meantime, I need everyone to stay calm. And the police are going to need statements from all of you before you leave here. So, ummm…"

Ellie let her gaze slide around the diner. "Uh, everyone has a pen, right?"

Nods met her question.

"Okay, great, so, turn over your placemat and write down where you were between five-thirty and now. Any details you remember about who was with you, or anyone who was missing. Just write down everything you can remember before you forget."

Paper placemats flipped over on the tables as guests started busily writing their statements. "Good work," Mia whispered, squeezing Ellie's shoulder.

An ambulance siren blared as it approached the diner and skidded to a stop out front. Two paramedics hopped out, shouldered their gear, and raced inside. They dropped to their knees next to Lana and began to assess her as fellow guests looked on, scribbling notes and rubbernecking at the scene.

"What a nightmare," Ellie said, rubbing her fingers against her forehead.

"It's okay," Mia said, wrapping an arm around her shoulders, "Rickie will figure it out."

"Rickie? Oh, yeah, speaking of, what's with the weird nickname?"

Mia pulled her arm away and twisted away from Ellie with a nonchalant expression. "It's nothing."

"Cookie? It's nothing?"

Mia rolled her eyes and shot Ellie a glance. "I'm sweet, like a cookie."

"Oh, for heaven's sake," Ellie said with a groan.

"What? It's the first time in a while I've felt…desirable."

"Mia, you're a gorgeous woman. Come on, you look a decade younger than you are. You're in great shape. You're attractive."

"All things that you are, too."

"I'm not saying I'm not. I'm just saying—"

Mia laid a hand on Ellie's arm. "I know. Not to jump on the first bandwagon because someone's giving me attention. I get it. I love that you're looking out for me, but I like Rick. It's not just a rebound thing."

Ellie sucked in a breath. "I hope not. You deserve the best."

"So do you."

"Don't get me started with a relationship, I don't want it." She shot a glance toward the alcove hiding the body. "Not now that we're smack dab in the middle of yet another murder investigation."

"Let Rick handle it, Ellie."

Ellie nodded before she slid her gaze to her guests. "Yeah. But this is not what I needed on my opening weekend. And I wonder if it has any connection to the shooting last night."

"You think it does?"

Ellie lifted her shoulders into a shrug as she crossed her arms. "Maybe. Is someone dead set on ruining my opening weekend?"

Mia wrapped her finger around a blonde wave in her hair. "Enough to commit a murder?"

Ellie cocked her head. "They shot at me, right?"

"A potshot is a lot different than actual murder," Mia said.

"What other reason could there be? He's a guest in town. Motive is going to be hard to nail down unless it was aimed at me. What are the chances he made an enemy that quickly who would murder him?"

"Maybe he had an in-town connection. We can't assume he's never been to Salem Falls, before," Mia argued. "He could have been here lots of times. Maybe he visits regularly."

"You have a point," Ellie said as another car pulled up to the diner. Maddie's brunette bob bounced inside as she gathered her things and emerged from the car.

With her bag jouncing off her hip, she climbed the stone steps and pushed through the diner's door. "Hey, Ellie, how you doing, honey?"

"I've been better. But I'm better than the poor man outside of the restrooms. And her." She thumbed toward Lana who the paramedics loaded onto a stretcher.

"Hey, Maddie," Nathan said as he approached them, "the body's back here."

"Well, time for me to check out the stiff," Maddie said, hefting the bag higher.

Ellie pressed her lips together into a tight-lipped smile and nodded. She spun to find Val trailing behind the paramedics who wheeled Lana to the ambulance outside.

"She's okay," Val reported, "they're just taking her for tests to make sure there's no concussion."

"Oh, good. Does someone need to go with her?"

Val turned the corners of her lips down as she shook her head. "Nah, they'll keep her overnight. The shock of her husband's death is enough to warrant some observation."

Ellie shook her head again. "How awful. How could this happen?"

"Hey, Val?" Rick said. "Can you come here for a minute?"

Val squeezed Ellie's shoulder before skirting past her. She spoke a few minutes with Rick before he directed her to the alcove. She leaned in before she turned back and nodded at him.

"What do you think they're talking about?" Ellie asked.

"I'll find out tonight," Mia answered.

"Mia, please tell me you're not dating the Sheriff just to

keep tabs on investigations."

"I'm not! But it comes in handy when there's a crime that's been committed." She offered Ellie a wink as she tossed a lock of hair over her shoulder.

Ellie's lips curled on the edge in amusement despite the shake of her head. Rick spoke for another moment to Val before he headed toward Ellie and Mia. "All right, we're going to take statements from the folks here before we send them back with you. None of them can leave town right now, and we'll tell them that. But we want them out of the diner so we can do our work."

Ellie nodded. "Understood. They can stay at the B&B as planned, though any further festivities with the game will be canceled."

Rick nodded before making his announcement. "Folks, if I could have your attention. Right now, we have an active crime scene. And we need to take statements from all of you. Either Deputy Hawk or I will meet with each of you. After that, you'll be able to return to the B&B. We ask for the time being that you don't leave town."

A few gasps went up from the crowd.

"You don't think we could have anything to do with this, do you?" Carol shouted.

"Right now, I can't say anything definitively. And that's why until we get some information, I'm asking you all to stay in Salem Falls. Ellie already has your accommodations set up for the weekend. I suggest you try to enjoy them until you hear otherwise."

Murmurs ran through the guests as they whispered to each other while Nathan and Rick called Danny and Rose up to speak to them first.

Ellie sucked in a breath as she eyed the crowd, and her heart skipped a beat. She twisted to face Mia. "Wonder if we'll be sleeping under the same roof as a murderer?"

CHAPTER 12

"*L*ana," Mia breathed as she scrunched her features.

"You think?" Ellie asked. "I was wondering the same thing. But then her reaction to his death–"

"Was probably faked! She needed a way out and quick. So, she faked a fainting spell and got herself a ride out complete with bodyguards and a chauffeur."

"I'd hardly call the paramedics bodyguards and a chauffeur, but you have a point. She conveniently got out of any questioning whatsoever."

"Which gives her plenty of time to get her story straight." Mia arched an eyebrow before she patted Ellie's arm. "Wait here. I'm going to tell Rickie."

"I'm coming with you!" Ellie hissed as she hurried to follow Mia toward Rick, who had just finished taking a statement from Carol.

"Hey, Sugarbear," Mia said as she grabbed his elbow and tugged him toward her.

Rick twisted to face her. "Yeah?"

"We just had a thought. Lana, the dead guy's wife, got out of here pretty quickly after she supposedly hit her head. And

117

she was no peach earlier today either. I got the impression she didn't want to be here. Maybe had some reason to off her husband."

Rick narrowed his eyes as he tapped his pen on his notepad. "Did she threaten him directly?"

"No, not directly. But she's a real diva. And who else would want to murder someone who just got to town?"

"I'll keep it in mind. But we need to be open to all ideas at this point until we get some concrete evidence that points us in the right direction."

Mia nodded as she squeezed his arm. "But you definitely need to talk to Lana. Before she can come up with a cover story."

"Yeah, we'll get someone over there."

"I could–"

Rick shook his head. "No."

"But–"

He shifted his weight and sighed, flicking a warning glance at her. "I said no. I don't want either of you ladies involved in an ongoing police investigation. Look what happened the last time. You accused poor Hazel, and then nearly got yourself killed."

Ellie held up her hands. "Fine by me. I had enough getting shot at last night, thanks. I don't need to be on another killer's radar."

"Oh, yeah, which reminds me," Mia said, flicking her eyebrows up, "could this be Andy?"

Rick wrinkled his brow. "Andy? The grocer Andy?"

"Yeah. I mean, he's the most likely suspect for who shot at Ellie. Maybe he went one step further to ruin her business opening. Nothing puts a damper on your opening weekend like a murder."

Rick waved a hand in the air. "Okay, that's it."

"Huh?"

"No more accusations. No more involvement in this case. Give your statements to Nathan and then head back to the B&B. Let us do our jobs."

"I'm just suggesting–"

"I know what you're doing, Cookie, and I don't want you involved. If you keep it up, I'm not going to tell you anything about this case. I don't want you two creeping around on your own with a murderer on the loose."

"Fine," Ellie said with a nod. "Like I said, I've already been shot at. I don't want to be involved with another murderer."

"And it could be a separate incident entirely. We have no proof of anything about who shot at you or who killed Zane."

"So, you haven't found anything yet?" Ellie asked.

Rick huffed and shot her an irritated glance.

She held her hands up and shook her head. "Just asking, sorry."

"As soon as we know anything, I'll tell you. But not if you're going to run around and put yourselves in harm's way."

"We'll probably do that if you *don't* tell us," Mia threatened.

Rick clicked his tongue and pressed his lips into a thin line. "You're lucky I like you."

She tugged the corner of her lips back in a half smile before she pecked his cheek. "I like you, too." With another quick kiss, she waved her hand at Nathan before she flitted toward him, dragging Ellie with her. "Rickie said to give you our statements."

"Oh, right, sure." He flipped to a new page and pressed his pen against the blank paper. "Where were you when the murder happened?"

"In the booth with Ellie, Mac, and Jake. I heard Scarlett scream. We thought it was part of the fake murder game thing. But then she said someone had been murdered and called you."

"Do you remember anyone specific missing from the party?"

"Ummm," Mia said. "Not really. People were milling around all night. Some people were out of their seats to get food or use the restroom."

Nathan flicked his gaze to Ellie. "What about you?"

"No one specific, but I wasn't paying a ton of attention. Carol may have been up getting food. Umm, Anna was gone, Jim, Lana, and Danny, maybe? I'm not sure where they were though. I just remember a lot of empty seats."

"Got it," Nathan said as he scrawled the names down on his notepad. "Thanks."

Mia lifted her chin and lowered her eyes to study the notebook. "Does that match what you've already heard?"

"What do you mean?"

"I mean does everyone's stories jive? Have you ferreted out the liar yet?"

Nathan flipped the notebook closed and shoved it in his pocket. "I can't comment on an ongoing investigation."

"Oh, come on, this is me you're talking to," Mia said.

"Yeah, exactly," Nathan answered, wagging a finger at her, "Rick will kill me if I big-mouthed it to you."

Mia's shoulders rose to her ears. "He's going to tell me anyway."

"Then it's on him. Not me." Nathan pressed his lips together and backed away a step.

Mia heaved a sigh and crossed her arms. "Unreal."

Ellie's lips curled on the corners, and she grabbed Mia by the elbow and dragged her closer to the guests. "Hi, folks. I think everyone has given their statements, so we'll shuttle you all back to the B&B now. In light of what happened tonight, we will forego any further murder mystery activities."

A groan went up through some of them, and Ellie held her hands up. "I know this isn't the weekend you expected, but the town's festival is still going on tomorrow, so you can enjoy that. And I promise I'll make it up to you. But for now, there's dessert back at the B&B and comfy beds."

The group of guests exchanged glances before Carol and Ed rose from their seats. "Come on, folks, there's still a murder to solve."

"Oh, no–" Ellie began when the din of chairs scraping and guests hurrying away from their tables cut her off.

The crowd filtered outside past Ellie and Mia and climbed aboard the waiting bus. Ellie heaved a sigh and shot a glance at Mia. "Looks like we'll have our work cut out for us with this crowd."

"Hey, maybe they'll solve the murder and give you a great review."

Ellie flicked her eyebrows up as she held back a laugh. "Five stars. The murder mystery was so realistic."

Mia chuckled, grabbing Ellie's hand and tugging her toward the door. "Come on. We'll get through it."

They pushed into the cool fall night and boarded the bus. Whispers split the otherwise quiet ride back to the B&B.

Carol led the group off the bus and into the foyer. "I saw a sunroom earlier which would be a lovely place to reconvene and compare notes. Anyone wanting to poke into this mystery, join me in twenty minutes there."

She twisted to face Ellie as the group dispersed to their rooms to change or drop off their belongings. "I believe you said there was hot chocolate or tea that could be made in the evenings?"

"Yes," Ellie said with a nod, "but I've really got to caution you about digging around. The Sheriff was very clear about leaving the investigation up to him."

"Oh, fiddlesticks," she said with a wave of her hand, "we're just going to compare notes. Maybe even give him a good start on a suspect list. Now, where are your mugs?"

"I'll take care of it," Ellie promised.

"One batch of hot chocolate coming up!" Mia said with a smile before she followed Ellie upstairs. "I'll dump my purse and meet you in the kitchen."

"Sounds good," Ellie said as she pushed into her bedroom, finding an excited Lola wagging her entire behind while rearing back on her hind legs and reaching for Ellie.

"Ellie! Ellie! You're home!" Lola shouted.

"Yep, I'm back."

"Well, did you off somebody?" Cleo inquired, opening her green eyes to slits as she lounged in the middle of the bed.

"No, but someone else did."

Cleo shot her a glance. "Explain."

"Someone killed one of our guests at the diner."

Lola stopped dancing around, and her tail slowed to a slight wiggle. "But that was supposed to happen."

Ellie hung her purse on the clothing rack across the room and kicked off her shoes in favor of slippers. "No, Lola, they weren't supposed to actually die."

"So, they died like Susie?"

"Yes, and no. They died for real like Susie, but they didn't drown."

Cleo shook a paw in the air before she licked it and dragged it over her face. "Wow, it's almost like…it's cursed."

Ellie puckered her lips and shook her head. "Stop it."

"What?" Cleo shot back. "I wonder how Sheriff Rick is taking it. He runs a real tight town, you know. Yeah, right."

Ellie wandered to the bathroom in search of a hair tie. "I'll be interested to see what he comes up with. I don't envy him this investigation."

Cleo shouted from the spot on the bed, "He's clueless. He'll never solve it."

Ellie returned tugging her long hair through the colorful scrunchie. "We'll see."

"Oh, by the way, we had a bit of excitement here, too," Cleo said as she stood and arched her back, flattening her ears against her head.

Ellie froze and stared at her. "What's that supposed to mean? What did you do?"

"I didn't do anything," Cleo answered, settling onto her haunches.

Ellie flicked her gaze to the dog who wagged her tail. "Lola?"

"That other dog howled. Max, was it? I tried to tell him it was okay, but he didn't want to hear it."

"Oh, is that all?" Ellie said, resuming her shamble across the room.

"Is that all?" Cleo cried. "That's enough. The entire time you were gone listening to that howling. Sounded like a dying werewolf. I'd much rather have been prowling around the diner, eating hamburgers and watching someone get offed. Who's the stiff, anyway?"

"Zane," Ellie answered. "And it wasn't much fun."

"Zane the pain?" Cleo and Lola asked simultaneously.

"Uh, I guess."

"That's what his wife called him," Cleo said. "Zane the pain. Said she'd be better off if he was dead."

Ellie froze with her hand on the doorknob and whipped around to face the animals. "What? Are you sure that's what you heard?"

Cleo bobbed her head up and down. "Yep. She said, 'Zane

the pain. You've always been the bane of my existence. I don't know why I married you. I'd be better off if you were dead!'"

"It's true," Lola said with a wiggle of her tail, "she said that."

"And now he's dead. Hmmm, I wonder who killed him?" Cleo murmured as she stared into space.

Ellie arched an eyebrow as she considered the new information. "It certainly seems like she had a motive."

"Did Sheriff Rick drag her out in handcuffs?" Cleo asked.

"No. She fainted when she heard the news and smacked her head off of the table. She's at the hospital now."

"No, she isn't." Cleo slid her eyes closed and shook her head.

"What do you mean?"

"I mean I'd bet one of my nine lives she's gone. You call the hospital, and you'll find out that she's skipped out. Gone-zo. Disappeared. Vanished. Poof. Vamoose."

Ellie held up a hand. "Okay, okay, I get it. Though I'm not certain about that."

Cleo tilted her head. "Go ahead and try it. You'll see."

"Mmm, I'm sure. And when they ask how I knew, I'll tell them the cat told me."

"I bet they'd be impressed," Cleo answered.

Ellie patted her side. "Come on, Lol, I'll let you out."

"Okay," Lola said as she shuffled after Ellie.

After a quick stop outside, they made their way to the kitchen where Mia already stood at the stove heating a large pot of chocolaty liquid.

"Mmm, smells good," Ellie said as she sniffed at the steam curling from the warm milk.

"I can't wait to hear what these guys come up with."

Ellie fished mugs from the cabinet above the coffee pot. "I'm afraid to find out."

"Hi, ladies," Kylie said as she bounded into the kitchen

with her husband, Jim, in tow. "Are we ready for the meeting?"

"Hot chocolate's almost ready!" Mia said with a grin.

Ellie set out marshmallows and whipped cream on the counter near the stove along with the mugs. "Help yourself."

"Thanks," Kylie said as she ladled the hot liquid into two mugs before spraying a generous dollop of whipped cream onto the top of each. "So, who do you think did it?"

"I have not even given it any thought," Ellie answered. "It all happened so fast. I just can't believe it, honestly."

"I wonder if someone used the cover of your party for this exactly. Which means it's premeditated." Kylie wrapped her hands around her mug and raised her eyebrows, flicking her gaze between the two women.

"I mean–"

"Oh, this looks divine," Carol interrupted as she bustled in. "Ed'll be down in a minute. But I'll grab two mugs for us."

"Hi, Carol," Kylie said. "Ready to compare notes?"

The older woman spooned marshmallows into the steaming milk as she bobbed her head up and down. "Am I ever. This is so interesting. I can't wait to do some sleuthing at the festival tomorrow."

"Ugh, you two can have it," Anna said as she shuffled into the kitchen in a fluffy robe and pink bunny slippers with her more utilitarian sister behind her in button-down flannels and a sturdy pair of orthopedics. "I'm not even certain we should be discussing it."

"You're right, Anna," Ellie said. "Maybe we should just enjoy our evening. The porch is lovely–"

"Nonsense," Carol said with a wave of her hand. "There's no crime in sharing information."

"Well, it is an ongoing inv–"

"Carol's right," Ava said with a grin. "Where's your sense of adventure?"

Anna sipped at her hot chocolate after ladling it from the pot and crinkled her turned-up nose. "It died with Zane."

"Joking about the deceased? Edgy," Ava said, elbowing her sister.

"Okay, people," Carol answered as Ed trudged into the room. "Most of us are here outside of Danny and Rose. Should we head in and get down to business?"

"We're here!" Danny said as he and Rose piled into the kitchen.

"I don't know how much help we'll be, but we're happy to participate," Rose answered.

Ellie doled out two more mugs of the sweet, warm beverage to them before everyone shuffled into the now dimly lit sun porch and found seats.

She flicked on a few lamps, bringing a warm light to the space as Carol began the discussion. "We need to establish who was gone from their seats when the murder happened. Those people are suspects."

"Wait, wait, wait," Danny said, waving a hand in the air, "why? Just because you're out of your seat doesn't mean you offed somebody."

"No, but it gives you the opportunity. Then we need to look at motive."

Kylie shrugged a shoulder. "How would we know anyone's motive? We don't know each other, and we don't know anyone in town."

Carol poked a finger at her. "That's where sleuthing comes in. We'll meet people from the town. We can grill 'em about their connections to Zane."

Ellie shot Mia a confused glance with a wrinkled nose. "Is she serious?" Ellie mouthed.

Mia shrugged a shoulder as Jake slipped into the room, leaning against the door jamb. He waved at Ellie and wiggled his eyebrows.

"So, who was missing?" Ava asked. "I was in my seat. Anna was at the buffet."

"I don't remember Anna being at the buffet," Rose said.

Anna glanced up sharply at her. "Yes, I was!"

"You weren't. You came from the bathroom," Carol said. "You were clinging to the hot officer."

"I…I wasn't *in* the bathroom. I wandered there when all the commotion started. I was at the buffet." Anna gave the statement a curt nod.

"What were you getting then?" Rose asked.

"Huh?"

"What food were you getting? Another slider? More salad? Fries? If you were at the buffet, what were you getting?"

Anna set her mouth into a thin line and glared at the newlywed. "What are you accusing me of?"

"Nothing. I'm just asking. If you were at the buffet, you would remember why and you would tell us."

"Why should I? I should just openly share information after you accused me of murder?"

"Whoa," Danny said, leaping from his seat, "I don't think Rosie accused you of murder. She's merely trying to nail down the details of your alibi."

"Oh, so I need an alibi now?"

"I don't know, you tell us," Jim chimed in. "You seem really interested in hiding something."

"Why in the world would I kill Zane?"

"Maybe you were having an affair with him," Kylie said.

"Oh, come on. Maybe *you* were," Anna spat back, jabbing a finger at Kylie.

"Hey, you can't accuse my wife of sleeping around with someone else's husband."

"She just accused me of it!" Anna shouted.

"Okay, okay, okay, that's enough folks," Ellie said as she

stalked to the middle of the room, waving her hands. "This is a police investigation. We really should not be involved in it at all."

"I disagree," Carol answered. "And I think this has been rather enlightening."

"Wonderful, but before it turns into anything more than a discussion, I think we should disband. You're welcome to ponder the mystery all you'd like, but I think this conversation should stop."

"I agree," Anna said with a huff as she rose to stand. "I'm not sticking around for any more of this."

She stormed from the room. Ava drained the last of her hot chocolate and followed her sister with a smirk.

Kylie grimaced and flung a hand in the air. "Yeah, I'm out, too, before I get accused of infidelity again."

"Rose, Danny," Carol said as she stood, "care to compare notes? We can meet in my room."

"Sure," Rose said with a nod.

"Wow," Ellie murmured as everyone disappeared from the room. "That was intense."

"No kidding," Mia said. "Wonder how true any of it is."

"I don't know about that," Jake said with a wiggle of his eyebrows, "but I've got some juicy information if you'd care to hear it."

CHAPTER 13

*M*ia grabbed Jake's arm and tugged him into the sunroom before she shoved him into a chair. "Spill, kid."

"Wait, wait!" Ellie leaned her head into the kitchen, straining to listen. She straightened and shook her head. "I hate to be a pain, but I'm a little worried about the walls having ears."

Mia lowered her voice to a whisper. "Where do you want to go? Out? Do you think it's safe outside or should we go into town?"

"We can use the sunporch off my bedroom."

"Good idea," Mia said, grabbing Jake's hand and tugging him up to stand.

They wound through the house and up the stairs. Lola picked up her head as Ellie flicked on the light and led the others into the room. She waved them inside before she secured the door.

"Hi, Jake!" Lola said, leaping to her feet and wagging her tail.

"What in the blue heck is this?" Cleo asked, her eyes wide as saucers. "We're being invaded!"

She slinked from the bed and thudded onto the floor before she disappeared into the dark hole under the mattress.

"It's just Mia and Jake." Lola leapt off the bed and pattered over to the young reporter.

"Hi, Lola," Jake said, rubbing her ears. "How do you like having a B&B?"

"It's okay. I don't get to go out too much yet because I'll bark at everyone."

"I bet you bark at everyone," Jake said with a grin.

"She literally just said that, dummy," Cleo called.

"It's through here," Ellie said, ignoring the chatter from the pets as she led them to the small porch across the room.

The wicker rockers creaked as everyone found a seat. Lola sat at Jake's feet for a few minutes before she settled down with a sigh.

Mia leaned on the arm of her rocker toward Jake. "Okay, whatcha got, kid?"

"I hung around the diner on Scarlett's orders until the police left. They've got a list of people they want to question again from the guests here along with a list of people from town."

"Did they say who?" Ellie asked.

Jake flipped his notebook open but shook his head. "No names. They were cautious, but I do know they want Scarlett fingerprinted."

Mia's eyebrows shot up. "Really? Wow!"

"I don't think she's a suspect, but since she found the body, they want to rule out any fingerprints that may be hers. She says she didn't touch anything, though."

Ellie pulled her leg up onto the chair and set it rocking gently. "Is she going to comply?"

"I think so. She said she has nothing to hide. Plus, it'll make a juicy story when she reveals she had a 'hand in the investigation.'"

Mia rolled her eyes. "Ugh, please."

"She'll use the entire fingerprinting trip to try to wrangle more information," Jake said before he scanned his notes.

"The knife used to commit the murder was from Val's kitchen. So, Val and everyone at the diner with access to the kitchen–which is basically all employees–are being questioned. They're looking into any connections they can find between the vic and anyone else on the scene."

"That makes sense. Wonder if they'll get any information from Lana. Or maybe someone will admit to knowing him," Ellie said.

Jake nodded, tapping his finger against the paper. "They're going to talk to the wife. And also, it looked like two or three sets of prints on the knife."

Mia and Ellie shared a glance. "That's a lot of prints."

"Yeah, though there was mention about the prints not giving them a clue about the murderer because the person could have used gloves."

"Good point," Mia said. "Which would mean it was premeditated."

"It almost had to have been premeditated, right?" Ellie asked.

Mia shifted in her seat causing the wicker to creak. "What makes you say that?"

"Well, I doubt he was robbed, right? And who would just randomly murder him in the middle of a diner?"

"Someone who had a psychotic break?" Mia suggested.

"It *could* happen, but the likelihood is low, I think. This has to have been someone who knew him."

"Okay, knew him," Mia said, poking a finger at her, "but that doesn't mean premeditated."

Ellie let her head rest against the puffy pillow on the chair. "Good point. We need to look at Zane's connections. Maybe someone didn't intend to kill him but killed him in a fit of rage."

"Like a jilted lover," Mia said.

"Or a business partner," Jake added.

"Right. I wonder if we can do a quick search on him to find anyone who may be related." Ellie pushed herself up to stand, waving a finger in the air. "I'll grab my laptop."

Jake tugged his phone from his pocket as she hurried to the nightstand and grabbed the device.

"People search shows Lana, Robert, and Beverly as possible relations," he said as she plopped into the chair.

"I don't know how you use your phone to do that. It'd take me forever to type everything in."

"So, no one other than Lana," Mia said, tapping her chin, "who I still think is a good contender for this."

"We really need to know whose prints are on that knife. That'll go a long way to telling us about premeditation or prior connections, I think," Ellie said, popping her laptop open. She stared at her screen for a moment, reminded of the search she'd started but hadn't finished.

"What were you looking up?" Mia asked as she glanced at the screen.

Ellie rolled her eyes as she opened a new tab. "Locations of the train robberies. I was trying to figure out if it was possible that all the stolen items were in Salem Falls."

"I think it is," Jake answered while Ellie tapped around on her keyboard.

"What makes you say that?" Mia asked.

Jake tapped his phone's black screen. "I looked it up, too. The robberies were not that far from here. Furthest was near Pittsburgh, which is a good distance back in that day, but not unfathomable."

"Look at you, Ace Reporter," Ellie said with a sly grin.

He chuckled, shoving a lock of hair from his forehead. "I actually paid attention in journalism classes."

"Okay, so the stuff could be here in Salem Falls," Ellie said, drumming her fingers against her laptop.

"Or in this house."

"Or in this house," she repeated with a nod. "But where?"

"Hidden," Cleo said from the bedroom.

"Hidden where?" Ellie asked.

"Secret room," Mia said. "Are there plans for this old place?"

"Maybe in the office. Field trip?"

"Okay," Mia said with a grin and a head bob as she leapt from her seat.

"Jake, you coming?"

He rose and shoved his phone into his pocket. "Yeah. I want to see if there's a secret room. That'd be lit."

Mia eyed him, her nose wrinkling. "Super dope, right?"

"It's not working for you, hon," Ellie said as she clapped her on the back. "Just date yourself and say super cool."

Mia followed her across the bedroom. "We're *not* that old!"

Ellie chuckled as she unlocked the door and swung it open. "Uh-huh. The internet wasn't invented when we were born. This kid's lived with it his entire life."

"I'm not *that* young," Jake said, rubbing his neck. "I mean, yes, I've grown up with the internet, but I'm not a kid."

"You're a baby," Mia said as they piled into the hall with Lola in tow.

Ellie froze as she took a step toward the stairs leading to the third floor. She held up a hand and raised a finger to her lips before she tapped it toward the lower level. Lola's mouth formed an O, characteristic of her impulse to bark. Ellie waved and hand at her and hissed, "No!"

The dog's lower lip bobbed up and down a few times until Ellie squatted down next to her and rubbed her ears to keep her quiet.

Mia crinkled her brow as she tiptoed to the banister and turned her ear toward it. Hushed voices rose from the living room.

"Who is it?" Ellie mouthed.

Mia raised her shoulders in a shrug.

The voices rose a bit and they got pieces of words.

"...don't care!" someone hissed.

"We can't just leave," the other answered.

"We can. They can't keep us here."

"Right, because that won't look suspicious."

Mia's eyebrows shot up, and her jaw dropped open. "We need to find out who this is."

"...can't pin anything on us," the first voice answered.

"Really? We'll be the first people they look at when we disappear."

Mia pushed away from the railing and skirted around Ellie. She eased onto the first step and tiptoed down to the landing. With a wince, she set a foot on the first step. It creaked, splitting the otherwise quiet air.

Mia slid her eyes closed as the hushed whispers stopped short. She pressed her lips together and hurried down the stairs before swinging into the sitting room. Her shoulders slumped, and she twisted to face Ellie and Jake with a shake of her head. "Nothing."

"Get back up here," Ellie whispered.

Mia bobbed up the steps, still shaking her head. "Sorry. I thought I could spy on them."

Ellie wagged her finger at her friend. "You gotta watch out for that first step. It's a dead giveaway."

"Should have warned me *before* I went down there," Mia said as Ellie led them down the hall toward the stairs.

"I couldn't do a thing. You went running away like a super spy."

"I did not run like a super spy," Mia answered. "We should have sent Jake. He's probably light on his feet."

Jake batted her arm. "Oh, sure. Send me into the lion's den."

Ellie climbed the steep stairs. "No one's going into the lion's den. No one is going anywhere near these people. One of them could be a murderer!"

"But which one? And why? And where is this treasure? We have too many mysteries," Mia said as they pushed through the door into the office.

Ellie stuck her hands on her hips and scanned the space. "Okay, there's the desk, the file cabinet, and the cabinet there. Who wants to explore what?"

"I'll take the desk," Mia offered, skirting around it and plopping into the chair.

Jake crossed to the cabinet and settled into a cross-legged seat on the floor. "I got this cabinet."

Ellie tugged open the drawer on the file cabinet and rummaged through the files. Lola plopped to the floor with a deep sigh, settling her head on her front paws.

"Here's a map," Mia said, catching everyone's attention, "but it just looks drawn."

Ellie lifted her chin and peered over the desk lamp at the paper Mia flashed. "Oh, yeah, that was Aunt Susie's layout from the B&B reopening plans."

Mia slapped it down onto the desk with a sigh. "Too bad she didn't note where the treasure was."

"Nope, sorry. I don't even know if she knew about it."

"She never mentioned it?" Jake asked.

Ellie winced, ceasing her motion with a finger caught between two hanging folders. "I hadn't seen her in a long time. I still feel really bad about that."

Mia leapt from her seat and hurried toward her to wrap her in an embrace. "Aw, Ellie. I'm sure she understood. You had a life pretty far from here."

Ellie patted her friend's hand. "Thanks. I know that, but it seems selfish now. I hadn't seen her since I was a kid. In four decades, I couldn't make it to visit once?"

Mia stroked her hair. "Don't beat yourself up. People lose touch, especially when they live far away."

Ellie sucked in a breath before she blew out a long sigh. "I guess. Nothing to be done about it now, anyway."

"Hey, you knew her, Jake," Mia said with her arm still wrapped around Ellie. "Did she ever mention the treasure?"

Jake jutted his lower lip out and shook his head. "Not to me."

Mia slumped and sighed. "Back to the search."

Ellie continued her perusal of folders as Mia shuffled back to the desk and tugged another drawer open.

"Nothing but stationary in this one," she lamented.

Ellie slammed her drawer shut and rolled open the bottom one. "I came up empty on my first drawer, too."

"I've only found antiques," Jake noted.

Ellie's heart skipped a beat, and she snapped her gaze toward him, wondering if he'd found the treasure.

He held up a VHS movie as he chuckled.

"Very funny, kid," Mia answered. "Some of us still remember renting those at the supermarket."

"Or the minimart," Ellie said.

"Be kind, rewind," Mia answered with a wink.

"What are you guys talking about?" Jake asked.

Ellie wandered toward him and slid the bulky cassette from the sleeve. She tapped the plastic window on one side. "Nothing was worse than when you rented a movie and you popped it into your VCR only to find the credits rolling when you pressed play. Then you had to rewind the entire thing to start from the beginning."

"And it took a little bit," Mia answered.

"Yeah. Like the popcorn was gone by the time you started the movie amounts of time."

Jake stared down at the plastic tape as Ellie handed it back. "That's awful."

"Our lives were rough," Ellie said as she shuffled back to the file cabinet drawer and continued rifling through it.

"No kidding," Jake said as he swung the door closed. "There's nothing in here."

Ellie blew a piece of hair from her face as she slid the drawer closed. "Nothing here either."

Mia flung her hands in the air. "I'm empty, too."

Ellie tugged herself up to stand using the corner of the cabinet. "So much for finding plans to lead us to the treasure."

"Maybe they filed building plans with the town," Jake suggested. "I'll try inquiring on Monday."

"Okay, thanks," Ellie said as Mia's phone chimed.

She slid it from her pocket and toggled on the display. "It's Rick."

"Anything interesting?" Ellie asked.

Mia's jaw dropped open, and she flicked her gaze up, shifting it between Ellie and Jake. "He said Lana is missing!"

CHAPTER 14

"What?" Ellie asked, her jaw falling open.

"What's wrong, Ellie?" Lola asked.

Mia's fingers pounded across the keyboard as she answered her beau. "I'm asking what he means. Like did someone take her or did she check herself out or what?"

They waited in silence for the next chime of Mia's phone.

"Well?" Ellie questioned.

"Missing. She didn't check herself out, she's just gone. One minute she was in the hospital bed and the next minute the nurse went in to check on her and no Lana."

Ellie chewed her lower lip. "So, she could have walked out on her own."

"Or someone kidnapped her," Mia answered. "I mean… maybe? Kill her husband, kidnap the wife."

Ellie narrowed her eyes as she parsed the statement. "That seems backward."

"What do you mean?" Mia asked.

Jake rubbed the back of his neck as he stared into space. "You'd think they'd kidnap one of them and do a ransom demand instead of kill one and kidnap the other."

"Right," Ellie said. "What is the point of the kidnap?"

"Maybe it's not for ransom. Maybe she has something they want, like information. So, they kill the husband to make sure she cooperates."

Ellie puckered her lips and shrugged. "Maybe."

Jake crossed his arms. "Then it's no one here. As far as we know, everyone's in the house."

"That we know of," Mia answered.

"Yeah, true. Two people were just out of their rooms. They could have gone out. More people could be gone."

Mia climbed from her chair and pounded her knuckles against the desk. "Let's knock on the doors and find out."

"What?" Ellie said, screwing up her face. "No!"

Mia stamped a foot on the floor, causing Lola to let out a low rumble. "Come on. How else are we going to know who's out?"

Ellie shushed Lola before she responded. "I'm not disturbing people at my B&B by pounding on their doors."

"Tell them you're asking if they need anything like towels or something," Mia suggested.

Ellie shook her head and waved a finger in the air. "No. Not at this time of night."

"Oh, come on, it's like eight-thirty or something."

"Some people like to relax. I don't want to disturb the guests."

"One of whom may be murdering someone *right now*." Mia stuck her hands on her hips. "If you don't do it, I will. And then people will wonder why I'm knocking on their doors and not you."

Ellie crossed her arms and scrunched her face.

"Do it," Jake said with a chuckle.

"You two are the worst influences. Fine." Ellie flung her hands in the air and shook her head.

Mia clapped her hands and bounced on her toes. "Yay! Let's find out who's a murderer and who isn't."

Ellie rolled her eyes as she spun on her heel and stalked from the room. She hurried down the stairs, her legs feeling like jelly as she approached the first door. Mia and Jake hovered at the end of the hall. Mia bit her lower lip as she nodded and bent to rub Lola's ears. Jake offered her a thumbs up.

Ellie shook her head and pounded on the first door. She waited, rocking on her heels and staring at the dark grain of the wood.

"Try again," Mia whispered.

Ellie pounded on the door again before she pressed an ear against it. She pulled away and shrugged. "Nothing."

"Whose room is it?" Mia asked as she crossed to the next door.

"Carol and Ed."

"Hmm," Mia murmured, drumming her fingers on her forearm.

Ellie pounded on the next door. She sucked in a breath and waited. After a second knock, she shook her head. "Danny and Rose are also out."

Mia flicked her eyebrows up. "Two more on the suspect list."

Ellie paraded down to the next door and banged on it. "Nothing. This is Anna and Ava's room."

"Another two," Jake said.

"The entire B&B is on the suspect list," Ellie said with a sigh.

"Not true," Mia answered as Ellie knocked at Jim and Kylie's door. "We're not on it."

The door swung open, startling her and Jim squinted into the hall light. "Something wrong?"

"Just making sure you have everything you need."

He glanced over his shoulder before he nodded. "Oh, uh, yeah. Yeah, all good, thanks."

"Great," Ellie said as the door began to close. "If you–" She threw her hands in the air. "Okay."

"One innocent person," Mia said.

"Just because he's here doesn't mean he's innocent."

"Well, he's not meeting Lana," Mia answered as they bypassed the missing woman's door and continued to Ellie's room.

Ellie waved them into the room. Lola raced inside and leapt onto the bed. "Unless he already met with her. Or he called her."

"Why would he call her?" Mia asked, regaining her seat on the private porch.

Ellie plopped into the wicker rocker with a sigh. "Tell her to leave? Maybe they're in cahoots."

"Okay, so where is everyone else?" Mia asked, jabbing a finger against the brown woven chair arm.

Ellie shrugged. "Walking the dog."

"Murdering someone else," Jake said.

"Running away from the crime," Mia answered before she sat straighter. "I think we should go back to the diner!"

Ellie screwed up her face. "What?"

"The perp always returns to the scene of the crime. We should go there to see who comes back."

"I don't know if that's actually true," Ellie murmured. "I mean, will someone really show up there tonight? For what purpose?"

Mia chewed her lower lip as she tried to come up with a reason. "Ummm."

"No reason," Ellie answered. "The police have already been there. And unless it was related to the diner, there's no reason to return."

Jake lifted one shoulder in a shrug. "Plus, they could

return to the scene of the crime tomorrow morning when the diner opens and no one would know. It would be kind of stupid to break in now."

"Stop making sense," Mia said with a frown. "I wanted to go get into my all-black outfit and do some sleuthing."

"Nothing's stopping you from getting into your catsuit. We can go out for a walk and see who we find," Ellie suggested.

"You're on! Everyone get into your sleuthing outfits, and let's go see what we find!" Mia dashed from the room, earning a grumble from Lola as she swept past.

Jake shot Ellie a confused glance. "Sleuthing outfit?"

Ellie turned the corner of her lips down as she set her rocker in motion and shrugged. "I don't know. I'm wearing this."

"You're going to stick out like a sore thumb," Cleo called. "Everyone will see you coming."

"We'll take Lola with us," Ellie said, ignoring the cat. "She'll be our excuse for the walk."

"Sounds good to me. I wonder where everyone is. And I wonder if Scarlett found anything in her snooping." Jake pulled his phone from his pocket and tapped around on it.

"She would have made an excellent ambulance chaser, she should have gone into law," Ellie said with a laugh.

Jake flicked his eyebrows up and barked out a laugh. "She's something. She will hound the police for a statement, show up at crime scenes, the works."

"Are there many crime scenes in Salem Falls?"

"No, but if there is, she's all over it." Jake's phone chimed, and he clicked on the display. A scoff escaped his lips. "She's trying to find out more information on Lana's disappearance."

"She's at the hospital?"

"Drove there right behind the police."

They exchanged a glance, smiles playing on both of their lips. "Ambulance chaser."

Mia pushed through the door a moment later and struck a pose, hand on one hip as she used the other to flick her ponytail over her shoulder. "Ready."

Ellie scanned her up and down, noting the black leggings, black long-sleeve t, and black sneakers. "You sure you don't want a ski mask to complete the look?"

"No, I'm sleuthing, not robbing a gas station."

"You can't go wrong in all black," Cleo called from under the bed.

"Oh, excuse me," Ellie said with a groan as she pushed herself to stand. "We figured we'd take Lola with us as our excuse."

"Good thinking. I can creep on people if we need to," Mia answered.

"Come on, Lola, let's get your leash."

"Leash?" Lola asked. "I'll just walk."

"Don't want you jumping all over any of the guests we find out there."

"I won't," Lola said as she leapt off the bed.

"Yeah, right," Cleo shouted after them as they left the room.

"We're not taking the chance you get too rambunctious. Besides, this is good training for you to learn to walk on a leash so we can go into town more often."

"I hate that collar. I like to be naked."

Ellie swung around the railing at the bottom and headed for the kitchen pantry. "You're not going naked."

Mia chuckled behind her. "It's really funny how you talk to them like they can understand."

"Sometimes, I think they can," Ellie said.

"What does she mean, Ellie? I can understand you. And I answer all the time."

Ellie gave Lola a wide-eyed, amused glance. "She doesn't know you can talk, does she?"

"Doesn't seem like it," Lola answered.

Mia gave the dog's shoulders a rub. "Of course, you can, big girl."

Lola offered Mia's hand a lick before Ellie slipped the collar around her neck and snapped the leash onto it. "Okay, ready to go."

Lola shook all over, her floppy ears slapping off her head before she settled into a seat.

"Come on, Lol," Ellie called, tugging on the leash.

With a sigh, she rose to her feet and lumbered behind them. "Fine. I hate this collar, though."

They met Jake on the porch out front, finding him talking to Carol and Ed, who sat in the rockers with their poodle lounging at their feet.

Lola's tail wagged as she spotted the dog, but she hid behind Ellie's legs.

"Do you want to say hello, Lola?"

"Uh-uh."

"Come on, it's okay," Ellie said as she took a step toward the other dog. Lola wagged her tail as she tentatively approached the poodle.

"Hi, I'm Lola."

"Max," he answered, rising to his feet.

Lola shook off her leash from hanging on her shoulder. "I'm going for a walk, but I don't like my leash."

"Were you out for a walk with Max?" Ellie asked.

"Yes. Just around the property. It's a beautiful piece of land. I'll bet it's just amazing in spring and summer."

"Oh, it is," Ellie said. "I spent the end of summer here and it's beautiful. I can't wait to see springtime here."

"Oh, you haven't been here that long?" Carol asked.

"No. I came out after my aunt passed away and willed me the place. She died over the summer."

Carol's features pinched. "Oh, I'm sorry for your loss."

"Thank you."

Mia leaned back against the railing, cocking her head. "So, what about you two? First trip to Salem Falls or have you been here before?"

"Subtle," Jake whispered in Ellie's ear.

"We passed through here once many moons ago," Carol said with a chuckle. "Ed and I were just married and on our way to Bar Harbor for our honeymoon. Oh, what a trip that was. We drove from Ohio. Can you imagine?"

"What's that about a fifteen-hour drive?" Jake asked.

"And then some," Ed answered with a chuckle. "You're talking fifteen hours straight through, and speeding at the time. They didn't allow you to go seventy miles an hour back then. It was fifty-five, no more!"

Carol chuckled. "And of course, we wanted to be leisurely."

"Yeah, not that leisurely."

"We ended up with a flat tire and had to stay the weekend here."

"At this B&B?" Ellie asked.

"Oh, no. This wasn't open, at least not to our knowledge. We stayed at a little place on the outskirts. Nothing was open, and we had to wait until Monday for that tire repair. But we had a lovely time here and always said we would come back."

"Only took us forty years," Ed said, slapping his thigh.

"At least you got back here, and I'm so pleased you picked my B&B to stay at," Ellie answered with a grin. "Well, we'll let you enjoy your evening. Come on, Lola." She tugged at the dog's leash as she stepped toward the stair.

"Bye, Max," Lola said. "Have a nice night."

"Have a nice walk, Lola," the poodle answered as he settled his head on his paws.

The trio bounded down the three steps to the lawn below with Lola in the lead.

"So, Carol and Ed have been here before," Mia said with a raise of her eyebrows.

"Yeah, a hundred years ago," Jake answered as they strode toward the corner of the house.

Mia shoved her hands into the tight pockets of her athletic pants. "So? Maybe a hundred years ago they made some lasting connections. And then it led to murder."

"That was dramatic," Ellie said as she tugged the leash to pull Lola away from a bush she sniffed.

"Could be," Mia answered with a shrug.

A couple approached from around the corner. In the dim walkway lights, Ellie made out Danny and Rose. Their clasped hands swung between them as they approached.

"Hey, you two," Ellie said. "Out for a stroll?"

Lola sniffed in the air at the pair. Rose held a hand out toward her. "Are you Lola?"

"Yes," Lola answered with a tentative wag of her tail.

Ellie patted the dog's head. "Yep, this is Lola. How do you like the property?"

"It's really pretty. We were just sitting back by the stream. It's so relaxing."

"I think so, too," Ellie agreed with a nod.

"So, have you been out this way before or is this your first time in Salem Falls?" Mia asked.

"I've never been," Danny answered. "But Rose has."

Mia's eyebrows shot up as she slid her gaze to the redhead. "Oh?"

Rose nodded as she slipped her other hand around Danny's. "My family used to come here every summer when I was a kid."

"Oh, really?" Ellie asked.

"We had family in the area." Rose shoved a hand in her pocket and lifted a shoulder.

"Do you still?" Mia asked.

"No. My uncle died years ago. And we stopped coming."

"Sorry to hear that," Ellie said. "Well, enjoy your evening."

The couple said goodnight, and they went their separate ways.

Ellie cracked Mia across the arm. "Why don't you just ask them if they killed Zane?"

"Should I have?"

"No!" Ellie scolded.

"But I got the info. She came here often. Lasting connections that led to a murder, perhaps?"

"Wait a minute," Ellie said with a shake of her head as they rounded the back corner of the house. "Wouldn't it be a lasting connection to Zane, not Salem Falls?"

"Or both. Maybe they were both connected," Mia said with a shrug.

"Is that someone sitting over by the fire pit?" Jake questioned.

Mia froze, and Ellie squinted into the darkness, searching for any dark figures. Whispered voices gave them away.

"Someone's there!" Mia whispered.

"Hello?" Ellie called out.

"Hi," Ava's voice answered. "Sorry, I thought we were allowed to sit out here."

"Oh, you are. Just didn't want to startle you." Ellie wandered over, tugging Lola along with her. "Do you want me to get the fire pit going?"

"No, no, it's fine," Ava answered. "We'll be going in soon. Just wanted a little fresh air before bed."

"You sure?"

"Yep."

Anna remained quiet, her arms crossed over her chest as she stared blankly ahead.

Ellie shifted her eyes back and forth between them, trying to eke out any information from their dimly lit faces. She slid into one of the Adirondack chairs. "Enjoying yourselves?"

"The murder kind of dampened our time here," Ava answered.

"Yeah," Ellie said. "I understand that. But there's plenty of fun still to be had tomorrow at the festival."

Anna leapt from her seat, her hands balled into fists. "Who wants to have fun after someone's been killed!" She stormed away from the fire pit toward the house.

Ava puckered her lips and rose from her seat. "Good night, everyone." She scurried after her sister, wrapping an arm around her as they disappeared around the corner.

"Wow, that was a reaction," Mia noted.

"Tell me about it," Ellie answered.

Mia drummed her fingers against the low-slung chair's arm. "Maybe a little too much of a reaction."

"What do you mean?" Jake asked, sinking into the seat vacated by Ava.

"I mean she seems pretty upset. Maybe the guilt is eating away at her."

"You think Anna had something to do with the murder?" Ellie asked.

Mia lifted her shoulders, flailing her arms in the dim moonlight. "Maybe. She seems pretty upset."

Jake's face lit up as he toggled on his phone and tapped around.

"What are you doing?" Mia asked, lifting her chin to peer over the top edge of the device.

"Making a note to check into any connection between Zane and Anna."

Ellie waved a finger at him. "Any of the guests, really."

"Right. I'll dig around and see if I can find anything, but it may take a while." He narrowed his eyes before his thumbs pounded across the display again. "Better idea. I'll turn Scarlett loose on it. She'll spend the entire night tracking information."

"Good use of resources," Ellie said with a nod. "With any luck–" Her voice cut off, and she snapped her gaze over her shoulder to the house.

"With any luck what?" Mia asked.

Ellie waved her hand in the air. "Shhh. I heard something."

"What?" Mia hissed as she leaned forward.

Ellie thrashed her hand through the air before she clamped a hand around Lola's snout to stop her from barking. Jake spun to face them. "I heard it, too. Sounded like a voice."

"Sounds like Toby."

The voice grew louder as a dark figure crept around the edge of the house. "…know that! Don't you think I know that!"

He paused, his shoes scraping against the steppingstones planted in the grass.

"No. No! I just…Look, just make sure you find Lana before she blows this whole thing to bits!"

CHAPTER 15

"OMG!" Mia breathed.

"Whatever, I already told you..." Toby's voice trailed off as he disappeared around the side of the house.

"Did he just say something about Lana?" Mia questioned.

"That's what I heard," Jake said with a nod.

Ellie slumped back in the chair. Lola leapt up on the chair's arm. "Ellie, are you okay?"

"I can't believe this. Toby has a connection to Lana?"

Jake glanced over his shoulder before toggling on his phone.

"What are you doing?" Mia asked. "Do you have one of those voice enhancers on there?"

"Huh? No. I was going to tell Scarlett to skip the connection search, though calling those dogs off may be impossible."

"What? Why?" Mia asked. "We have to know!"

Jake let his lips fall open before he flicked his gaze to Ellie. "Well..."

"If it's on my account, don't call her off. We have to know. I just...once again, I'm shocked by Toby, and not in a good way."

Mia grabbed her friend's hand and patted it. "Sorry, El."

"It's fine. It's just more evidence that what I did was right."

"Okay, if you're sure. Because if he has a connection to Lana or Zane, Scarlett will find it. And she won't let it go."

"I'm sure. It has nothing to do with me. And if he's into something he shouldn't be, I don't want him under this roof."

Jake shoved his phone into his pocket with a nod. "Okay. Don't say I didn't warn you."

Mia slapped her hands against the wooden arms and rose. "Come on, let's finish our walk. Although, everyone's accounted for."

"Except Lana?" Jake said as they stood, and Ellie tugged Lola along with them.

Mia peered into the darkness. "Hey, do you think she'll come back here?"

"Do you smell anyone, Lol?" Ellie asked.

"No. I don't smell anyone out here now."

"What do you think, Lola? Will we find Lana?" Mia asked as they strolled to the opposite corner of the house.

"No, I just said no. No one is out here. Ellie, tell her."

"She's not barking, so she must not smell anyone."

Jake shoved his hands into his pockets as they rounded the corner. "I'm surprised she let Toby sneak up on us."

"Hey, I did not! You stopped me from barking," Lola complained.

"I caught her before she could bark and ruin it for us."

"Ruin it?" Lola asked.

"And now we got the information that Toby knows Lana."

They approached the front of the house. "*And* knows someone else who knows Lana. He told the person he was talking to that they had to find Lana."

"I wonder if we can find out who he was talking to?" Mia asked. "Jake, can you find out who he was talking to?"

"What? No," he said with a shake of his head, his

eyebrows crinkling as they approached the warm lights of the porch. "Why would you think I could?"

Mia shrugged and climbed to the now-empty porch. "You're good with technology. I figured you could yeet it or something."

Jake scratched his head before sliding a lock of hair behind his ear. "That's not even…it doesn't make sense."

Ellie let Lola off her leash to sniff around the yard for a few moments and stared into the night as she waited, brow furrowed. "Doesn't yeet mean throw?"

"Yeah," Jake answered. "She literally said she thought I could figure out who he was talking to by throwing…something. His phone? I don't know."

"I thought yeet meant something else." Mia shrugged. "Plus, I thought there was some cool reporter hack or something."

"What reporter hack would I have to get someone's call list?"

"Oh, oh!" Mia said, bouncing on her toes. "We can call the phone company and get a list of his calls."

Jake scoffed. "With a warrant."

"I can get that," Mia said.

"What? You're not even a cop."

"She's dating one, though," Ellie said as she hugged her arms around her midriff. "But I don't think he's just going to let you paw through someone's phone records."

Mia shot her a haughty glance. "We'll see about that."

"You're terrible," Ellie answered with a laugh.

The crunch of gravel drew her attention to the driveway. She called Lola onto the porch as she peered into the darkness at the car rumbling toward them.

"Is it Lana returning from her trip to the scene of the crime?" Mia whispered.

Ellie crinkled her nose and shook her head. "Their car is

here."

"Oh, right. Who is it?"

The vehicle reached the gravel lit by the porch lamps. Ellie's shoulders slumped as she spotted the light bar on the roof. "It's your paramour."

"Huh?" Jake asked.

"It's Rick," Ellie explained.

"Yeah, my paramour," Mia said with a raise of one shoulder. "Your vocab could use some work for a reporter."

"I'll be sure to use that word when I report in the future."

Rick climbed from the police cruiser with a deep sigh.

"Hey, boo!" Mia called with a smile.

Rick shambled across the space and climbed the stairs. "Hey, Cookie, no time to chat. I'm here on official business."

"Oh, hot," Mia said with a half smile. "Are you ready to make an arrest, Sheriff?"

Ellie screwed up her face. "Ew. Please stop flirting in front of other people. It's weird."

Rick pressed his lips together, his hands falling to his belt. "I'm not sure yet. Ellie, is your ex-husband on the premises?"

Ellie's heart skipped a beat. "Toby? Yeah, he came back a little while ago. Hey, listen, umm, we overheard something you maybe should know about while he was on the phone."

"I'll get it later. Right now, I'd like to see Toby."

Ellie offered him a dubious glance before she swung open the screen door. "I'll get him. Come on in."

They shuffled through the door into the foyer. Ellie mounted the stairs with Lola following behind her.

"Do you think Toby did it?" Lola asked as they reached the landing.

Ellie offered a tentative smile at the group downstairs before she hurried up the remaining stairs to the second-floor hall. "I don't know, but I'd be surprised if he did."

"Really? He seems like a jerk."

"I know. But a murderer? A jerk is pretty far from a murderer."

"Not *that* far," Lola contended as Ellie climbed the stairs to the third floor.

"Shh, pipe down before someone thinks I'm crazy."

"Why would they think that?"

"Because I'm talking to a dog. Just shush for a minute," Ellie said as she raised a closed hand to knock at Toby's door.

Lola's tail wagged as Ellie's knuckles drummed against the wood. She patted her thighs, jiggling her knees back and forth as she waited. A knot tied her stomach.

The door swung open a moment later, and a shirtless Toby stuck his head out.

"Someone's here to see you."

"Who?" he asked as he tugged a flannel shirt on and buttoned it.

"Sheriff," Ellie answered before she spun on her heel.

Toby grabbed her elbow, pulling her back to him. "Wait. What does he want?"

Ellie wrangled her arm away from his grip. "To talk to you."

"About?"

Ellie squashed her eyebrows together as she studied Toby. With his jaw muscles tensed, and his lips in a thin line, his agitation was obvious.

"I don't know, Toby. He showed up and asked for you."

Toby huffed out a sigh, running his fingers through his hair. "That's all he said?"

"That's all he said. He's in the foyer." She took a step down the hall.

"El, wait," Toby called. "Can you tell him I'm not here?"

Ellie twisted to face him, her features scrunched. "No, I can't. I told him you were here."

"Tell him you were wrong. You didn't see me."

"No, Toby, I'm not lying to the police for you. What's wrong with you?"

He flicked his gaze away from her, sticking his hands on his hips. "Huh?"

"What's wrong with you? Why are you acting like this?"

"Oh, I don't know, El. Maybe because a man was just murdered, and the police are asking for me. The cop who hates me, too."

"He doesn't hate you."

"Yes, he does," Lola said.

"He does. That little stunt of gathering the village here proved it. 'I run a real tight town, you hear?' He's after me. Of course, he wants to pin this on me. I'm the newcomer in town. They hate newcomers."

"That's not true. I'm new, and they don't hate me."

Toby shook his head and scrubbed his face. "I can't believe this. He's going to arrest me, mark my words."

Ellie thrust her hands out. "If you haven't done anything wrong, you don't need to worry."

"Unbelievable," he hissed as he pushed past her and stormed down the stairs to the floor below.

"He's upset," Lola said, her tail slowly moving back and forth.

"No kidding. But why?" Ellie crossed her arms as she stared after him.

"He thinks Rick is going to accuse him of murder. Even I know that."

"Come on," Ellie said, taking a step toward the stairs. "Let's go see what happens."

With Lola in tow, she hurried down to the second level. Shouts came from the foyer as she approached it. She grabbed the railing and peered over it.

"…no idea what you're talking about. I'm a cook there. Of course, I touched the knives." Toby flung his arms in the air.

NELLIE H. STEELE

Rick placed his hands on his belt again and shook his head. "Witnesses put the murder weapon in your hands no less than ten minutes before the murder occurred."

"I had to cut something. Of course, I had a knife in my hands."

"What did you have to cut?"

"What?"

Rick lifted his chin as he repeated the question. "What did you have to cut?"

"Lettuce. Onions. I don't know. I don't remember. I cut a lot of things."

Rick puckered his lips and sniffed. "Let's continue this down at the station." He reached for Toby's arm.

"Oh, hell no, man." Toby pulled back from the sheriff's hand, stumbling back a step and waving his hands in the air.

"There's no need to make a scene. We just want to go over the information."

"Look, I told you everything at the diner. That other guy, Nick, took my statement. I don't have anything else to say."

"Nathan," Mia said, settling her arms over her chest. "And if you don't have anything to hide, why not just go down and answer his questions?"

Toby narrowed his eyes at her. "Oh, you'd like that. You've probably been in his ear accusing me of everything. The only reason you're here is because I'm the new guy in town."

"I'm here because I have a knife that several witnesses place in your hands moments before it ended up in someone else's chest."

"And I told you I had nothing to do with that."

Rick bobbed his head up and down with puckered lips. "Mmm-hmm, you did." He leaned forward, raising his eyes to Toby's face and lowering his voice to a whisper. "I don't believe you."

"No, of course, you wouldn't. You already hate me because I'm a newcomer. Everyone hates big bad Toby because he cheated on his wife and then moved into sleepy Salem Falls."

"Moved? I thought you were just passing through?" Mia asked.

Rick held a hand up, shushing Mia before he leveled his gaze at Toby again. "That's not the reason at all. Now, we can take this down to the station, or I can arrest you and we can have the same conversation but in handcuffs. Your choice."

Toby scoffed, crossing his arms over his chest as he widened his stance. "Arrest me? On what grounds? Because I, the cook at the diner, happened to chop tomatoes."

"So, now it's tomatoes?" Rick said, squinting his eyes at Toby.

"Unbelievable. You can't arrest me. And I'm not going anywhere with you. I have rights."

A shuffling noise sounded behind Ellie, and she whipped around to find Carol, wrapped in a fluffy robe, approaching the railing. "Something wrong? Sounds like a commotion."

"Follow-up questions from the sheriff," Ellie whispered.

Carol raised her eyebrows and peered down at the scene as it continued to unfold.

"I can arrest you, and I will unless you come down to the station and answer my questions."

Toby thrashed his head back and forth. "No."

Rick huffed out a breath as he reached for his handcuffs. "You leave me no choice here. Toby Larson, you are under arrest for the murder of Zane Cartwright. You have the right to remain silent. Anything you say can and will be used against you in a court of law. You have the right to an attorney–"

"This is bull!" Toby shouted as he danced away from Rick who approached him with handcuffs. "I demand to know on what grounds you're arresting me. You have no proof of anything. This'll never get past a judge."

Rick flicked his eyebrows up. "I've got your hands on the murder weapon minutes before the murder, and I've got you meeting with the deceased last night. That proof enough for you?"

CHAPTER 16

*E*llie's jaw dropped open as Rick slapped the handcuffs on Toby's right wrist and twisted him around backward.

"Oh my word," Carol whispered. "I wonder how he knew the man."

Ellie settled her features into a frown. "So do I."

Chaos still reigned downstairs as Toby objected to the arrest. He flicked his gaze up to Ellie, catching her eye. "El, you gotta help me. I didn't do this. You know me."

"I thought I did," Ellie said with a shake of her head.

"Call an attorney. Mel, or whatever his name is."

"Ha!" Mia barked. "I don't think Mac's going to help you. No one's going to help you. You're a killer!"

"You always were a stupid–"

"Hey," Rick growled, tugging Toby back sharply and turning him toward the door. "I'd watch what I say unless you want a few more charges piled on top of first-degree murder."

"This is harassment. I'll have your badge. I'll sue–" Toby's

159

voice trailed off as Rick paraded him out the door to the waiting cruiser.

"Wow," Ellie said, burying her face in her hands.

"Oh, Ellie," Mia said before she hurried up the stairs, pushing between Carol and her friend and wrapping Ellie in a hug. "I'm so sorry you saw that. I thought you were with a guest or something."

Ellie lifted her head and inhaled deeply, flicking her gaze to the almost-empty foyer. "It's fine. I'm okay. I just...never thought Toby would be arrested for murder." A fleeting smile crossed her face. "Then again, I never thought he'd cheat on me with a waitress, leave me, then come crawling back because she did the same thing to him."

"Oh, honey. I'm sure Rick'll sort everything out."

"Doubt it," a sassy voice said from behind. Ellie twisted to find Cleo slinking from the bedroom.

"Yeah, I guess so. I just...can't believe he did it."

Mia pushed a lock of hair behind Ellie's ear. "Can't or don't want to?"

Ellie considered it. "Both. I don't know. It feels surreal. Although, he really wanted to avoid talking to Rick."

"Really?" Carol asked.

Ellie flicked her gaze to the woman, suddenly aware of her presence. "I guess no one would want to just after a murder."

"No one with something to hide, that is," Carol answered.

Ellie offered her a shrug. "Well, I'm certain the police have it handled."

"Yep," Mia said, lifting her chin. "Rick is a good cop. He'll handle it. Rest assured."

Carol offered them a cryptic smile and a curt nod. "We'll see. Thanks for the information, ladies." She spun on a heel and shuffled back to her room.

"Wow, she's intense," Mia said with a wrinkled nose.

"I really didn't want to say much more in front of her."

"Let's get a cup of hot chocolate and talk in private. Why don't you head into your bedroom? Jake and I will meet you there."

"I can help make hot chocolate. I'm not a Victorian housewife who needs to lay down, you know."

"No one said you are. But it's totally fine to take a few minutes to yourself."

Ellie lowered her gaze to the hardwood floor as she sucked in a breath. "Maybe a minute or two would be good."

Mia squeezed her arm and nodded before she spun and bounced down the stairs. "Hot chocolate, kid. You grab the fixings, I'll heat the milk."

Ellie chuckled at the conversation as they disappeared in the hall before she turned and shooed Lola into the room.

Cleo followed behind them. "So, the old ball and chain got pinched, huh?"

Ellie clamped her lips together as she sauntered to the sunroom, flicking a glance over her shoulder at the cat. "He's not the old ball and chain, anymore. I divorced him, remember?"

Cleo leapt onto the arm as Ellie collapsed into the cushioned wicker rocker. "I thought he divorced you."

Ellie shot her an irritated glance.

"What?" the cat asked. "It's true, isn't it?"

"Yes, it's true. Thanks for reminding me, Cleo."

"No problem, anytime. Happy to help. Listen, we need to talk."

"About?"

"A few things. First of all, I don't know how you feel about the old man after he left you, but if you think he's innocent, you better start sleuthing."

"I think Rick can handle it." Ellie set the rocker in motion before she pulled her legs onto the seat.

Cleo leapt to her feet, wobbling on the arm. "Whoa! Will you watch what you're doing? I nearly fell!"

"You're a cat. You'll land on your feet."

"Really?" Lola asked.

"Of course, I will," Cleo answered, "but the blatant disregard for my safety is concerning. Maybe I should have a talk with Sheriff Rick. Not that it would matter. He'd probably arrest the wrong person."

"We don't know he arrested the wrong person," Ellie said.

"He did," Cleo assured her. "Don't say I didn't warn you when an innocent man goes to the slammer."

Ellie rolled her eyes. "Toby's hardly innocent. He knew Zane, and he probably hid that from the cops. So, he has some explaining to do at the very least."

Cleo stared at her with narrowed eyes for a moment. "The second thing I wanted to talk to you about was–"

"One steaming hot chocolate to settle your nerves," Mia sang as she shuffled across the room and delivered the warm mug to Ellie.

"Hi, little kitty," she said with a pat on Cleo's head. "Did you crawl out from your hidey hole to visit with us."

"Idiot," Cleo said as she leapt off the chair and slinked past Jake to hide under the bed.

Mia sighed as she sank into the rocker next to Ellie. "She loves me."

"I love you," Lola said.

Mia offered the dog a smile and patted her head. "And you love me, too, right, Lola?"

"I just said I did. Ellie, I don't think Mia can hear too well."

"She does love you," Ellie answered. "And Cleo, too."

"I do not," the cat shouted from under the bed.

Jake sipped at his hot chocolate before he took a seat. "So, uh, I hate to bring up a bad topic, but…someone was arrested for Zane's murder."

"Toby," Ellie said while she chased a marshmallow around the frothy beverage. "In some ways, I can't believe it."

"You don't think he did it?" Mia asked.

Ellie shot her a glance. "Do you?"

Mia shrugged and sipped at the steaming liquid. "Maybe."

"Mia, you've known him for decades. Do you think he murdered a man?"

"He's been doing a lot of strange stuff lately, El. Maybe this is some kind of mid-life crisis, and he got in over his head and was desperate to get out."

"You really think he's capable of murder?" Ellie asked.

"I think none of us knows what we're capable of until we're put into a position where we find out."

Ellie's shoulders slumped, and she wrapped her fingers around the warm mug before taking a sip.

"So, I was actually going in a different direction than questioning if he did it," Jake said, tapping his fingertips against his mug.

All eyes turned to him, and Ellie raised her eyebrows, prompting him to continue.

"An arrest was made. Scarlett is going to want this all over the front page tomorrow." Jake wrinkled his nose as he shot Ellie a concerned glance.

"Okay?" she said.

"I can imagine this may be uncomfortable for you since he's your ex-husband. I can try–"

Ellie cut off his statement with a wave of her hand. "He got himself into this. It has nothing to do with me. Don't put your job at risk to try to protect me. It'll all come out anyway, especially if he's guilty."

Jake wrapped both hands around his mug as he bobbed his head up and down. "Okay, fair enough. I'm not sure I could have avoided it anyway. Scarlett is going to know, and she's going to run with it."

"That may be the best thing," Ellie said after another drink.

Jake offered her an incredulous glance. "Uhhhh, I'm not so sure about that."

"If anyone's going to get to the bottom of this, it's Scarlett. She's going to find out his connection to Zane and maybe that will shed some light on the situation."

"Ohhh," Mia said, patting Ellie's arm, "good thinking. She'll do a little digging on our behalf."

Jake slid his phone from his pocket. "Speaking of, let's see if she's found anything yet."

Ellie waved a finger in the air. "Ask her first, then spill your news."

Jake nodded as he tapped on his screen before he clicked off the display. "Sent."

Ellie sucked in a breath as she studied the dark chocolate liquid tinged with the remnants of melted marshmallows in the blue mug. "Do you–"

A chime interrupted her statement. "Got an answer," Jake said, toggling on his phone. "She says, 'Still digging. HBU?'"

"HBU?" Mia asked.

"How 'bout you," Jake and Ellie answered.

Mia swatted at Ellie. "Ohhh, look at you knowing the kid's slang."

"I yeeted it," Ellie said before she stuck her tongue out.

"I am never going to live that down, am I?" Mia asked.

Ellie shook her head as a smile played on her lips. "Nope."

"Okay, I let my info slip to Scarlett, this should be–and she's answered already."

Mia leaned forward with a grin. "What did she say?"

Jake read from his screen. "OMG, seriously? What's the evidence? Did you see the arrest? Did you get pictures of the arrest? Did Ellie see the arrest? Did you get a statement from the police? Did you get a statement from Toby? Did you get a quote from Ellie?"

Ellie screwed up her face. "How did she type all of that so fast?"

"You'd be amazed at her skills," Jake answered as he tapped around on his phone.

"What are you telling her?" Mia asked.

"Witnessed arrest. No pics, no statements."

His phone rang a second after he sent the message. Ellie winced as Scarlett's shrill voice blared from across the room.

"Ho-Ho-Scarlett, hold on," he said as he waved a hand in the air. He pulled the phone from his ear and poked at the screen. "I've got you on speaker."

"Who else is there?"

Jake flicked his gaze to the other two women, and Ellie offered him a nod.

"Ellie and Mia."

"Do they know the information?"

"They witnessed it, too."

"Tell me everything. What happened? Was there a confrontation? How did the arrest go down? Was there trouble? Did he deny it?"

"Okay, okay, okay," Jake said, interrupting her long line of questions. "He says he didn't do it. He gave some questionable answers. Rick said he was spotted with the deceased last night–"

"Whoa, okay, that's information we need to know. Ellie, how did your husband know the vic?"

Ellie leaned forward in the chair. "I don't know. I'm surprised, to be honest."

"Would you say shocked?" Scarlett said.

"Uh, I guess so, yes. I don't want to believe he could be a murderer."

165

"…numb with shock after her long-time husband… okay, what else?"

Ellie scrunched her features and shot Mia a glance, mouthing the words, "Numb with shock?"

Mia rolled her eyes and shrugged.

"Uh," Jake continued, "I think that's about it. We have no idea how Zane and Toby are connected, but they were seen together last night."

Ellie stood from the chair and hurried into her bedroom.

Lola followed her, a slow wag to her tail as she stopped at the nightstand. "What are you doing, Ellie?"

A smile curved Ellie's lips upward as she waved a paper in the air. "A-ha!"

She hurried back into the room, finding Jake bobbing his head up and down as Scarlett requested a full description of the arrest sent to her immediately.

"I'll send it right over to you," he said before signing off the call.

Ellie dangled the paper pinched between her thumb and forefinger.

"What's that?"

"The note Toby dropped when he came home the other night."

"The unreadable one?" Mia asked.

"Yes. Do you think it's connected to the murder? Do you think this came from Zane?"

Mia tapped her lips. "Does it look like Toby's handwriting or not?"

Ellie squinted down at the unreadable mess. "No, it's not his handwriting."

"Oh, do you have a sample of Zane's?"

Ellie shot her a glare. "No. Why would I have Zane's handwriting? And even if I did, the last time we did hand-writing comparisons it ended in disaster."

"It ended with us solving a murder." Mia poked a finger at her with her eyebrows raised.

"And me almost getting offed."

"Well, that too, but still…"

Jake rose and approached Ellie, squinting at the paper she held. "Can you make anything out on the note?"

"I couldn't. Maybe your eyes are better than mine."

He grabbed the paper and studied it. "It's completely smeared."

Ellie wrinkled her nose. "I know. But Toby was really interested in finding it. I don't know if he knew it was destroyed or not, but he asked if I found a paper."

"Did you tell him you did?"

"No," Ellie said with a shake of her head, "I fibbed. It's useless anyway, so I figured it wasn't that big of a deal."

Jake pulled the paper closer to him. "Does this look like it says pendant?"

Ellie smacked her hand off the chair's arm, startling Lola who let out a bark. "No barking! That's exactly what I said. It can't be coincidence right?"

Jake tugged his phone from his pocket and snapped a picture. "It could be, but it's kind of weird that a note would show up with the word pendant on it a few days after the discussion about Pizarro's Pendant."

Mia straightened. "Do you think the murder could be related to the hidden treasure?"

Ellie scrunched her eyebrows together. "Really? How would Toby even know?"

"Maybe Zane knew and told Toby. Asked him to poke around while he was here," Mia answered.

Ellie stared into space, sucking in a breath as the wicker creaked underneath her. "How would Zane know?"

"Maybe he has a connection to Salem Falls."

Jake handed the note back to Ellie. "We need more information. Maybe Scarlett can find a connection."

"We need to do more than wait on Scarlett," Mia said, leaping from her seat.

"Like what?" Ellie asked. "Do you want to take another walk around the house in your catsuit or visit the scene of the crime?"

Mia stuck a hand on her cocked hip and arched an eyebrow. "No. I want to search Lana and Zane's room."

CHAPTER 17

*H*eat washed over Ellie. "Are you crazy?"

"No," Mia said with a pout. "We need info! And we know where there may be a treasure trove."

"We have no idea if there's any information in their room and also, that's a gross violation of privacy."

"It is not," Mia answered.

"It is so. I can't just waltz into their room and go through their stuff," Ellie claimed.

Jake tilted his head. "The legalities are really unclear. You do own the B&B. Technically, it's your room."

Mia crossed her arms and cocked her head. "See, even the kid agrees."

"I can't believe you two. You're terrible influences."

"I can go in," Lola said.

"That's useless," Cleo answered from her hiding spot. "You're better off sending Sheriff Rick."

Ellie pointed a finger at Mia. "Maybe you should text Rick and see if he wants to search their room for clues or something."

"I wasn't serious. He won't find any clues either," Cleo retorted.

Mia wrinkled her nose. "First of all, he's busy questioning your ex, and we need answers from Toby. And second, I'm sure he needs some kind of legal paperwork to do that."

"Umm, so do we."

"No, because Jake said it's your property."

"Jake isn't an attorney."

"He's a reporter, so, close."

Ellie screwed up her face. "How is that close?"

"He is probably always scrounging around on other people's property looking for scoops. He'd have to know how far he can go."

"I mean, I'm not doing that like ever. Salem Falls doesn't have that many scoops, and I don't prowl around on other people's property."

"See?" Ellie thrust a hand toward him. "He doesn't prowl around on other people's property."

"But this is your property."

"I don't want to mess up a murder investigation *or* get arrested," Ellie said with a shake of her head.

Mia pressed her lips together in a thin line as she tugged her phone from her waistband.

"What are you doing?"

"Asking Luke if you can go into a guest's room."

"What? Mia!"

Mia shushed her and finished her typing, sending the message on its way. "We need legal advice. He's an attorney. And he helped you out before, right?"

"Yeah, for a dollar. Which is still weird. Why? What's the deal with you and Luke?"

Color rose in Mia's cheeks as she tugged her lips into a wince. The chiming of her phone interrupted any answer she might have given. "He answered."

"That was quick," Jake said. "On a Friday night, really late."

"He owes her big time," Ellie said. "We have no idea why, but apparently this favor she did him is the gift that keeps on giving."

"Okay, Luke says guests have a reasonable expectation of privacy–"

Ellie slapped her hand against the chair's arm. "Thank you, told you."

"*But*," Mia continued, "if they are engaging in something illegal or disturbing other guests you *can* enter the room without permission."

"They aren't disturbing other guests. Zane is dead, and Lana is missing."

"Well, technically, the death disturbed other guests," Mia answered.

"Also, they *may* be doing something illegal which led to the murder," Jake added.

"You two. You are really bad influences," Ellie said as she climbed to her feet.

Mia grinned. "So, we're going in?"

"I think only I should go in. And tell Luke if this backfires on me, he's representing me since it's on his advice I'm doing this."

"You can't go in yourself, you may miss something."

"Neither of you are owners," Ellie said. "What if–"

Mia waved a hand in the air. "What if, what if. What if you were in there already, and we casually strolled by, found the door open, and went in to talk to you."

"Fine, let's go. I guess we may as well put that catsuit to use."

They shuffled from the room with Lola in tow.

"I've got the spare key downstairs. I'll run down and grab it." Ellie hurried down the stairs as Mia stooped to pet Lola and prevent the dog from following. She made her way to the pantry and unlocked the small safe there to retrieve the master key for the bedrooms.

"You know who else's room we should search?" Mia whispered as Ellie climbed the last few stairs to the second floor.

"I don't even want to know."

"Toby's. He could be hiding something major."

"Let's get the illegal one over with first. I feel like I have more right to search Toby's room than the others."

A thud sounded behind one of the doors as they passed it, and Ellie froze. She snapped her gaze to the door, brow crinkling. Was someone listening to their conversation?

"Is that Carol's room?" Mia hissed.

Ellie nodded and pressed a finger to her lips before motioning for them to continue down the hall to Zane and Lana's suite. She approached the door and leaned back, scanning up and down the hall before she slid the key into the lock and twisted it.

The door popped open, and she raced inside. Lola and the others followed her. Ellie eased the door shut with a wince and flicked the lock.

Lights bloomed to life as Mia flicked the switch on the wall. "Whoa."

Ellie spun to face the room. "Geez."

Jake tripped over a wayward shoe lying in the middle of the floor. "They are not neat travelers."

Ellie wrinkled her nose at the clothes strewn around the room, the half-empty suitcase flung open on the holder, and the makeup scattered across the vanity in the en-suite bathroom. "They haven't been here long enough to make this much of a mess."

"Apparently, Lana and Zane know how to get it done,"

Mia said. She crossed to the open suitcase and rummaged through the contents.

Ellie crossed her arms as Lola sniffed around at the various items in the room. "Umm, I don't think pawing through luggage is protected under the law."

"We have to," Mia argued. "It's not like they are going to leave a giant clue laying out for us to see."

"If my B&B is shut down two days after I opened–"

"Relax, El, no one's going to catch us." Mia shifted a few more items around before she scanned the room for another location to search.

Jake tugged open the top drawer on the nightstand. "What, no Bible?"

Ellie pursed her lips as she swung open the cupboard door. "The Gideons haven't been here yet."

Mia dropped to her knees and peered under the bed. She winced as she twisted to reach underneath and tug out another suitcase. "Ew, who puts a suitcase under the bed?"

"Hey! I cleaned thoroughly. It's perfectly fine to put your suitcase under the bed here."

"Still…they don't know that," Mia said with a shrug as she flung the top open and rooted through the items. "Nothing but clothes."

She flipped it shut and sighed, collapsing back on her heels.

Ellie's stomach jittered as she scanned the room. "Maybe we shouldn't be here."

"We need information," Mia argued.

The events replayed in Ellie's mind as she glanced into the bathroom before she shuffled toward the bed and sank onto it. She drummed her palms against her thighs. One of the room's occupants had just been killed. The other had disappeared. What if they were hiding something? "I think we should leave."

"But Ellie…" Mia said, smacking her hand off the top of the suitcase. She paused, staring down at the black nylon fabric.

"What?" Ellie asked, spinning to face her.

Mia grabbed the zipper to the top compartment and opened it. She fished inside before she pulled out a series of printed papers and held them up. She unfurled them and studied the contents. Her jaw dropped open.

Heat prickled Ellie's skin as she eyed Mia's reaction to the papers. "What's on them?"

Without a word, Mia flicked them around for the others to see.

Jake stooped lower to read them. "Is that–"

"Information about the treasure hidden in this house," Ellie said.

Mia flattened the papers against the suitcase. "From that weird, ancient website."

"Do you think it's a coincidence?" Ellie asked.

"Yeah, maybe they were reading up on Salem Falls and stumbled across that," Jake suggested.

Ellie considered it before she nodded. "Right, exactly. Probably just some reading material for while they were here."

Mia shot Ellie an unimpressed glance. "Yeah, right. They just happened to find information about the treasure. And then they printed it. And then one of them ended up dead after meeting with Toby who had a list with the word pendant on it, and the other is missing."

Ellie winced. It was a red flag. Maybe they should inform the police.

Mia climbed to her feet and waved the papers in the air. "This is a clue. This murder is connected to your treasure."

"My treasure?" Ellie asked. "It's not *my* treasure."

Mia folded the papers, creasing them with her nail before

she shoved them under her arm. "We need to find this treasure before someone else gets hurt."

Ellie's stomach turned. Would the curse strike again? She rose to her feet, waving her arms in the air. "Whoa, whoa, wait a minute. We have no idea this is related at all to the murder."

"Uh, I think it is. This is evidence." She poked her fingers at the paper. Do you think Toby knew anything about the treasure?"

"I don't know. He hasn't said anything to me."

"Not surprising." Mia drummed her fingers against her forearm. "Hey! You should go talk to him about it. See if he'll spill anything now that he's under duress."

Ellie screwed up her face, not wanting any part of Toby's current mess. "No! I'm not getting involved with this investigation."

"Come on, El, Rick will let you in to see him because you're family...sort of."

Ellie pressed her lips together and crossed her arms. "I'm *not* going to ask Toby if he was treasure-hunting with the deceased."

"Come on," Mia whined.

"You go," Ellie said with an arch of her eyebrow. "I'm sure Sugarboo will let you in."

"It's Sugarbear and I'm sure he would, but Toby won't tell me anything. He hates me."

"He doesn't feel much better about me. He hated me enough to cheat."

"But he came running back the second he needed something."

Ellie shook her head, refusing to take part in any of this plan. "Hardly a testimonial to our relationship."

"I'll do it," Jake volunteered.

All eyes turned to him, and a grin formed on Mia's face.

Ellie fluttered her eyelashes as a series of emotions shot through her. She couldn't send the kid in to do her job. "No. That's too much. You shouldn't get involved."

Jake shrugged. "I'll say I'm doing it for the paper. Getting the scoop. Allowing him to tell his side of the story."

"No, no, no, no, no," Ellie said, sticking her hands on her hips. "I can't let you do that. You shouldn't be involved with this mess."

Jake's phone chimed before he could answer. He glanced at the screen before he flashed it toward the women. "Whether I should have to or not, it's now my official job to do it."

A message from Scarlett blazed on the screen. *Head over to the station, see if Peach will let you talk to the perp*.

"Who's Peach?" Mia asked with a wrinkled nose.

"Rick," Jake said as he pounded against the virtual keyboard to type his response.

Mia stiffened, color rising in her cheeks. "Why does she call him Peach?"

"He's from Georgia." He snapped his gaze to a visibly upset Mia. "Georgia Peach."

"Oh, right. I thought maybe…"

Jake tugged the corners of his lips down as he stowed his phone. "They're not dating. It's not a pet name. Scarlett would think dating a cop is beneath her."

Mia's upset turned to ire at the statement. "Rick's a nice guy."

"Yeah, but he's a cop. And Scarlett's…Scarlett. Anyway, looks like I'm heading to the station."

"Wait, what should we do in the meantime? Go to the diner? Search for the treasure?" Mia asked.

"Maybe nothing," Ellie said. "I think we should just cool it, and let Rick handle things."

"You're right. We should look for Lana."

Ellie blinked at her friend. "Are you kidding? Where would we look?"

Mia shrugged. "We can't just sit here!"

"I wasn't planning on it. I was going to get some sleep."

Mia waved a hand at her. "Who can sleep with all this going on?"

Exhaustion coursed through her, and she stifled a yawn. "Me, I can."

"Fine, I'll go myself. You go to sleep."

"Ugh, you're awful. I can't let you go alone. But we're taking Lola with us for protection."

Mia bounced on her toes, tapping her fingertips together. "Can we take Cleo, too?"

"Cleo hates the car."

"Aww," Mia grumbled with a wrinkled nose, "I totally think the cat sleuth would be cool."

"You wrangle her into a carrier. By the time you're finished, we may be taking a trip to the hospital instead of wherever you plan to go searching for Lana."

"I wouldn't put her in a carrier," Mia said as they made their way out of the room and down the hall. "I'd just let her walk around. Her keen night vision may spot something we don't."

Ellie offered Mia a stony stare.

"I'll ask her!" she said in response before darting into Ellie's room. "Oh, Cleo!"

Ellie smirked at her friend's exuberance with the cat before she twisted to face Jake. "Let us know if you find anything out from my illustrious ex."

"I will. I'll text you. Though they may not let me see him."

Ellie traced the outline of a floorboard with her foot, scuffing it against a groove. "I really don't want to visit him, but…if you need me to come out for your scoop, let me know."

"It may be easier for me to talk to him. Unless they won't let me."

"Good luck," Ellie said as he started down the stairs.

"You too. Keep me updated if you find anything."

"Yep," Ellie said as Mia pranced out with Cleo behind her.

"Field trip," Cleo shouted.

"Text us the deets, kid!" Mia called over the railing.

"Yep. I'll yeet them to you," Jake answered as he headed out the door.

"Shh, people are trying to sleep." Down the hall, a door creaked closed, softly latching.

Mia shot Ellie a knowing glance. "Doesn't sound like it."

Ellie started down the stairs. "No wonder with your carrying on."

Lola and Cleo raced down the stairs ahead of her with the cat calling, "Shotgun!" as she approached the door.

"I can't believe you convinced Cleo to come," Ellie said, swinging her purse strap over her shoulder. "We're taking your car."

"Definitely. It's way better than yours for slinking around town."

They stepped on the porch with the pets racing in front of them. "Slinking?"

"My car is black. We can hide super easily."

"You are really into this sleuthing thing."

"I'm thinking of becoming a PI," Mia said, the yellow running lights lighting her face as she pressed her key fob to unlock her doors.

Ellie swung her door open, and the cat leapt into the front seat. Ellie gave her a questioning glance before she tugged open the back door and shooed Lola inside. "Really?"

Mia lifted a shoulder before sliding behind the wheel. "Maybe. I mean, who knows? It would be great because I could work with Rickie."

"I guess we'll test your skills out tonight," Ellie answered as she shoved at the cat. "Move over."

"Get in the back. I called this seat," Cleo answered.

"I'm not riding in the back, Cleo, move over. Sit on the console."

"Come on, kitty," Mia said, patting the rubbery top of her armrest. "This is a nice spot for you."

"Don't ruin this for me," Cleo answered as she climbed onto the cube and sat down, wrapping her tail around her legs.

"Okay," Ellie said, strapping into the seat. "Where are we going to find clues?"

Mia fired the engine and clicked off the emergency brake before she shifted into gear. "I figured we could start at the cemetery."

Ellie screwed up her face as the car lurched forward. "What? Why would we go to the cemetery?"

"I don't know. It seems like a plausible place for clues."

"How?" Ellie asked with a crinkled nose as they pulled onto the road.

"In the movies, people are always at cemeteries. An owl hoots in the distance. Spooky shadows are cast over the tombstones. And villains lurk in the darkness."

Ellie stared at her friend, features frozen into a confused expression. "Thanks for that, Vincent Price."

"'Cause this is Thriller," Cleo sang, lifting a paw in the air. Ellie gave her an unimpressed glance.

"What's a thriller?" Lola asked.

"It's MJ. Get some culture, pooch."

"I can't help it. Anyway, at least we're doing something." Mia swung the car onto another road and slowed as they approached the fenced graveyard.

"What's an MJ?" Lola asked.

Ellie let her gaze rise to the ceiling, wondering if she'd

make it through the trip with her sanity intact. Mia's brakes squealed as she brought the car to a stop and leaned over to crack open the glove box. She grabbed a flashlight from inside and wound it.

"You have a windup flashlight?"

"Yeah, Rick gave it to me. So, I don't have to remember to change batteries." She clicked it on and aimed it into the foggy cemetery.

Ellie let her head bounce against the headrest as she waited for Mia to complete her scan. A gasp drew her attention. "Someone's in there!"

CHAPTER 18

"*W*hat?" Ellie asked, leaning forward and peering into the foggy darkness. Headstones poked up from the ground but she failed to identify the person Mia claimed to see. "Where?"

"Right…" Mia huffed out a breath and shook her head. "They went behind a building. Dang it."

"Are you sure someone is in there?"

"Yes, I'm sure."

Cleo bobbed her head. "I saw them. With my excellent night vision. Two people…or maybe zombies."

"Where are the zombies?" Lola scurried across the backseat and stood at the window, her tail shaking.

Mia popped her door open. "Come on!"

"I'm not going into the ceme–" Ellie began when the slamming door cut off her statement.

"Go, Ellie. Find out what's going on," Cleo said. "I'll wait here."

Ellie clicked her seat belt off. "Why don't you go? You're the super sleuth."

"Oh, right, sure, send the innocent black cat into the

graveyard at midnight. I could be captured and sacrificed. Do you know what people do to black cats in cemeteries at night?"

"Fine, fine. Stay here with Lola."

"I want to go," Lola said.

Ellie signaled for her to sit down, climbing from the car. "Just wait here."

Lola leapt at the window, tail wagging as she stared at Ellie's departing form. A weak whine emanated from the car. Ellie twisted to spot Cleo swatting at the dog and shook her head. "Those two."

"Aren't you glad we brought them along?" Mia asked as she tugged the unlocked gate open. It creaked on its hinges, and an owl hooted in the distance.

Mia froze and flicked a finger in the air. "There's the owl."

Ellie glanced up to find the large bird perched high in a tree as she slid through the opening onto the cobblestone path. "Next up, spooky shadows."

Mia bobbed her head up and down in response.

Leaves rustled on the trees, a few of them falling to the ground. Ellie inched forward toward a mausoleum looming over them.

A shriek resounded, and both women came to an abrupt halt. Mia winced, eyes wide as she clamped a hand around Ellie's forearm and squeezed. "What was that?"

"The villains," Ellie whispered.

Mia's jaw dropped open. "Really?"

Ellie squashed her eyebrows together and slid her eyes closed as she focused on the sounds in the cemetery. Wind whistled through the trees scattered around, swishing the leaves. The owl hooted again in the distance. And another muffled shriek sent her eyes popping open.

She flicked her gaze to Mia and shook her head. "No, it's Cleo."

With her lips pressed into a firm line, she glared at the car parked near the gate. A black paw waved in the air inside.

"What is she doing?"

"Smacking Lola around for something or another. Lola's probably barking or grumbling."

Mia pressed a hand to her chest. "She scared the crap out of me."

Ellie tugged her arm back from Mia's grasp. "If that scared the crap out of you, maybe you shouldn't be a PI."

"If I was a PI, I'd be prepared. With like a weapon or something," Mia said as they continued forward.

Ellie squinted into the darkness as she swung left and threaded through the tombstones. "I don't see anyone."

"Someone's in here," Mia hissed.

"Where did they go? What are they doing in the cemetery in the middle of the night?"

"Who knows? Secret meetings betwixt murderers?"

"Did you just say betwixt?" Ellie asked as they approached a large weeping angel statue. She frowned at it, hurrying past as a chill swept over her.

"Yeah. It sounded pretty cool, right?"

"Sounded kind of ridiculous, but we are standing in the middle of a cemetery in the middle of the night searching for a missing woman after a murder, so I guess it fits. Why are we here, anyway?"

"I told you," Mia answered with a huff, "bad guys always meet in cemeteries."

"I thought we were looking for Lana, not bad guys."

"What if Lana is the bad guy?"

Ellie considered it, flicking her eyebrows up. "Maybe she did kill her husband, but then why did she leave the hospital and go to the cemetery of all places?"

"To meet her co-conspirator, no duh."

"Which is who?"

"Whom," Mia said.

"Is it? Wait, is it who or whom? I never know."

"It's who when it's the subject of the sentence and whom when it's the object," Mia answered.

"Was it the subject or the object?"

"Object, so it should be whom."

"Are you sure?" Ellie paused under a large oak and grabbed her phone, toggling it on. The bright screen lit up the surrounding area, disturbing the owl perched above. It sailed from the tree, diving toward their heads before it pulled up and flapped its wide wings, flying toward the moon.

Both women screamed as the creature dipped toward them, instinctively covering their heads. Ellie's heart hammered until she identified the bird as it flitted into the distance.

"That stupid owl," she murmured as she straightened and her pulse returned to normal, "scared me half to death."

"Yeah, me too. So, is it who or whom?"

"Never mind," Ellie said, shoving the phone into her pocket. "What person is Lana meeting with? Who else is involved in this murder?"

"Or whom else?"

"And which one of them actually stuck the knife in Zane's chest?"

"Good question. If we find the people lurking around in here, maybe we'll know. I saw them right up by that mausoleum."

"Let's keep going. I think the path circles around it and continues to another row."

Ellie nodded, and they ambled toward the large stone building flanked by two angels with swords. Ellie's gaze rose up to the top. "Wow."

"St. Michael the Archangel," Mia said. "Defend us in battle."

"Apparently, this guy needed a lot of defense."

"Whose tomb is it?" Mia wound up her flashlight and clicked it on, searching for the information. Her jaw dropped as she read it.

"Who is it?" Ellie asked.

Mia spun wide-eyed and faced her. "It's Charles Portsmith. The former owner of your B&B. The plaque says he was buried with guardians to keep him safe from the curse that killed him."

"Wow, they took that pretty seriously." A shudder passed through Ellie as she studied the muscular angelic forms with their swords ready for a fight.

"What's weirder is why there were two people lurking here." Mia waved her flashlight around the mausoleum before she climbed the stairs between the two statues. "But they definitely were."

"How do you know?"

"There are muddy footprints on the steps here. They lead inside."

"Seriously?"

"Yes, seriously," Mia said, "look for yourself."

Ellie leaned forward and stared at the mud-caked steps. "How do we know this is fresh?"

"Looks fresh." Mia scraped a few bits away, squashing them underfoot. "It's not crusty and dry."

"What would someone be doing here?" Ellie glanced around the area in search of anyone lingering as her pulse quickened.

"Should we go in and find out?"

Ellie winced but nodded. "I guess so, though I'd rather not."

She steeled her nerves and trudged up the stone steps,

passing between the two drawn swords. Mia twisted the knob and pushed the metal door inward. It creaked on its hinges, sending a nails-on-chalkboard noise into the night air and turning Ellie's flesh into goosebumps.

"I don't like this." Ellie wrapped her arm around her midriff.

"It's not that bad. It's not like his body is going to be laying out all rotten and gross."

"Forgive me for not wanting to creep into a crypt in the middle of the night."

"Scared of ghosts?"

"No. That's the house on First Street that's haunted, remember?"

Mia took a step into the mausoleum. "It's hardly reportable to say the cemetery is haunted, that's just a given."

Icy air wafted past Ellie as Mia disappeared into the stone structure. With another shiver, she glanced over her shoulder, searching the darkness, for what she didn't know, before she pushed herself to slip through the open door and into the tomb.

Mia's weak flashlight beam swept around the interior. Ellie wrinkled her nose as it highlighted thick cobwebs. A black spider scurried away from the sudden burst of light, tucking itself into a dark corner.

"Okay, no one is in here, let's go," Ellie said.

"Wait!" Mia exclaimed as she wound her flashlight up again. "We haven't even looked around."

"Who wants to look around? Not me. I don't want to see any more spiders or worse. There are cobwebs everywhere. And I've already seen the main attraction." She patted the thick stone coffin in the center of the space. "Here's Charles."

"Why was someone in here?" Mia asked aloud as she skirted around the casket.

Ellie batted at a stray spiderweb that floated closer to her.

"We have no idea someone was in here. You're surmising based on some weak evidence."

"It's hardly weak evidence. Fresh mud on the stairs means someone was in here recently."

"Okay, so?" Ellie asked. "It doesn't have anything to do with Zane's murder or Lana's disappearance."

Mia shined the light at her. "We don't know that."

Ellie held up a hand, squinting against it. "It makes no sense at all. Why would the killer come here? And what are the chances even if they did that they picked this tomb in particular?"

Mia pressed her lips together and narrowed her eyes as she paused in search of a response.

"Let's just go before I see something worse than a spider."

"There's nothing worse than a spider in here. Well, other than the killer who was probably in here a few minutes ago." Mia swung the light at Ellie again. "OMG, Danny and Rose were out. Do you think they were the ones in here? They could be the killers!"

"Why would the newlyweds be the killers? Plus, so were Anna and Ava *and* Carol and Ed."

"If they are newlyweds. Maybe they're faking that. And yeah, it could be *any* of them."

"Why would it be any of them, and why would they fake their marriage?"

"Bad business deal with Zane. Nefarious ties to Lana." She shined the light at Ellie again. "The treasure."

Ellie narrowed her eyes again and stepped to the side to escape the bright beam. Something touched her face, and she swung her arms wildly to free herself from any unwanted insects.

Mia doubled over laughing as Ellie shook her hair. "It's not funny. There could be a spider in my hair. And we have no idea the treasure is real."

"Zane did have information on it. Maybe he planned to look for it and so did the newlyweds, so they killed him."

"That's far-fetched, but–" Her words cut off as Mia's flashlight dimmed until it died.

"Oh, shoot," Mia said in the blackness. A thin sliver of light painted the floor where the door opened to the outside.

"That's our cue."

"Wait, I'll just wind it up again," Mia said as Ellie moved toward the door. A shadow blotted out the little bit of light before the hinges creaked.

"Hurry up, there's a cloud blotting out the little bit of moonlight we had."

The winding sound stopped, replaced by Mia's voice. "Cloud? There were no clouds tonight."

"Well, obviously one cropped up because the sliver of light is gone. The moon must be behind a cloud."

The winding resumed. "I'm telling you there were no clouds. You probably knocked the door closed with your conniption fit."

Ellie huffed into the darkness. "It wasn't a conniption fit. There was a cobweb on me. And I didn't knock it shut. It's still–"

The light beam illuminated the space as Mia flicked the flashlight on again. "It's still what?"

Ellie's heart skipped a beat as she stared at the metal door. "It's shut! How did it close?"

Mia sidestepped around the coffin toward the door. "You probably knocked it."

"I didn't," Ellie insisted as she wrapped her hand around the brass knob and twisted it. She tugged back, but the door didn't budge. Her eyes went wide, and she shot a panicked glance at Mia. "It won't open."

Mia's brows pinched. "What do you mean it won't open? It has to open."

She nudged Ellie to the side and grabbed the knob. With a twist of her wrist, she pulled back on the door, leaning at an extreme angle as she pressed her lips together. "Stupid thing must be stuck."

Ellie pushed her aside. "Move over, let me try again." She grabbed the doorknob and twisted one way, then the other while rattling the door in the jamb.

"I bet the metal is catching somewhere. Probably hasn't been opened much since they built it. We'll try together."

Ellie nodded as Mia cupped her hand around Ellie's and together, they tugged back on the door. It never budged.

Mia let go and wiped a bead of sweat from her brow.

Ellie stared at the dark metal as she wrapped her arms around herself and a quiver entered her voice. "We're stuck in here."

CHAPTER 19

"We can't be stuck," Mia said with a scoff.

"Really? Tell that to the door. We're stuck. Trapped in a tomb."

"It's fine. We're not stuck. We both have our phones and–"

Ellie waved a hand in the air. "Shh, listen."

Mia slid her head forward as she stared at the floor. "What?"

"Lola's barking. I can hear her in the distance."

Mia pressed her ear against the door. Her eyebrows shot up after a moment. "I hear her! Although, it doesn't do us much good. She's stuck in the car."

"Not that," Ellie said. "She must see someone. She's barking at something."

"She barks at everything. It could be a branch or a leaf."

"Or it could be the people you saw lurking around here. What if they locked us in?" Ellie's eyes went wide, and she grabbed the doorknob again and tugged wildly.

"How would they lock us in?" Mia asked.

"A key? A bar? A chain? I don't know how villains lock people in places normally."

Mia wrinkled her nose. "That seems far-fetched."

"Really? *That* seems far-fetched? You're actually saying this to me after dragging me to a cemetery and into a crypt and you think the so-called villains you saw lurking around a graveyard at midnight locking us in is far-fetched?"

Mia shook her head and set the flashlight on the coffin before tugging her phone from her pocket. "We're not trapped. So, it was a weak effort on their part. All we have to do is call someone."

Mia flashed her phone's bright display at Ellie and poked a finger at the bars at the top. "We're above ground, so we have signal and everything."

"Okay, great. Call Rick," Ellie said, pressing a hand to her head.

Mia winced and shot her a glance. "Uhh, I mean, I'd rather not."

"What do you mean, you'd rather not? Why not?"

"First of all, he's super busy questioning a suspect. So, I don't want to interrupt his important work."

"He could send Nathan."

"Secondly," Mia answered, ticking another point off on her fingers, "I'd really rather not let Rick know that we're trespassing in a cemetery at midnight."

Ellie's features fell into an unimpressed frown. "Seriously?"

"I mean, it's going pretty good with him, so I'd rather not have him mad at me if at all possible."

Ellie heaved a sigh and crossed her arms as the light died again.

Mia wound up the flashlight again. "Call Mac."

Ellie slid her eyes closed as she shook her head and fished her phone from her purse. She found Mac's number and dialed. The line trilled a few times before she heard his recorded voice on the other end. "No answer."

Ellie puckered her lips and stared down at her list of contacts.

"Who else do we know who may be up?"

"I can't believe this," she said as she pressed the call button next to one of the contacts. The line trilled a few times before Jake answered.

"Hey, Ellie, did you find something?"

"No. We need some help if you're done with Toby."

"Haven't seen him yet. I'm still hanging around in case they let me in, but so far it's a no-go. What do you need?"

"We got stuck, and we need you to spring us. You may need some tools or something, I don't know."

A scuffle sounded on the other end of the line before Jake spoke again. "Sure thing. Where are you? Did you blow a tire or did the engine die or what?"

"No, no, we're not stuck on the road."

"Oh, where are you?"

Ellie licked her lips and stuck a hand on her hip, lifting one shoulder in an attempt to feel less ridiculous. "We're... inside a mausoleum at the cemetery."

Silence met her words. "Huh?"

"We thought we saw someone lurking around in the cemetery. We came in to take a look and ended up stuck inside the crypt of Charles Portsmith." She rolled her eyes at their own stupidity.

"Right, okay, umm, just give me a few minutes to get out there." The sound of a car door slamming punctuated his statement.

"Thanks, Jake."

They ended the call, and Ellie blew out a long breath. "Jake's coming."

"Oh, good. Did he talk to Toby?"

"No, they wouldn't let him. He was hanging around in case they changed their mind, but so far, no one but the cops are talking to Toby."

"See, I told you Rick was busy. And soon enough we'll be out of here and moving on to the next location."

Ellie slipped her phone back into her purse, snapping her gaze sharply to Mia. "Next location? I think it's time to call it a night."

"What? We have more questions than answers now!"

"Not really."

"Yes, really. We know someone was lurking around this tomb. And how odd is it that it belonged to the very man who had the treasure, to begin with."

"So, what? They were searching for a clue in his coffin?"

Mia spun and grabbed the flashlight, aiming it at the stone enclosure. "Doesn't look like they opened it."

"Thank heavens. We're not opening it either."

"What if the treasure's hidden in there?" Mia asked.

"Leave it hidden."

"I don't know if anyone but you is going to think that."

Mia squatted down and studied the sealed top. Ellie's stomach rolled as she considered the body inside. Was it surrounded by treasure?

Her thoughts were interrupted by a loud bang. She leapt in the air, pressing a hand to her chest. "Ellie?" Jake's voice called.

"Jake!" she answered, allowing her pulse to return to normal. "You can't sneak up on us like that. We're too old to be startled."

"You're not *that* old. Although you did watch VHS, so I guess maybe you are."

Ellie stuck a hand on her hip. "Very funny. Can you get the door opened?"

"No. It's chained shut."

"Wait, what? Are you serious?" Mia approached the door, pressing her ear against it. "Did you say it's chained shut?"

"Yeah. The chain is wrapped around the knobs and then locked. I can't get it open without cutting it."

"Well, cut it!" Mia shouted.

"I don't have cutters. And the hardware store isn't open. I'm not sure any hardware stores around here are open."

"Listen, Jake," Ellie called, "there are some tools in the shed at the B&B. It's locked, but there's a spare set of keys in the pantry."

"Okay. Oh, wait, I don't have keys to the B&B."

"It's unlocked. Not everyone was back in the house when we left, so I left the door open."

"Okay, I'll grab the tools and be right back."

Ellie sucked in a breath as she nodded at the statement.

"Don't go away," he added before he chuckled.

"Very funny," Ellie groaned.

"Stick to your day job, kid," Mia shouted.

"Hey, just remember who's rescuing you at midnight from a mausoleum."

His footsteps receded as he returned to his car. Ellie stretched her neck and set her hands on her hips. "Well, at least he can get us out."

"Yeah, and I didn't have to call Rick."

"Maybe next time we should rethink trespassing," Ellie said.

"Someone else didn't. Someone was in here. Someone who may be a guest at your B&B."

"We have no proof of that."

"You said it yourself. Not everyone was in their room when we left. Totally possible the newlyweds were here in the cemetery and locked us in here. *Or* Carol and Ed. *Or* Anna and Ava."

"Again, why?"

"Because they're after the treasure. This all comes back to the treasure. It has to!" Mia ticked points off on her fingers. "Think about it. Zane had information on the treasure. Now Zane is dead. Charles had a direct connection to the treasure."

"And he, also, is dead," Ellie noted with a smirk.

"Very funny. He had a connection to it, and someone was lurking around in his mausoleum. And we have a connection to the treasure and are now locked inside."

"Okay, maybe it's all related. But we have no proof of anything."

"Which is why we are here. We have to get proof."

Ellie heaved a sigh. She'd never convince Mia to stop digging. Although, truthfully, she wanted answers, too. She sucked in a deep breath and leaned back against the stone coffin as she considered her answer. The top shifted. She flailed her arms as she toppled back further than expected.

"Ellie!" Mia said in a hushed tone. "You opened his coffin!"

"I didn't mean to. Help me close it."

Mia shot her a glance.

"What? Help me close it."

"What's the rush?"

Ellie's jaw dropped open. "Are you serious? I defiled a man's grave."

Mia bobbed her head up and down. "Yeah, sorta. But, I mean, it's already open now. What's the harm in giving it an extra shove and checking out the inside for a clue."

"That's gross. He's probably rotted in there. It's been like a hundred years."

"I'll just take a peek. Help me push this to the side a little."

Ellie offered her friend an unimpressed stare before she held her hands up. "Fine."

Together, they inched the stone lid sideways enough to

peek into the coffin. Mia wound up the flashlight before she shined it inside. Suit pants ended in shiny dress shoes. Ellie ducked to peer further up, finding a rotting body, hands clasped over his belly inside.

She wrinkled her nose as her lips formed a grimace. "Nothing in there but a dead guy."

"Really?" Mia asked, dipping lower to glance inside. She straightened with a sigh. "You're right. Just a dead dude. Unless…" Her eyes widened and the corners of her lips turned up.

"What?"

"Do you think there's a clue in his pocket?"

"Ew, I don't know, and I'm not going to find out. If you want to paw through the clothes of a dead man, you go right ahead. I'm out."

Mia stared into the coffin again before she shook her head. "Probably he doesn't."

"Okay, let's put the lid back on. I'm not leaving his grave disturbed."

"Why not? You're already cursed. Maybe that'll reverse it."

"Very funny, just grab the edge and help me put this back in place." Ellie wrapped her fingers around the ornate corner and tugged, her nose scrunching as her shoulders burned with effort. "Are you pulling?"

"Yeah, I'm pulling," Mia grunted. "It's not moving."

Mia let go and stumbled back a step, running a hand through her hair. "Put your butt against it again."

Ellie glared at her as she let up on her tugging.

"What? It worked the last time. Go around to the other side and try pushing while I pull."

"Fine," Ellie said, skirting the corner and pressing her backside against the edge of the lid. She dug her feet into the stone floor and pushed. The lid inched over.

"A little more," Mia said with a groan.

Ellie scrunched her face. Sweat beaded on her brow as she gave the lid another shove.

"Okay, stop!" Mia called. "It's in place side to side, but we need to push it down to cover his feet.

Ellie whipped her hair off her neck, fanning herself. "Whew. It's hot in here."

"You're having a hot flash."

"I am not. It's hot. I'm doing all the work here." She let her hair cascade down over her shoulders again before she inched her way around the stone rectangle and positioned herself at the top.

She gave it a hard shove. "I can't budge it. I need help."

Mia circled around to join her. As Ellie sidestepped her way over to make room, her foot caught on something. She stumbled forward, grasping the lid to balance herself.

"Whoa, you okay?"

"I tripped on something. Put the light down here." She poked a finger toward her feet.

Mia aimed the now-weak flashlight beam toward the floor. It glinted off something before dying. She wound it up again and aimed the now-brighter light.

Ellie furrowed her brow. "What is that?"

"Looks like a plaque. Maybe it says his dates of death or something."

"Why put it up here? No one would ever see it."

"Probably so no one tripped on it like you just did."

Ellie squatted down and study it. "Give me the light."

Mia passed it to her and she aimed it at the bronze plaque. Black lettering dotted it. She squinted down at it. "Ugh. It's no use."

She dug in her purse for a few minutes before she pulled out a pair of readers. "Can't see a thing in this light."

After sliding them on her face, she peered at the writing

again. Her jaw flapped open and she shot Mia a surprised glance.

"What's it say?"

Ellie swallowed hard as she traced the letters on the bronze plaque. "It says, 'To my descendant, use the clock to find the pendant.'"

CHAPTER 20

*M*ia dropped to her knees and stared at the plaque. She wrinkled her nose and whipped the reading glasses off Ellie's face before holding them up to her own eyes. "Wow. It's definitely a clue about the treasure."

"Sure sounds like it."

"I wonder if the other person or persons in here tonight found it."

"I don't know." Ellie pulled her phone from her purse and snapped a picture of the plaque. "What does it mean?"

"Obviously, we have to use the clock to find the pendant."

Ellie rose to stand, studying the image on her phone. "No kidding. What clock? Where?"

"There's a clock in the center of town. Maybe it's that one."

"Maybe. How do we use it to find the treasure?" Ellie clicked off her display and slid the phone into her purse.

"We'll swing by and check it out as soon as we're done with our sleuthing for Lana," Mia said as she rose to stand and tugged at her shirt.

"Okay. Let's finish closing up poor Charles's tomb."

"Wait!" Mia said, freezing with her hands stuck out on either side. "What if he has the clock inside his casket?"

"I didn't see a clock inside there."

"What if it's in his pocket? Like one of those ones that hang from a chain?"

"That's a pocket watch, not a clock."

"It's still a clock."

"I'm not sure it would be described as a clock."

Mia whipped her phone from her pocket and tapped around. "Clock. A timekeeping device. So, it could be."

"Fine," Ellie said, sticking her hands on her hips, "do you want to climb in there and look."

Mia wrinkled her nose. "No, let's hope it's the one in the town's center."

"That's what I thought." She braced herself against the lid and gave it a shove. "Come on, help me."

Mia leaned into a lunge and pushed. The lid slid closed, and Ellie blew out a sigh of relief, swiping at the sweat that had formed on her brow. "Now, to escape this place."

"You're right," Mia said. "Why would he put this plaque here, and then bury the clock with him? That makes no sense."

"I'm glad you agree that pawing through someone's casket is ridiculous."

"Ladies! I'm back!" Jake called from outside.

"Oh, thank goodness," Ellie said after a sigh of relief. She hurried around the coffin to the door. "We're here. Did you find everything you need?"

"Yeah. I got the bolt cutters. Here goes nothing."

Ellie pressed her ear to the door before a loud snap sounded followed by the rattling of chains. A moment later, the door swung open. Cool night air rushed in, sending a shiver down Ellie's damp spine.

She heaved out another relieved sigh as she stepped into the dim moonlight. "Thanks, Jake."

"Anytime," he said as Mia stepped out of the mausoleum.

"Thanks, kid." She stooped to study the chains. "These were wrapped around the knob?"

Jake nodded. "Uh-huh. And locked."

"So someone locked us in that mausoleum on purpose." Mia straightened and shook her head.

"Who?" Jake asked.

"We don't know. Mia saw someone lurking around in here, and we came in to check it out. She found muddy footprints leading inside. We went in, and that's when someone locked us in. We never saw them."

Jake scratched his head. "That's odd. Why would someone be here and then lock you in?"

"Because of the treasure," Mia answered.

"The treasure?" Jake asked.

Mia dipped her chin at Ellie. "Show him what we found?"

Ellie slid her phone from her purse and toggled it on before pulling up the image of the plaque. "This was inside Charles's mausoleum."

"Use the clock to find the pendant," Jake read. "Do you think someone was looking for that?"

"We don't know, but isn't it odd that I saw them around the crypt belonging to Charles Portsmith, found muddy footprints leading inside, and then someone imprisoned us in there?"

"Yeah, I do think it's odd. Why did you come here anyway?"

"You always check cemeteries after a murder, everyone knows that," Mia answered.

Jake scrunched his features. "Uh…"

Mia waved a hand in the air. "Never mind. We were here

and happened to spot something. Here's the bigger question: is this all related?"

"The murder and the treasure?" Jake asked.

Mia bobbed her head up and down. "Yeah. It makes sense, right?"

"Does it? Zane had some information on the treasure, but why kill him?"

"To get to it first!" Mia exclaimed.

"Maybe. Who else is looking for the treasure, though?"

"Could be anybody. Someone from the town, one of the guests. Maybe even Lana."

Outside of the hooting of the owl, silence fell between them.

"Come on, we've got more sleuthing to do," Mia said, grabbing Ellie's hand. She tugged Ellie down the path toward the entrance. "You coming, kid?"

After scooping the bolt cutters off the ground, Jake hurried after them. "Yeah. You got room or do I need to drive myself?"

"We have room. If you don't mind sitting in the back with Lola."

"I don't mind. I'll leave my car here. Pop your trunk, and I'll toss these inside." He waved the bolt cutters in the air as they slipped through the creaky gate.

He stowed them in the trunk as Mia and Ellie slid into their seats.

"Where have you been?" Cleo asked, leaping onto the console.

"I saw two people running around out here. I yelled and yelled but you didn't come," Lola said.

"I heard you barking, Lola. But we were stuck inside the mausoleum. Someone locked us in. Did you see anybody?"

"I just said I did."

"Did you recognize them?"

"No, I saw two people but it was dark. They had hoods on," Lola answered as Jake slid into the back seat. "Jake!"

"Hi, Lola. Oh, you brought Cleo, too."

Mia fired the engine and flicked him a glance through the rearview mirror. "Kitties like to sleuth."

"But kitty hasn't been sleuthing," Cleo shot back. "She's been stuck in the car with the loud, barky dog, powerless to do anything or find out who locked you up."

Ellie ran a finger down the cat's head as she ducked away. "I'm glad you two were safe in the car."

"Safe in the car?" Cleo exclaimed. "Total waste of my talents. I could have identified them, tracked them, and this entire mess would be over."

Mia swung the car around, leaving Jake's crossover behind as she rumbled down the road. "Next stop: the diner."

"Oh, can we get a burger?" Lola asked.

"It's closed, dummy," Cleo answered.

"Oh," Lola said. "Then why are we going there?"

"To investigate." Cleo slid her eyes closed.

"I wonder if there are any security cameras in or around the cemetery," Jake asked as Mia swung the car onto the road toward the diner. He tugged his phone from his pocket and tapped around on it. "I'm asking Scarlett."

"Oh, great. She'll want to know why," Ellie said, her head smacking off the headrest.

"She says she doesn't think they have security. They've never had problems there before. And yep, she asked why."

"Did you answer her?" Mia asked, killing her lights as she approached the diner and slowed the car to a crawl.

"Yeah. I said you'd spotted someone lurking around in there."

Ellie shot a glance over her shoulder. "That's not going to satisfy her. She's going to want to know what we were doing there."

"Probably," Jake said, stowing his phone in his pocket. "I'll look at the texts later."

Mia slid her car into the empty lot and turned off the engine. She peered through the windshield into the darkened diner.

"Someone's in there," Cleo said.

Ellie squinted, leaning closer to the windshield. "I don't see anything."

"I'm telling you, someone's in there," Cleo said. "Lola, back me up."

Lola glanced out the side window. "I can't smell anyone."

"Not with the windows closed," Cleo answered. "Crack a window."

Jake climbed forward, leaning closer to Cleo as he studied the interior of the diner. "Do you think it's true people return to the scene of the crime?"

"I think–" Mia began when her voice cut off. "OMG, someone's in there!"

Cleo heaved out a sigh. "I told you. No one ever listens to the cat."

Mia grabbed her door handle. "I'm going in."

"Wait!" Ellie said, grasping her by the arm. "We have no idea who that is. It could be the murderer!"

"Even better," Mia said, leaning toward the door.

"No! Not better. What if they strike again?"

"Okay, then we all go. And we take Lola."

Lola's tail wagged. "Maybe I can get a burger."

"I'm not sure that's a great idea. We could be confronting a killer. I don't want to expose Lola to that. What if she gets hurt? Or one of us gets hurt?"

"No one's going to get hurt because, by the time we decide, the person is going to be long gone."

"It could just be Val or someone else cleaning up after the incident," Jake said. "Maybe it's no one."

"And maybe it's the killer." Mia yanked the handle and kicked open the door. The interior light glowed to life.

"Oh, great," Ellie said as she hurried out of the car door. "Now, they'll know we're coming."

Cleo slipped out onto the pavement next to her, making a dash toward the diner. Jake popped open his door and scurried out before he slammed it shut, trapping Lola in the car.

"Take the back entrance, kid. We'll try the front."

"Oh my goodness, no!" Ellie shouted as her heart hammered. "We shouldn't be sending him alone. That could be a killer in there."

"I'll go with him!" Cleo shouted as she darted around the corner of the building in front of Jake.

Ellie followed Mia up the stairs to the diner's front door. "Mia, this is so stupid."

Mia yanked on the handle. "Locked." She pressed her nose against the glass, shielding her face with her hands as she stared inside. "They're over by the restrooms where the murder happened. It has to be the murderer!"

She banged on the glass. The figure startled and whipped around to glance at them, still hidden mostly by shadows. "Hey, you! We can see you in there. You're surrounded! Give it up!"

"Mia!"

"What? They are!"

"And that could panic them and lead them to do something stupid." The figure darted from the alcove's bathroom and fled toward the kitchen. "Like that, see?"

"They won't get anywhere. Jake's back there."

Ellie hurried down the stairs as Mia jimmied the door again. "I'm going around."

"Good idea," Mia said. She trailed behind Ellie as they rounded the building.

Ellie hobbled around the front corner. "Oh, my stupid hip

is killing me. I should have worn better shoes if I knew I'd be chasing a murderer."

"Probably hurt it pushing Charles's coffin lid back in place."

"Probably," Ellie said with a wince as they rounded the bend. The back door to the diner flew open as Jake reached it. It smacked him in the face and knocked him backward. He stumbled a few steps before he lost his balance and collapsed to the ground.

The dark figure dashed out and loped across the gravel lot toward the tree line.

"I'm all over it!" Cleo shouted, her green eyes gleaming in the dark night before she dashed after the runner.

"Jake!" Ellie shouted. "Cleo!"

Mia changed direction, hurling herself toward the escaping figure. "I'll go after them. Help Jake."

Ellie pressed a hand to her forehead as a wave of emotion shot through her. She hurried toward Jake and knelt next to him. "Jake?"

He didn't answer. She pressed two fingers against his throat, breathing a sigh of relief as a steady thumping thrummed. She patted his cheeks. "Jake, come on, wake up."

Ellie sat back on her heels and dug through her purse in search of her phone. She keyed in the emergency number. Her thumb hovered over the call button when a groan escaped from Jake's lips.

She shoved the phone back into her bag and leaned over him. "Jake? Can you hear me? Are you okay?"

His eyes fluttered open, and his features scrunched. "Yeah, yeah, I can hear you."

"Are you in pain? Should I call an ambulance?"

"No," he answered, pressing the palm of his hand against his forehead. "I'm okay. I just have a killer headache."

"I think I should call the paramedics."

Jake pushed himself up to sit. "No, I'm fine."

"You could have a concussion. You were out for a few minutes."

"Really, I'm okay. I don't need to go to the hospital."

Feet crunched gravel as someone approached from the woods. Ellie rose to her feet, fishing for her phone in her purse again. "Who's there? I've already called the police."

"Chill out, Ellie," Mia choked out. "It's me."

She approached the diner and doubled over as she tried to catch her breath.

"Did you find anything?"

Mia straightened, tossing her blonde hair over her shoulder. "No, all I did was pull my hamstring."

"At least that's all that happened. You shouldn't have run after them. First, because you're over fifty, and second because they could be a killer and could have hurt you."

"Okay, first, I'm fifty, not over. And speaking of hurt, how's the kid?"

"I'm fine," Jake said, rubbing at the red mark on his forehead.

"He's not. We really need to visit the hospital and make sure he doesn't have a concussion."

"Right. Okay, next stop is the hospital. Once he gets checked out, we'll try the clock and see if we can find anything."

"I really don't–"

"Listen, kid, we could all use some downtime here. And maybe an ice pack if I can wrangle one from the nurse."

Ellie closed her purse and stretched out a hand to help Jake to his feet. "That sounds like a good plan. Maybe Scarlett will dig something up in the meantime, and we'll have a new angle to work."

"Okay," Jake said as he climbed to his feet. "I'll go for the sake of you ladies resting."

"Good decision, kid," Mia said as she clapped him on the shoulder. "Let's go. Maybe we can even get a sandwich."

"I doubt the cafeteria is open this time of night," Jake said as they walked around the building.

"I meant from the nurse. If you ask them really nicely, sometimes they'll give you a sandwich and some jello."

"Only you would love hospital jello," Ellie said with a shake of her head before she stopped. "Wait, has anyone seen Cleo?"

"Cleo?" Mia asked.

"She ran after the person in the diner with you. But she didn't come back."

"Maybe she's waiting at the car," Mia said.

"Oh, maybe. Yeah, she's probably sitting on the hood waiting for us to come back and carry on with sleuthing."

Mia wrapped her arm around Ellie's shoulders as they continued around the building to the front lot.

Ellie squinted at the car, searching for the small cat. "It's impossible to see if she's there. Why couldn't she be light-colored?"

They reached the car without finding any trace of her. Ellie leaned over and checked underneath. "Cleo?"

"Cleo!" Mia shouted. "Come on, kitty kitty. Train's leaving!"

"She's not here." Ellie planted a palm against her forehead.

"It's okay, Ellie, we'll find her," Jake said. "I'll grab a flash-light and go into the woods–"

"No," Ellie interrupted. "No, there's a predator on the loose out there. No one should go into the woods."

"I'll go around back and call her," Mia said.

Ellie nodded as she tugged her door open and stuck her head inside. "Have you seen Cleo?" she whispered to Lola.

"No. I haven't seen anyone."

Ellie's shoulders slumped as she ducked out of the car and

slammed the door shut. She hurried around the side of the building, following the sound of Mia's voice to the edge of the woods. She joined in shouting for the little cat as she swept her cell phone's flashlight back and forth.

After a few minutes of calling, she let her hand fall to her side and shook her head. "It's no use. She's lost. Cleo is lost."

CHAPTER 21

*E*llie squatted down as her legs turned weak. The little cat had run off into the woods chasing after a burglar, possibly a murderer, and had disappeared. She never should have taken them with her. What was she thinking?

"It'll be okay, El, we'll find her. Maybe she's just chasing a firefly or something."

Ellie blinked back the tears in her eyes as memories of Lola chasing after a dangerous person flitted through her mind. The dog had been missing for a while and had managed to hurt her foot in the process.

Surely Cleo was savvy enough to stay away from the person. She hated people. Possibly not, though, if she was trying to make her contribution. The cat had too much brazenness for her own good.

"Hey," Jake said as he joined them, "I'm really fine. I don't need to go to the hospital. We can stay and look for Cleo."

"You should get checked out," Ellie said as she rose to stand.

Mia nodded. "Maybe we should take a quick run there, then come back, and she'll be here waiting."

Ellie pressed her lips together as tears stung her eyes. "I can wait here in case she comes back. I don't want her to be alone."

"We'll stay," Jake said.

"I can stay," Mia answered. "We can call the paramedics–"

Jake waved his hands in the air. "That's ridiculous. I don't need an ambulance."

Ellie rubbed at her temples. "Actually, if you're sure you're okay, would you two mind running back to the house and grabbing her treat jar? Maybe she'll come back if she hears me shake it."

"Yeah, sure, of course, Ellie," Mia said, squeezing her arm. "Anything you want."

"I'll stay here with you," Jake said. "You shouldn't be here alone."

"The kid's right. I'll take Lola and head back for the treats. Do you want me to leave her there or bring her back with me?"

"Umm, bring her back. Maybe she can sniff out Cleo."

"Good idea. Okay, I'll be back in a jiffy. Don't solve any mysteries without me." Mia grinned at them before she jogged toward the front parking lot, cursing under her breath about her hurt hamstring.

Ellie wrapped her arms around her, sucking in a breath as she tried to convince herself the cat was fine. "Thanks for staying with me."

"Sure," Jake said. "I'm sure we'll find her."

"Every time one of these incidents pops up one of my pets goes missing. Last time, Lola had to go to the vet."

"Hopefully, Cleo will be luckier. She's a pretty smart cat."

Ellie offered a quiet chuckle. "I'm surprised she didn't come back just because you said that. Are you sure your head is okay?"

"Yeah, it's fine. Even the headache is starting to go away."

Jake's phone chimed, and he pulled it from his pocket and toggled on the display. "Update from Scarlett."

"Did she find a connection between Zane and anyone in town or any of the guests?"

"Yeah, she did," Jake answered, scrolling through the long text. "Zane and Kylie are cousins."

"What? Are you serious? They didn't act like they knew each other that well."

"She says they are, and she's still digging. No connections to anyone else who is a guest at the B&B or any town residents thus far."

"Okay, so maybe there's a family feud, and Kylie or Jim is the killer."

Jake tapped around on his phone, bringing up a notepad. "Jim was not in his seat during the time of the murder, according to my notes."

"They were in their bedroom when I checked on them earlier. They were the only ones."

"Keeping to themselves because one of them just committed a murder?"

Ellie stared into the dark woods in front of them. "Maybe. Did it look like it could be Jim or Kylie who was just in the diner?"

"I'm not sure. All I saw was the door coming at me."

"It was too dark from the front to catch many details. Why would they come back here?"

"Guilt? The knife is in processing, so it's not to get rid of the murder weapon."

Tires on the pavement reached their ears before the squeal of brakes. A few moments later, Mia appeared with Lola in the lead. "Is she back yet?"

"No, we haven't seen her. Did you get the treats?" Ellie asked.

Mia waved the bag in the air. "Her favorite. Greenies."

"Thanks." Ellie swiped them and crinkled the noisy container before she shook it. "Cleo! Come on and get your treats!"

She waited a few seconds, straining for any sound of the animal. She tried again, rattling the treats in the bag. "Cleo! Treats!"

"I don't smell her, Ellie," Lola said as her gaze darted around.

"She's not coming," Ellie said with a sigh.

"Maybe she can't hear you," Mia answered. "Let's go into the woods and try it."

Ellie grabbed her phone and toggled on the flashlight. "Okay. Yeah. Lola doesn't seem to smell her. Maybe she'll catch a whiff if we get on her trail."

"Right. Come on, Lola." Mia tugged on her leash as she picked her way between the trees.

"Lola, if you smell Cleo, let us know."

"Okay, Ellie," Lola answered before she set her nose to the ground and sniffed.

"She went this way." Lola pulled Mia's arm to the right.

"Wonder if she caught a whiff," Mia asked as she hurried to follow behind Lola. "She's pulling hard."

"Let's hope so," Ellie said as she shook the bag again. "Cleo, come on out. Come get your treats."

Lola stopped, her tail slowly wagging back and forth.

"What is it, Lola?" Jake asked when he caught up to her. "Do you smell Cleo?"

"No, I lost her scent," she answered. Her nose wiggled in the air as she sniffed the wind.

"Cleo!" Ellie shouted again. "Come on, girl!"

"I think she lost the trail." Mia pulled on Lola's leash to move her to the left. "Try here, Lola."

Lola sniffed around in a pile of leaves before she lifted her head and stared into the darkness. She set her nose to the ground again and sniffed, pulling Mia along with her.

"I found her again. This way."

"She's on to something again," Ellie said.

Mia held the leash tightly as Lola strained against it. "Hopefully it's not a wild animal."

"Cleo!"

"With all the shouting, I think we'll scare them off before we get too close," Jake said.

"Hey, there are no bears around here, are there?" Mia asked.

Jake shrugged. "I don't know. I don't usually run around in the woods at night."

"Well, have there been any sightings? Someone in this town probably wanders through the woods after dark. Or maybe someone caught one rummaging around in the diner's dumpster?"

"No, Val's never reported any bears."

"Good," Mia said with a sigh as Lola continued to tug her forward.

"The scent is stronger," Lola said, pausing for a moment before she continued forward. "She's been here recently."

"Keep following the scent, Lola. You're doing good." Ellie crumpled the bag again, calling for the cat.

"Come on, Lola, sniff her out, girl," Jake said.

"I'm trying. I think she's close. I smell her. Smells like… litter and cat food." Lola lifted a paw and sniffed in the air again before she darted toward a tree. "I smell her here."

"Cleo!" Ellie rattled the treats in the bag again. "Treats! Come on, girl."

Lola sniffed around the base of the tree before she sat down. "She's here. I smell her."

Ellie swept the flashlight beam around in search of the small cat. "Cleo!"

"Come on, Lola, get up, girl," Mia said, jimmying the leash.

"No, she's here. I smell her here," Lola answered.

"She won't go, Ellie. I don't know what's wrong with her."

"She thinks Cleo is nearby, I think. I wonder if–"

"El-Ellie," a small voice cried.

"Cleo?" Ellie gasped, swinging the beam around wildly. "Did anyone else hear something?"

Jake shook his head, sweeping his cell phone's light near the base of the trees.

"Cleo!" Ellie called again.

"I'm here," a tired voice called out. "It's bad, though. I'm in pretty bad shape."

Ellie's heart beat faster, and she spun in search of the small cat. "Cleo, where are you?"

Lola leapt to her feet. "Oh, no, she's hurt!"

"Cleo, sweetie, where are you? Are you hurt?"

"She's hurt, Ellie," Lola answered. "She said she's in bad shape."

"Up here," Cleo breathed out. "In the tree. Oh, the agony."

Jake flicked his phone's flashlight higher. "I heard a meow!"

"Oh, no. She's in the tree. I wonder if she got hurt," Ellie said, her throat closing as a lump formed.

They searched the branches above them. Jake swept the light beam around until two green eyes glowed back at them.

"There." He jabbed his finger in the air.

Ellie followed the line and found Cleo huddled on a branch. The fur on her back stood up and her tail feathered out like a wire brush. A pitiful meow escaped her.

"Cleo," Ellie said, her heart still pounding as she pressed a hand against her chest. "Thank goodness we found you. Come down from there."

"I can't. It's bad, Ellie. I may be dying."

Ellie waved the treat bag in the air. "Come on, Cleo."

"I can't. Not even for a Greenie. It's terrible. I never thought it would end like this."

Mia handed Ellie the leash before she heaved herself up on a branch.

"Careful, don't hurt yourself."

"I'm fine. I can still climb trees. I'm coming for you, kitty. Auntie Mia's gonna rescue you."

Another wretched mewl sounded at Mia's words.

Jake lowered his flashlight. "Maybe I should run back for a towel to wrap her in."

"Maybe. Oh, be careful, that person from the diner could still be out here."

"Will do," Jake said as he trotted off toward the car.

Mia reached the branch Cleo sat on and shimmied her way toward the cat. Cleo offered another howl, and Mia froze. "Sorry, kitty. Is the shaking hurting you?"

Ellie squeezed her lips together as her mind ran through the things that could be wrong with the animal. She hoped they weren't serious enough to warrant anything extreme. "Why did you have to run off after that person?"

"Someone had to do it," Cleo said, her voice weak and breathy. "Tell them I was brave until the end, will you?"

Tears formed in Ellie's eyes. Mia continued to ease her way toward the cat. Cleo backed away as she approached.

"Easy, kitty, easy. I'm going to help you."

"Just leave me to die," Cleo answered.

Mia stopped her motion, freezing as the muscles of her jaw tensed and her nostrils flared. In one swift motion, she leaned forward and scooped the cat into her arms. Cleo let out a wail and a hiss as Mia tucked the cat under her arm and made her way back toward the trunk.

The black cat struggled and wriggled. "Let me go, you brute. You're hurting me worse!"

"Easy, Cleo, let her help you."

Mia winced as she reached the end of the branch and slid down to the next one. "Owww, she's clawing the heck out of me."

"I'm sorry," Ellie said, wringing her hands.

Jake trotted back up with a towel in hand. "Got it. How bad is she hurt? Is she bleeding?"

"I don't feel any blood," Mia answered as she continued down the tree toward the ground.

"She's fighting her and crying a lot." Ellie slid a hand onto her forehead as she bit her lower lip.

Mia reached the ground and Ellie hurried forward toward her. Jake scooped the cat into the towel and wrapped her tightly before handing her off to Ellie.

"Is she okay?" Lola asked.

"It's okay, Cleo. We got you. Let's go. I'll call Dr. Meyer on our way and see if he can come in."

"Right," Mia said, collecting the leash from Ellie.

"Wait, wait!" Cleo shouted as she wriggled in the towel. "Dr. Meyer?"

The little cat squeezed an arm out of the wrap and climbed up, leaping from the towel. She stalked around, then shook a paw, shooting a glare at Ellie. "Let's not go that far."

"Whoa," Jake said. "Well, it looks like she's walking okay."

Cleo shook her head and sat down on the ground, licking a paw before she raked it over her face. "I'm fine, idiots."

"Cleo!" Lola bounded toward the cat and sniffed at her head.

Cleo ducked away, batting at the dog. "Get off of me, you lug."

Ellie sobered, setting a hand on her hip as she shook her head at the scene. "She's fine."

"I'm so happy you're okay, Cleo."

"Are you sure you're okay, Cleo?" Ellie asked. "Lola had to go to the vet after her escapade with the killer."

"I'm fine. It's a miracle. I have been healed." The cat rose to all fours and arched her back before she stalked toward Mia and rubbed against her legs.

"Aww, you're welcome, kitty. She was just scared, Ellie. She's okay."

"Mm-hm," Ellie said, taking Lola's leash back from Mia as Cleo flicked her green-eyed gaze to her. "All right. Back to the car before anyone runs off and gets lost again."

"I wasn't lost," Cleo claimed as Mia scooped her up. "Hey, put me down."

Mia crushed the cat tightly against her body as she wriggled. "Uh-uh, kitty. We're not taking any chances."

"I hate you so much. Just when I was starting to like you, you do this."

Ellie struggled to hold in laughter as she spun back toward the car. The snapping of a twig made her freeze. She arched an eyebrow and glanced at Jake and Mia. "What was that?"

Mia tugged the corners of her mouth back. "Sounded like someone behind us."

"Yeah, but who?"

Jake bit his lower lip as he flicked his gaze between the two of them. "The murderer?"

CHAPTER 22

*E*llie gulped as they stood staring into the darkness around them. Another twig snapped. Lola pulled the leash taut as she leapt toward the noise with a high-pitched squeal.

"Ellie! Someone's out there," she shouted before letting out another few loud barks.

"Easy, Lola," Ellie hissed, pulling her back. "Stop barking."

"But someone's there."

"There's a killer out there! And the dummy is holding on to me so I can't run. I'm gonna die!" Cleo wailed. "Get off me, dummy. I'm way faster than you."

"Hello?" Ellie called.

Mia glared at her, her jaw hanging open. "What are you doing?" she mouthed.

Ellie raised a shoulder in the air. "Maybe they'll just surrender."

Leaves rustled, and Lola belted out a few more barks. "Shh, quiet," Ellie said, tugging the dog back toward her.

"Who's there?" Mia shouted, keeping the cat pressed close

against her. "Show yourself. We have a weapon, and we're not afraid to use it."

"Mia," Ellie hissed, "why would you say that? We do not."

"We do. I'll turn the cat loose on them. With these claws, they'll never survive it."

"You're an idiot," Cleo said.

Jake swept his light around as more leaves rustled.

A figure poked their head out from behind a tree trunk. "Don't shoot."

"We don't have a weapon. Just come out," Ellie said.

Mia made a face at her as Lana held her hands up and inched sideways, squinting against the bright light of Jake's phone.

"Lana?" Ellie asked, her jaw dropping open. She blinked a few times, making sure her eyes were not deceiving her.

"Yeah, it's me. I was the one you saw in the diner."

The trio exchanged glances before turning their attention back to Lana. "What were you doing there?" Mia asked.

Lana stared at her feet, her lips pressed together in a tight line.

Ellie's stomach rolled with each passing second as she wondered if they'd hear a murder confession in the next few seconds. What would they do? Call Rick? How would they handle it? And would Lana turn violent with them?

"I–I…" Lana stammered before she sank her head in her hands while her shoulders shook with sobs.

Mia winced and shot a glance at Ellie. Jake slid his head forward and offered Ellie a questioning glance.

"What?" she mouthed.

"Do something," Mia murmured, signaling with her head toward the still-weeping Lana.

"Why me?" Ellie hissed.

"Just go," Mia said through gritted teeth.

Ellie rolled her eyes before she tugged on Lola's leash, slowly approaching Lana. She grimaced as she reached a hand out, leaving it floating in the air for a moment before she gently patted the woman's shoulder. "It's okay, Lana. Just talk to us."

The blonde threw her arms around Ellie, collapsing against her shoulder as she continued to cry.

Ellie shot a nervous glance at her companions before she let her hands touch her back. "Okay, it's okay. Whatever it is, it'll be okay."

"He's gone," Lana wailed.

"Uh, Zane, you mean?" Ellie asked. Was this a moment of guilt from the killer or was Lana genuinely stunned by his murder?

"Yes, Zane, who else would I be talking about?" Lana snapped, leaning away from Ellie as she wiped at the mascara-streaked tears running down her cheeks.

"Well, uh," Ellie stammered. She searched the faces of Jake and Mia for help.

"The thing is," Mia said, "what were you doing in the diner?"

Ellie screwed up her face. Why would Mia ask the weeping woman that question?

"I wanted to be near him again."

They stood in silence for a second before Ellie spoke. "Is that why you ran from the hospital?"

"I didn't run," Lana answered. "I just left. I was fine and the people just kept asking me how I felt and if I needed anything."

She wrapped her arms around herself and sucked in a shaky breath. "It was…aggravating. I just lost my husband in a violent crime, how do you think I am?"

She had a point, Ellie thought.

"I know Zane and I fought a lot. We didn't always see eye

to eye." She huffed out a laugh, sliding a lock of blonde hair behind her ear. "In fact, most of the time we didn't."

Her voice turned maudlin again, and she sniffed. "But I still loved him. He was my husband. I didn't expect it to end like this. I went to the diner because I just needed to see it again. I needed to see where he died. I needed it to be real because it doesn't feel that way. Not at all."

"Of course not. It's a shock," Ellie said.

"Yes, yes, it is. I can't believe she would do this to him."

Ellie's heart skipped a beat. "She? Lana, do you know who killed Zane?"

The corners of her lips tugged down, and her face twisted with disdain. "Oh, yes."

"Who?" Mia questioned.

Lana let her gaze slide from person to person in the group before she opened her lips to spit out the name.

A loud holler interrupted her. "MIA!" a loud voice boomed.

Leaves crunched behind them, and a bright light bounced from side to side.

Mia crinkled her nose. "Rick?"

He appeared in the small clearing with Nathan close behind him. The flashlight fell to Rick's side as he let his arm drop and closed his eyes for a moment.

"What are you doing here?" Mia asked.

"Officer Nathan! Help me! I'm hurt from being manhandled. I chased down the murderer, though. Now, I need to be cared for. Fed treats by hand and petted gently while I lay by a warm, crackling fire nestled in a soft blanket." Cleo reached a paw toward him with a forlorn meow.

"Got the whole crew, huh?" Nathan said.

Rick approached Mia and leaned his forehead against hers. "Thank heavens you're okay. I saw your car, and I couldn't get hold of you. I didn't know what to think."

"I'm fine. The cat ran off, and we had to find her."

Ellie shook her head at the limited information her friend passed along.

"And then we found Lana." Mia spun and pointed to an empty spot next to Ellie. Her eyes went wide, and her jaw dropped open. "Where'd she go?"

Ellie flicked her gaze to the spot where Lana had stood moments ago. "She was right here."

"She must have run off when she heard Rick," Jake said.

Ellie pressed a hand to her forehead. "Unbelievable. And she was about to tell us who the murderer was."

"Yeah, now we'll have to keep investigating on our own," Mia said ruefully.

"Investigating on your own?" Rick asked. "Now, wait just a minute, Cookie. I don't want you anywhere near this."

"It's too late, now, Sugar Bear, I'm involved."

"Can we pull back on the gross names while other people are present? It's just weird," Ellie said. "It's really distracting. And right now, we need to focus on finding Lana. She said she knew who killed Zane."

"Yeah, her," Rick said. "Which is why she keeps running from the law."

"He's so stupid," Cleo said with a shake of her head. "She's not the killer, dummy."

"I don't think she's the killer. She seems really upset by his death."

"Yeah, because she stabbed him. I'd be upset, too. She may have some guilt over it, but that doesn't mean she didn't do it."

"I don't know," Ellie said with a shake of her head.

Jake slicked a lock of hair behind his ear. "Yeah, I'd agree. She didn't seem guilty."

"People are excellent liars," Rick answered. "Which is why I don't want any of you near this. We've got a lot to unravel."

"Speaking of unraveling, is Toby still in custody?" Jake asked.

Rick set his hands on his hips. "He is."

"Can I-"

"No. We're still questioning him."

"Why?" Ellie asked.

"Because he's an idiot," Cleo said.

"I told you there's a lot to unravel."

Ellie crinkled her brow and tilted her head. "But you think Lana did it. So why-"

"Just trust me. I know what I'm doing," Rick answered, waving a hand in the air.

"Did you get the forensics back on the knife yet?" Mia asked.

Rick shot her a glance, pressing his lips together. "Preliminaries."

Mia's eyebrows shot up. "And?"

"He can't tell you. He doesn't know how to read it," Cleo said.

Ellie slid her eyes closed, her nostrils flaring as she held back a sigh.

"I don't know if I should tell you anything. You shouldn't know this stuff." He let his gaze fall on Jake. "Especially with him around."

"You can't withhold information from the press," Jake said. "Scarlett will dig until she gets it anyway. This is a major story in this town, and people will demand answers. You're better off just telling us instead of you getting slammed in the paper as the clueless sheriff."

Rick's jaw flexed as he stared at Jake who shrugged. "I'm just sayin'."

With a sigh, he adjusted his belt before he stuck his hands on his hips again. "Four sets of prints. Val, Toby, Anna, and an unknown."

Jake pounded his thumbs across his phone, listing the names in his note app. "I assume you cleared Val?"

"Pending confirmation, there's no reason to suspect Val of this. She has no connection to the vic and no motive. Also, several witnesses put her out in the diner at the time of the murder."

"Okay, so that leaves Toby–" Mia began.

"Who says he touched the knife to cut up tomatoes or onions or something. Could be a lie, could be the truth."

"Anna," Ellie added.

"Who could be our killer or who could have touched the knife when she saw the body."

Jake pointed at Rick. "And the unknown."

"Who could be Lana," Rick said. "Our killer."

"Or anyone else who is the killer," Ellie said.

"Right." Rick bobbed his head up and down. "Which is why I'd like to speak with Lana. She ran off for a reason. Guilt?"

"Upset," Ellie countered. "Her husband was just brutally murdered. It's a shock."

"Could be. Which means we still have a set of prints unaccounted for."

"And a killer is on the loose." Ellie tightened her grip on Lola's leash as a shiver shot down her spine.

Jake drummed his fingers on the side of his phone, his lips pressed together in a thin line. "I don't know if this helps you at all, but in the interest of sharing information, Scarlett did some digging and found out that Zane and Kylie are related."

"Kylie?" Rick asked.

Ellie answered, "MacAlistair. Another guest at the B&B. Apparently, she's related to Zane. Could her prints be the missing ones?"

Rick and Nathan exchanged a glance before Rick spoke.

"She's worth talking to, but we have nothing to bring her in on. It's not a crime to be related to the victim."

Ellie threw her hand in the air. "And Toby was seen with him the night before in a bar. What was he doing with the guy?"

"Says he just happened to sit next to him. He had no idea who he was." Rick shrugged.

Ellie's forehead crinkled as something about the story niggled at her. "Wait. What was Zane doing here last night? Where were they staying?"

Mia snapped her fingers and pointed to Ellie. "Yeah, and Lana said they had a long drive here. But they were here."

"You're right. So, who's lying?"

Rick shifted his weight, flicking his eyebrows up. "We have surveillance video showing Zane at the same bar as Toby. They leave at different times. Bartender says they spent over an hour talking, but he can't say about what because he didn't catch most of it."

Ellie chewed her lower lip as an unidentified emotion lodged itself in the pit of her stomach. She didn't want to do what she was about to suggest, but she couldn't stop herself. "Maybe it would help if I talked to him. Maybe he'd admit something to me."

Rick shook his head, lowering his gaze to the ground. "I hate to have you do that. I know you're not on good terms."

"It may even make things worse," Mia said with a frown.

"Or he may feel trapped and ask me for help."

"Ellie," Rick answered, "this is tough. It puts you in a real bad position legally."

Ellie lifted her shoulders to her ears. "I may not get anything from him, but maybe it'll give us a start. We just need one break."

Rick huffed out a sigh before his head bobbed up and down slowly. "He's your ex-husband. If you want to speak to him, I can't stop you. But he may refuse to see you."

"I'll take my chances," Ellie said with a nod.

They trudged through the woods to the diner. The police cruiser sat haphazardly behind Mia's car. She eyed it as she tugged open her door and set Cleo inside on the seat. "Wow, someone was in a hurry."

"I really wish you wouldn't do things like this."

"Get used to it, I am thinking of becoming a private eye." With a chuckle, Mia slid behind the wheel.

Ellie swapped seats with Jake, and lifted Lola into the backseat, then climbing in after her.

"I hope you can get something out of him, El," Mia said as she shifted into reverse and waited for Rick to move the cruiser out of her way.

"I can't believe it's Lana. I just…didn't get that feeling from her."

"Maybe she's a terrific liar," Jake said.

"Do you think that? Either of you?"

"She seemed honest to me," Lola answered.

"I don't trust anybody. Maybe Nathan, but maybe not," Cleo answered.

Mia shrugged as she swung the car onto the road and aimed for the police station. "Maybe she is, but she seemed honest to me. Although, why did she disappear? Why not just tell the police who she thought did it?"

Ellie glanced out the window at the dark buildings of Salem Falls. "To be fair, maybe she thinks they'd arrest her and not listen."

"But they'd clear her right away once she told them the truth."

"Would they?"

Mia shot her a glance through the rearview mirror. "What's that supposed to mean?"

NELLIE H. STEELE

"It means just because she says this person did it, doesn't mean they'll find the proof they did or the motive. Even if it turns out that the person she's accusing is the other set of prints on that knife, it doesn't mean they're guilty."

"Right, the police could say they have no motive, but Lana does. Then suddenly she's being charged with a crime instead of the person she says did it."

"So, what?" Mia asked as they slid into a parking space outside of the police station. "Lana's going to confront the killer herself?"

"Maybe. We need to find her," Ellie said, sliding her forehead into her palm.

"Yeah, as soon as you find out if Toby will spill any beans." Mia kicked on the parking brake and swung her door open.

"You two wait here," Ellie said to Lola and Cleo. "I'll be right back."

"Send Nathan out to take care of me," Cleo called as Ellie slammed her door shut. She stared up at the building, recalling the first time she'd been inside it and learned her aunt had been killed. What would she learn tonight?

CHAPTER 23

*E*llie chewed her lower lip as she considered sliding into the backseat of the car and asking Mia to drive her back to the B&B. Her friend waited for her near the steps leading to the station's door. Jake offered her a reassuring smile.

She gave her head a slight shake. She'd talk to Toby for them. Maybe she could get some information for Jake.

She blew out a shaky breath, climbed the stairs, and pushed into the darkened office. Rick motioned for her to follow him back past the front desk. "Nathan's checking with him now to see if he'll see you."

Ellie nodded, unable to form words. This was the last place she wanted to be, but she needed information.

Nathan strolled toward them from around the corner. He bobbed his head up and down. "He said he'll see you."

Ellie blew out a long breath as she patted her thighs. "Okay."

"El, you don't have to do this." Mia grabbed her arm and squeezed.

Ellie offered her a fleeting smile as her stomach jittered. "I know. But we need to know what's going on, and this is the best way to get information."

Mia pressed her lips together and nodded. "Good luck."

Ellie sucked in a breath and flicked her eyebrows up as she glanced at Nathan. If she didn't go now, she might lose her nerve.

"Follow me," the dark-haired deputy said.

He led Ellie down the hall and around the corner. He pushed through the only door in the hall and motioned for her to enter.

Ellie swallowed hard and nodded at him as she skirted past him into the room. Toby sat at the lone table in the room, handcuffs still around his wrists.

Ellie offered Nathan a quiet "thank you."

He nodded at her. "If you need anything, just give us a holler." He shot a pointed glance at Toby. "We'll be right outside."

Toby shook his head as the door closed. Ellie inched to the chair opposite Toby and dragged it back with an irritating squeal of metal against concrete. She lowered herself into it, eyeing the man in front of her.

"You really set them up to hate me," he said.

She licked her lips as irritation flared her nostrils. "You did that all by yourself."

"Yep, I'm sure. That's why I'm sitting here in handcuffs for a murder I didn't commit."

"And if you're innocent, Rick will clear you."

"That small-town sheriff is looking to pin anything he can on me after you cried to him about me showing up on your doorstep."

Ellie shook her head, huffing out a sigh. "This was a mistake."

"Why are you here? I thought it was to help me because you felt guilty for getting me into this."

Ellie screwed up her face. "Getting you into this? I didn't get you into this." She pounded a flat hand against the metal table. "You showed up on *my* doorstep, begging for *my* help. I gave you a place to stay and even got you a job."

"Yeah, and on my first night on the job, there's a murder, and the local lawman is just itching to pin it on the new guy no one likes."

"He's looking to pin it on you because your fingerprints are on the knife, and you were seen with the victim one night before his murder."

Toby slammed his hands on the table. "I didn't kill him."

Ellie startled, squeezing her eyes closed as she pursed her lips.

"Hey, that's enough," Nathan said, bursting into the room.

"Sorry, won't happen again," Toby promised. He clasped his hands together and stared down at his lap as Nathan laid a hand on Ellie's shoulder.

"You okay?"

She patted it and nodded. "Yeah, thanks."

Nathan offered her a tight-lipped smile before he shuffled to the door and left them alone.

Ellie stared at Toby until he lifted his eyes to hers. "And that's another reason. What happened to you?"

"I've been arrested for murder. *That's* what happened to me."

"No, this other woman…she's changed you. You were never like this."

Toby slumped back in his chair with a sigh and shook his head. "Think what you want, but what did it was this murder charge. This is ridiculous. I've been here all night. I'm exhausted. And no matter what I say, they twist it all around and try to make me guilty."

"Are you?" Ellie asked.

"I can't believe you're asking me that."

"I can't believe you're not answering it."

"Do you seriously believe I killed that guy?"

Ellie leaned forward, balancing her elbows on the table. "I don't know what to believe, Toby. But I can't do anything to help you until you've been honest with me."

Toby scoffed, his shoulders rising to his ears. "What do you expect to hear? That I stabbed him in a fit of rage? That we argued over a beer the night before?"

"I'd like to hear the truth about that meeting. Because I don't think I have it yet. I don't think this was a chance meeting. What was he doing in town the night before he stayed at my B&B?"

"How should I know? The guy happened to sit next to me at the bar. We had a few laughs over baseball and that was that."

"Baseball," Ellie repeated, her head bobbing up and down. "Right. Well, then I guess that's all we have to discuss."

"Wait." Toby lunged across the table and grabbed her hand, tugging her forward. "You can't leave me here. You have to help me. Call a lawyer. Call Mud."

"Mac," she corrected.

"Whatever. I've got to get out of here."

"Why would I help you? Listen, if there's nothing to this meeting with Zane the night before, the truth will come out and it'll be over."

She wrenched her arm back from him and rose from her chair.

Toby pressed his lips into a thin line, his fingers rapping against the metal table nervously. "Wait."

Ellie's shoulders slumped, but she did not return to her seat. "What?"

His lower lip bobbed up and down for a second. Ellie lifted her eyebrows as she waited for the words to spill out of his mouth. Would it be a confession or something else?

The door opened again, and Nathan strolled in. "Someone else here to see you."

Toby straightened in his chair. "A lawyer?"

Nathan shook his head, setting his hands on his belt. A bleached blonde burst into the room amidst shouts from behind her.

"Ma'am, ma'am, you can't…"

Rick appeared in the doorway, his frustration obvious.

"Toby!" she shouted as she rushed to him.

Ellie heaved a sigh as the woman who broke up her marriage flung arms around her ex-husband's neck.

"Hey, Glo," he said. "I thought–"

"Never mind that," she said, cupping his hands in his face. "I came as soon as I heard."

Ellie crinkled her brow. Wasn't Gloria supposed to have been in Vegas with a new man? How did she hear about Toby's arrest?

"I came back and you were gone, baby. And then I heard about all of this." She glared at Ellie before she returned her attention to Toby.

Ellie screwed up her face. She had nothing to do with *this*. Why was the woman mad at her? With a roll of her eyes, Ellie stepped toward the door. "I'm done here."

"Sorry about that, Ellie," Rick said as he followed her down the hall. "She wouldn't take no for an answer, and she got away from me."

"It's fine. Perfect timing, actually. He tells me he's innocent and the meeting at the bar last night was just by chance. They talked about baseball."

Rick rubbed the back of his neck. "You believe him?"

Ellie shrugged as they turned the corner. Jake and Mia hurried toward them.

"OMG, El, can you believe that bi–"

Ellie held up a hand. "Yeah, I can." She blew out a breath

as she formed a response to Rick's question. "I don't know what to believe. I don't want to believe that Toby killed him, but I think the meeting is suspect. I don't think he's being truthful about that."

Rick nodded. "What's the connection, then? Why not be truthful?"

"He says you're twisting everything he says to make sure he's guilty." Ellie rolled her eyes. "If he just told the truth, maybe you wouldn't because you'd have the facts."

"I'm not–"

"I know, I know," Ellie said before he could finish. "You just do what you need to do. He's hiding something."

"Looks like we may be out of luck on that," Nathan said. "I think he's about to lawyer up."

"He asked me to get him an attorney. So, I'm sure she will."

"You know her?" Rick asked.

"Gloria Eggleton," Mia said, her tone filled with disdain. "She's the other woman."

"Gotcha," Rick said, shooting an apologetic glance at Ellie.

"Well, we'll get out of your hair and let you do your job. Good luck," Ellie said.

Rick nodded at her before he wagged a finger at Mia. "Don't get yourself in trouble, Cookie. You hear?"

"We'll be safe. We're just going to check out a few things related to the treasure."

"Surely that can wait until–"

"I'll never sleep," Mia interrupted.

Rick flicked his eyebrows up. "All right. Y'all be safe. We'll touch base in the morning."

"Thanks, Rick," Ellie said with a wave as she spun toward the front door. Her heart thudded against her ribs as she hurried toward it. A cold sweat beaded on her brow. She shivered as she stepped into the cool night air and descended the stairs to the car.

"You sure wanted to get out of there fast," Mia said as she unlocked her car with her key fob.

"Yeah, get in." Ellie yanked open the back door, pushed Lola over, and slid into the seat next to the excited pooch.

"What's up, El?" Mia asked after situating herself behind the wheel. Jake slipped his seat belt on and twisted to face her from the passenger seat.

"I have a really bad feeling."

"Why?"

Ellie's throat parched. She wished she'd brought a bottle of water with her as she swallowed hard and tried to voice her concerns. "Toby said Gloria left him, right?"

"Who is Gloria?" Lola asked.

"The bleach-blonde who raced in there like the building was on fire, and she'd left a million dollars cash inside," Cleo answered her. "But how do you know her, Ellie?"

She raised her tear-filled eyes to Mia. The woman flicked her blonde hair over her shoulder as she crinkled her brows. "Yeah." Her head bobbed up and down, picking up speed. "Yeah, he did. She cleared his bank account and took off with another guy."

"Ohhhh, she's the mistress," Cleo said.

"Toby's? Why did she come here?" Lola asked.

Ellie drummed her fingers on the cloth seat. "So, what's she doing here? How would she know any of this?"

"Maybe she kept tabs on him," Mia said with a shrug. "Stalked him on social media."

Jake cocked his head before he gave it a slight shake, looking unconvinced by the suggestion. "Why would you keep tabs on the person you robbed blind and then ran away from?"

Ellie poked a finger at him as her emotions settled.

"Exactly. And she runs in here and nearly breaks down the door to get to him?"

"So, what are you saying?" Mia asked.

Ellie shook her head, her gaze falling to her lap as another chill snaked up her spine. "I don't know, but something doesn't add up here. I can't put my finger on it, but something stinks in this whole situation."

Lola pawed at Ellie. "We still love you, Ellie."

"Yeah, even if the loser lied to you," Cleo answered.

Ellie stroked the dog's head and leaned forward to scratch under the cat's chin. "He's lying about something. Is it murder?"

CHAPTER 24

"OMG!" Mia exclaimed, bouncing in her seat. "What happened in that room, Ellie? Tell us everything."

"Nothing really happened, but none of this makes sense."

"Something happened. You just said you think Toby is lying about committing murder."

Cleo narrowed her eyes and shot Mia a glare. "I mean, she didn't say that."

"I didn't say that," Ellie answered, repeating the cat's words as Mia cooed over her.

"Who's a savvy little kitty?"

Cleo ducked away and leapt into the back seat. "Idiot."

"What are you saying, then?" Jake asked. "Something must have happened to make you distrust him. Was it only the other woman showing up or is there more?"

Ellie sighed, rubbing her sweaty hands up and down her pants. "He wouldn't tell me anything about anything. He said the bar thing with Zane was a chance meeting. I just get the feeling he's hiding something."

Jake slid a lock of hair behind his ear and fiddled with the seat belt strap around his neck. "Gut reaction or something he said contradicts an earlier statement?"

"Gut reaction. After two decades of marriage, I can just tell something is off."

Cleo pulled herself away from the window and flicked her gaze to Ellie. "How come you didn't know he was cheating, then?"

Ellie heaved a sigh. "Outside of the cheating. Maybe I'm wrong. Maybe I'm just bad at reading him these days."

Mia shook her head. "You're not wrong. If you think something is up, it is. And I agree. How did she know to come here? And why did she go racing in there like it was life or death?"

"What's her full name?" Jake pulled his phone from his pocket.

"Gloria Eggleton," Mia answered.

With a nod, Jake tapped around on his phone.

Ellie lifted her chin to peer at the glowing display. "What are you doing?"

"Sending it to Scarlett. If you want information, she'll find it." His phone chimed a moment later. He flashed the text for the two women to view.

Received. On it.

"Wow," Ellie said with a flick of her eyebrows, "she's efficient. Does she ever sleep?"

"Not to my knowledge, " Jake answered. "I'm starting to think she's an AI robot planted here for testing."

Mia fired the engine and tugged the shifter into reverse. "While the bot's working on tracking Miss Gloria's info down, let's check out that clock."

"What's the clue again?" Jake asked as the car glided backward.

Mia shifted and spun the wheel to aim the car at the town's center. "The pendant's in the clock."

"That's not it," Ellie said, bracing herself against the front seat as the car tilted to the side. She grabbed her phone from her purse and found the picture she'd snapped. "To my descendant, use the clock to find the pendant."

Jake scratched his head. "How do we use the clock?"

"That's what I'm saying," Mia answered as she swung the car onto Main Street, "if we're going to use the clock, it's got to be inside it. How else do you use a clock?"

"Maybe there's another clue on the clock or a direction marker," Ellie said.

"We're about to find out." Mia pulled the car alongside the square at the town's center.

"You can't park here," Ellie said.

"El, it's the middle of the night. And the cops are otherwise engaged. Do you really think Rick's going to race out here to give me a ticket for parking next to the curb at the town square?" Mia popped her door open and stepped into the cool night air.

"Maybe," Ellie said as she followed her, leaving the pets behind in the car. "It may be some kind of weird flirting thing."

"What? That's gross," Mia said, flicking her hair over her shoulder as she continued on toward the clock.

"You flirt super weirdly," Ellie said.

Mia shot a look behind her, flicking her gaze between Ellie and Jake who trailed behind them. "Do you think it's weird?"

"I am not getting in the middle of that one," Jake said with a shake of his head.

"See, the kid doesn't think it's weird."

"He doesn't want to say it's weird," Ellie said as they reached the tall clock in the middle of the grassy area.

Ellie turned on her flashlight and aimed it up at the large

clock while Mia rubbed her hands over the green metal post projecting it in the air.

"Do you see anything?" Jake asked.

"Nothing. But my vision's not super great at this stage in my life, so if you can read those tiny letters above the six, please let me know."

"Uhhh." Jake squinted up at the face, wrinkling his nose. "Greenock."

Ellie dropped the phone to her side. "Huh?"

"Greenock. That's what it says."

"What does that mean?" Mia asked as she stepped back and stared up at the face. "Is there a Greenock somewhere around here?"

She pulled her phone from her pocket and tapped around on it. "I don't see anything on the map. Oh, maybe there's a Greenock Street or something. Jake, do you know?"

"Not that I know of." Jake rubbed his neck as he moved his map around on his phone's display.

"Well, this has to be the next clue. So, what's Greenock mean?"

Ellie typed in her phone's search bar, then scrolled through the search results. She heaved a sigh and shook her head. "Greenock is the maker of the clock. Apparently, they make several of these types of display pieces."

"Where are they located? Is the treasure in their warehouse or something?"

Ellie scrolled to the fine print at the bottom, sliding her fingers across the screen to enlarge the tiny print. "Switzerland."

Mia let her head drop back between her shoulders. "Are you kidding me? So, the clue is useless."

Jake continued tapping on his phone. "Maybe this isn't the clock that was here when Charles died."

Mia hurried to Jake's side and peered over his shoulder. "Can you see old pictures or something?"

"So far, it looks like this is the clock that's been here for several decades."

Ellie wandered to one of the benches surrounding the tall time teller and collapsed onto it as it chimed the hour. "It's not right. Why would it be the clock in the center of town?"

"Because it's a landmark," Mia answered. "What other clock could it be?"

"Not this one. What did he do? Bury the treasure under the town square and no one knew about it?"

Mia bobbed her head up and down. "Maybe. I mean, maybe there's some kind of storage or bunker under here."

"Bunker? It was the 1800s, not World War 2."

"Well, the clue said the clock."

"Not this one." Ellie wrapped her sweater tighter around her and rubbed her arms against the chill of the fall night. "Let's just head home. There's nothing here."

Mia wrinkled her nose and studied the clock before she offered them a nod. "You're right. It's getting late. Maybe some sleep will help clarify things."

"Or maybe they'll have a breakthrough in the case overnight," Jake suggested. "I haven't heard back from Scarlett on the other woman angle yet."

Ellie rose with a groan and headed for the car. "Maybe she'll have answers in the morning."

"Can you drop me off at the cemetery? My car's still there," Jake said they piled into the car.

Ellie pulled her seat belt on and gave Lola a pat on the head. "Oh, gosh, I hate to have you driving back at this time of night."

"I'll be fine, Mom," Jake said with a snicker.

Mia started the car and eased away from the curb. "Very funny, kid. The thing is, though, if you get any actionable information, we can't…well, act on it, because you'll be all the way across town."

"I can just text you."

"He can yeet it to you," Ellie said with a grin, earning a frown from Mia. "Why don't you just stay at the B&B? I've got another space on the third floor."

Jake shot her a glance over his shoulder. "It's not Toby's, is it?"

"No. There's another one up there next to the library. I didn't rent it because it's on the smaller side and doesn't have a private bathroom. But you're welcome to it."

Jake puckered his lips for a moment before he glanced at his phone's display. "All right. If I know Scarlett, she'll have something in a few hours. Then we can get a jump on the information and follow up right away."

"Do you need to swing by your place and pick anything up?"

"Nah, I'll just crash in my clothes. It's fine."

"Oh, to be young again," Ellie said with a laugh.

"I remember those days," Mia answered. "Nowadays, if I don't get my pajamas on by at least six, I just can't handle the day."

"You and me both. At least I live where I work, so if I have to answer the door in my pajamas, it's okay."

"Man, I can't wait to get old," Jake said.

"Hey, we're not old, okay?" Mia answered as she swung the car onto the road to the B&B. "We're just…"

"Matured."

"Yeah, like a fine wine."

"Or cheese," Jake answered as the tires crunched the gravel of the driveway.

Cleo's green eyes popped open. "Where is the cheese?"

"Jake has cheese. He said cheese," Lola said.

"I love cheese. What kind of cheese is it?"

Ellie held back a chuckle as the car rolled to a stop in front of the darkened Victorian structure. "Come on, girls. Let's go get some rest."

"Yeah, I have been up far too long. That run through the woods took it all out of me. I hope I can even climb the stairs to the bedroom and jump onto the bed." Cleo leapt from the car as Ellie opened the door and darted to the porch to slink up the stairs and wait at the door.

Ellie stood and tugged at Lola's leash. The dog slid out of the car and sniffed around for a few minutes. She unhooked her leash and strode to the front door. She eased it open and crept into the quiet space.

"Sheets are already on the bed upstairs, but I'll get you an extra blanket," Ellie whispered as Cleo raced past her up the stairs.

"I'll be fine with what you've got on there," he said, giving Lola a pat on the head as she walked in with Mia.

"Let us know if you hear anything," Mia said. "Don't be shy about banging down my door. I want to follow up on this as soon as possible."

They said their goodnights and parted ways at the top of the stairs. Ellie slogged into her bedroom and peeled off her shirt before tossing it on the armchair. She slid into her flannel pajama top, wiggling her shoulders as she buttoned it to relieve the tension.

Lola leapt onto the bed as Ellie collapsed on the edge. "I am beat."

"Turn out the light," Cleo called from under the bed.

"Give me a minute," Ellie retorted as she snuggled under the covers. "We wouldn't have been this late if we didn't have to chase you down in the woods, you know?"

"I was hurt!" Cleo answered.

"You were not. Scared, maybe. But you weren't hurt."

"My pride was hurt. I thought I could catch that lady. She's not very fast, and I lost her."

Ellie flicked the light off. The gentle glow of the sliver of the moon cast tiny beams of light across the floor.

"You shouldn't have run after her. You're not a superhero, you know. You're just a cat who–"

"I'll stop you right there," Cleo answered, her green eyes gleaming in the dim light as she crawled from under the bed and leapt onto the mattress. "Just a cat does not describe me. It sounds like it isn't enough. I'm more than enough."

Ellie traced a finger between the cat's ears as she curled into a ball wedged between Ellie and Lola. "We know. You're Cleo. You're the best cat in the world."

"And don't you forget it," Cleo said before issuing a massive yawn. "Oh, speaking of forgetting things, I still have to tell you the important news."

"What important news?"

"The thing I was trying to tell you before, but we got caught up with Toby's arrest."

"Well, tell me now."

Cleo yawned again and tugged her chin toward her chest with a paw. "Not now. I'm too tired. I have to sleep a little."

With that, the little black cat let her eyes slide closed, a soft purring emanating from her chest as she slept.

Ellie rolled onto her back and sighed. "Can't be that important."

Lola popped her head up, and wagged her tail.

"Go to sleep, Lol, it's not important enough to interrupt her sleep."

With a sigh, Lola let her head rest against the mattress and closed her eyes. Ellie stared up at the ceiling, the events of the day floating through her head despite her exhaustion. Was her ex-husband guilty of murder?

The question echoed in her mind as her thoughts twisted

together, and she drifted off to sleep. A nonsensical dream blended together the events of her day. Somewhere a clock chimed the hour before it morphed into a portal. Ellie entered it, following the passage to an unknown end.

Air ruffled her hair. As she glanced over her shoulder to find the source, a gun fired. She ducked instinctively. A skeleton popped up from the ground. Its jaw bone opened and closed, repeating "find the pendant" over and over like a parrot.

Her body jolted as she backed away from the frightening sight. She tried to spin and run away, but something held her shoulders tightly. She wiggled back and forth, but couldn't free herself from the unknown force. Her body shook again, and her surroundings started to melt away.

She opened her eyes, blinking a few times before she recognized her surroundings. The pressure against her shoulders remained even after the dream. Something moved over top of her. Then a hand clamped down on her mouth.

CHAPTER 25

*E*llie issued a muffled scream as she struggled to pull the hand away and escape her attacker.

"Shhh," the hooded figure hissed.

Ellie felt around on the bed next to her in search of the animals. Where were Lola and Cleo?

"I got rid of the pets," the shadow whispered.

The hand smashed against her mouth muted her panicked response. Her heart thudded against her ribs. Had the poor animals been killed?

"They're fine." Ellie detected a female voice, but couldn't place it. "They're eating treats. Stop fighting me, I need your help."

Help? Ellie swallowed hard as she nodded.

The figure lifted her hand and raised a finger to her obscured lips before she threw back her hood. Blonde hair tumbled from the garment and cascaded over her shoulder.

Ellie kicked her feet to propel herself backward. "Lana?"

"Yeah, it's me. I need your help."

"What are you doing here? Why are you in my bedroom? And why did you wake me up like that?"

"I couldn't take the chance of you screaming when I woke you. So, I lured Cleo and Lola out with some treats. I'm sorry." Lana shook her head and flicked her gaze out the window. "But there's too much danger."

"Danger?" Ellie asked. "From the murderer?"

"Yes," Lana said, twisting to face her again. "I think I'm next on her list. You've got to help me."

"Okay," Ellie answered, shifting in the bed as she tried to make sense of the situation. "Help you how?"

"We have to find the treasure before it's too late."

"Treasure?" Ellie squinted at her in the darkness.

She bobbed her head up and down. "It's somewhere here. And if we don't find it before Kylie…"

"Kylie? Kylie is the murderer?"

"I think so. She's Zane's cousin. They had this crazy idea to come up here and find the treasure. I'm pretty sure she did it. Her or the other one."

"What other one?"

"He's got another cousin. Gloria. She's the one who told them about this. But then, suddenly, she didn't want any parts of it."

Ellie's heart skipped a beat. "Gloria? Do you mean–"

A knock at the door interrupted her words. Lana stiffened, shooting Ellie a warning glance. "Don't answer that."

"I have to," Ellie said. "It'll look odd if I don't."

Lana wagged her head again. "No, I–"

"I won't say anything about you being here. Wait here." Ellie threw her legs over the side of the bed and hurried toward the door. "Who is it?"

"Jake and Mia."

"No!" Lana hissed as Ellie turned the knob and pulled the door open.

"Shh, it's fine. They're friends."

"We have news!" Mia said, racing in with Lola, Cleo, and

Jake behind her. She stopped dead as she spotted the other figure in the room. "Lana!"

"Yeah," Ellie answered, closing the door and locking it. "I had a surprise visitor. She nearly scared me to death."

"Sorry," Lana said, "but I needed help."

Mia set a hand on her hip. "Help to get away with murder?"

"No, help to prove Kylie did it *and* find the treasure."

"That's the thing, though," Jake said with a shake of his head, "we have another suspect."

"Who?" Ellie asked.

"Gloria," Jake and Mia said in unison.

Jake nodded and continued, "She's related to Zane. And get this...they're all descendants of Charles Portsmith."

"You're kidding," Ellie said as her jaw hung open.

Jake shook his head, flashing the lit display of his phone at her. "Scarlett found the connection."

Ellie let her gaze float around the room as she pieced things together. "So, I wonder if Zane's meeting with Toby was less than a coincidence and more about the treasure."

"Did you say Toby?" Lana asked.

Ellie snapped her eyes to the woman and nodded. "Toby Larson, my ex-husband."

"Gloria's new squeeze?"

Ellie slid her eyes closed at the mention. The woman had squeezed Toby before he was available for picking.

"Yes," Mia answered as Ellie let her anger slowly simmer. "They were fooling around before Ellie and Toby were divorced. Sorry, I have no love lost for that...you know what."

Lana crossed her arms. "Neither do I. She started this whole thing. Said she had a connection up here that could help out. Then she told us to book here for the weekend.

After she convinced Toby to lay that guilt trip on you and poke around the house."

Ellie's heart skipped a beat, realizing she'd fallen for it hook, line, and sinker. Her blood boiled.

Mia set her jaw and flicked her gaze to Ellie. "Her connection was you. You unwittingly let that idiot stay here."

"After Zane heard about the treasure, it was all he could think about. He researched it and went back through records about the robberies, the whole nine. Gloria told him to come up early and give his information to her contact. He was supposed to meet them at a bar."

"That's when Toby came home with the list. I bet Zane gave it to him," Ellie said.

Jake stared down at the notes he'd typed on his phone earlier. "So, why did someone murder Zane? Was it one of the other guests who got wind of this plan and killed him for information?"

Lana pressed her lips together and shook her head. "It was Kylie, I know it."

"Why do you think it was Kylie?" Ellie asked.

"She and Jim are having some trouble with money. He lost his job recently. And their mortgage is sky-high. Once she heard about the treasure, it was all she talked about. Getting that money and getting their lives settled again."

Lana shrugged, tugging back one corner of her pink lips. "I felt bad for her. I still do in a way. But…I think she's guilty. I think she murdered my husband so she could find the treasure and keep it for herself."

"What about Gloria? Surely, she'll demand a share," Mia said.

Lana crossed her arms and lifted her shoulders again. "Yeah, but as far as I know, she and Gloria weren't fighting with each other."

"Were she and Zane fighting?" Jake asked.

Lana nodded, tears brimming in her eyes. "Yeah."

"Maybe you should sit down," Ellie said, wrapping an arm around the woman and leading her to a rocker on the sun porch.

Lana sank onto it, rubbing the length of her finger under her eye.

Mia eased into the chair next to her, perching on the edge. "I hate to press you, but…could you elaborate on what they argued about? It could be important for a motive."

Lana sniffled and nodded. "Money. She asked us for money when Jim was laid off. And we said no." She shook her head as she studied her hands in her lap. "I said no. I said we couldn't bail them out. I knew if we paid their mortgage, she'd keep asking for it. They always had a scheme for making money but they never did anything, you know?"

Ellie bobbed her head up and down, offering a sympathetic glance at the woman.

"They were going to strike it rich this way or that way, and then they'd pay us back. But I knew that would never happen. And yeah, Zane and I live comfortably, but that's from our own hard work. I didn't want to short ourselves and our future, you know?"

"You didn't do anything wrong," Mia answered.

"But I feel like I killed my husband. It wasn't Kylie, it was me. I put that knife in his chest the moment I said no. She just got so enraged. I've never seen her so angry." Lana buried her face in her hands as she sobbed.

"Did she threaten him?" Mia asked.

"Oh, yes," Lana answered, straightening as she wiped at her cheeks. "She screamed and yelled. Her face was purple-red, she was so angry. And she just looked at him with this hatred in her eyes, and she poked a finger at him." Lana jabbed her own finger in the air to mimic the scene. "And she said, 'You're going to get what's coming to you. You stabbed me in the gut with this, and someone's going to do that to you.'"

Mia's eyebrows shot up, and she raised her gaze to Ellie and Jake.

"Wow," Ellie answered. "I'm surprised no one picked up on that when you all arrived. I never suspected a thing."

"Well, she called and apologized later. Said she just lost her temper because of all the stress. But I never believed it. As soon as I heard Gloria's tale of this treasure, I knew there'd be trouble. I knew she'd find a way to get that money for herself."

Lana bent over as tears flowed down her cheeks again. "And she killed my Zane. I told him not to come. I begged him not to come."

"It's not your fault, Lana," Ellie said, patting her shoulder.

"We'll make sure she pays for this." Mia pulled her phone from her robe's pocket and tapped the screen before pressing it to her ear. "Hey, hon, it's me. We have some information that may help you…yeah…no, it's from Lana…yeah, she's here…uh, maybe…look either way, the thing is she says Kylie and Zane had a huge fight before they came and Kylie threatened him. You may want to check the prints against hers." She nodded. "Okay, I'll let her know."

Mia ended the call and returned the phone to her pocket. "Rick's sending a car over. They really need your statement. I hope that's okay. And they'd like to grab your prints to rule you out."

"No!" Lana leapt from her chair, her hands balling into fists. "No, it's not okay."

"Whoa," Ellie said, "it's okay, Lana. They just want to get all the information you just gave us."

Lana wrapped her arms around her waist, her features pinching. "No. They want to pin this on me. They *always* think it's the wife. They're going to think I'm just saying all of this to get myself out of trouble."

Ellie winced and shot a glance at Jake, then Mia. "I don't think so. All of this is provable, right? There's evidence."

"Yes, of course," Lana said, her eyes going wide. "And the evidence is in the coroner's office with a knife in his chest. It's my word against hers. And that little witch is going to lie."

Ellie opened her mouth, trying to find the words to calm the woman as they waited for Rick to arrive.

"I'm not going to stand for it!" Lana shouted before she dashed past Ellie, knocking her to the ground and racing out the door.

Ellie smacked hard into the floor, landing on her backside. "Ow!"

Mia raced after the woman. "Come on, kid! Let's run her down."

Jake crinkled his brow as he reached for Ellie. "Run her down? Is she serious?"

Ellie grimaced while she struggled to regain her feet. "Oh, that's going to leave a bruise. Mia can be a little overzealous."

A loud crash interrupted any further conversation.

Jake screwed up his face and started toward the door. "Seriously?"

Ellie hobbled behind him with Lola in tow. "Are you okay, Ellie? You look hurt."

"Only my pride."

"Is it bad? Do you need a doctor?"

Ellie chuckled and patted the dog's head. "No, it's just a figure of speech. Pride isn't a body part."

"Oh, right. Does your bum hurt, though?"

"A little," Ellie said with another wince. "What is going on out there?"

"They're busting up the house just like before," Cleo called from under the bed.

"No kidding." Ellie reached the door and pulled it open further when a screech split the air. Another few thuds sounded. She stepped into the hall as Lola tore out of the room past her, a shrill bark escaping from her.

"What is happening?" Ellie asked, racing to the railing and peering over. A crystal bowl lay in pieces on the hardwood below.

Lola barreled down the stairs toward the open front door inches from the broken container.

"Lola! Stop!" Ellie shouted before she scrambled after the dog.

The animal leapt from the stairs, skidded across the wood floor, and slammed into the small half-oval table. The blue vase on the top wobbled. A few of the carnation petals floated down from the flowers stowed inside the ceramic container.

"No!" Ellie cried as she clung to the railing. Her sore rump prevented her from hurrying toward the teetering object. She held out a hand in a desperate attempt to stop the vase from falling like a passenger pressing an imaginary brake in a car.

Her useless gesture did nothing. The vase lost its battle to stay upright. Ellie crinkled her forehead as it toppled over the edge. Water splashed onto the floor, stopping Lola in her tracks. Her furry face wrinkled, and her eyes widened. The dog glanced up a moment too late.

The flower holder smashed onto her head and shattered into pieces. Lola yelped as shards fell at her feet. The flowers tottered on top of her head.

She shot Ellie a panicked glance, white carnations framing her tan fur. "Ellie…"

"You're okay." Ellie hurried to the dog and ran a hand

over her fur, knocking the flowers to the floor and assessing any injuries. "You're okay. No blood. You're okay. Does your head hurt?"

"A little."

"Okay. We'll get you an ice pack and then check the web to see if you need medical care. Just be careful, let me pick you up. There are pieces of this vase everywhere. I don't want you to cut your paws."

Ellie rose from her crouch and slid her arms under the dog's stout body. With a cringe as her glute muscle pulled, she lifted the dog and turned toward the kitchen.

Mia emerged with a tea towel wrapped around her hand.

Jake followed behind her. "We'll see what Ellie says, but you may need stitches."

"What happened to you?" Ellie cried.

"I cut my hand. Stupid Lana smashed that crystal bowl. Then I fell trying to round the corner and chase her and cut my stupid hand. What happened to Lola?"

"She ran into the table and knocked the vase over. It cracked her right in the noggin."

"Okay, so we may need the vet and the hospital."

"I think I'm okay," Mia said as Jake tapped around on his phone.

"This site says to monitor the dog every thirty to sixty minutes. If she becomes lethargic or has trouble walking, she needs immediate medical care."

"Right," Ellie said with a huff as she slid between them and continued to the kitchen. "Let's see how she does when I put her down."

She eased Lola to the tile floor before she grabbed a baggie from a drawer and tugged open the freezer.

Lola stared up at them, flicking her gaze to each human face.

"Walk, baby," Mia said in a high-pitched tone.

Lola's tail slowly wagged. "Why?"

"Come here, Lola, and I'll get you a treat," Ellie said as she zipped the bag closed.

"Okay," Lola said, her tail wagging more. She tottered across the room toward Ellie who handed her a mini bone.

"She seems to be walking okay," Jake said.

"We'll keep an eye on her," Mia said as Ellie rubbed the dog's head again and set the icepack on it. She nudged her chin toward the now-bloody towel. "How about you?"

Mia tugged the corners of her lips back as she unraveled the towel. She sucked in a sharp breath as the fabric tore away from the wound. Blood rose to the surface, pooling in her palm. "I...I..."

She shot Ellie a panicked glance before her eyes rolled back in her head, and she plummeted head-first toward the floor.

CHAPTER 26

"Mia!" The ice bag dropped from Ellie's hand, rattling across the floor as she dove toward her fainting friend.

Jake lunged forward, bobbling his phone as he reached for the woozy woman. A groan escaped him as her dead weight collapsed against him. He thrust out a leg, steadying himself while Ellie grabbed Mia's other arm.

"Get her over to the chair and sit her down," Ellie said between clenched teeth.

"Yep," Jake said, his jaw hanging open as he clutched his phone between his chin and his collarbone.

The sound of crunching glass broke the silence as they plopped the still-unconscious Mia onto the hard seat.

Ellie's heart skipped a beat, and she shot a wide-eyed glance at Jake. "Someone's here."

He nodded before a voice called out.

"Police. We are coming in, and we are armed."

"Rick? It's us. Ellie and Jake...and Mia. We're in the kitchen."

Rick appeared a moment later, his weapon still drawn. He

rolled his head as he stared at the scene while shoving the gun into its holster. "What the heck is happening here?"

"Crazy stuff," Ellie answered as she patted Mia's cheeks.

Rick grabbed the radio attached to his shoulder and spoke into it. "This is Sheriff Crawford, I need a bus at Ellie's B&B ASAP. What happened?"

"She fainted," Ellie said. "She cut her hand. I don't know if the sight of the blood did it or if something else is wrong. She fell earlier. She said on her hip, but I don't know if she hit her head."

Nathan entered the room moments later. "Is she okay?"

Mia groaned and her eyelids fluttered.

"She's coming to," Ellie said as her friend's head rolled around. "Come on, Mia, wake up."

Her eyes finally opened, and she sucked in a deep breath. Rick bent closer to her, balancing himself on his thighs. "Hey, Cookie, how you feeling?"

She squinted her eyes, her forehead wrinkling. "What happened?"

"You fainted. How do you feel now?" Ellie asked, motioning for Nathan to retrieve a glass of water.

"Okay, I guess," she answered, her features pinched. "I don't know what happened."

"You fell for me…hard," Jake said with a grin.

"I doubt that, son," Rick answered.

"The kid's right. I swan-dived right at him."

"Must have had me on your mind," Rick said with a coy grin as he lifted the water glass from Nathan's hand and held it toward Mia.

"Thanks," she said with a wince as she stretched her hurt hand.

Rick glanced at her bloody palm. "What happened here?"

"Lana happened," Mia groaned.

Nathan glanced down the hall. "Speaking of, where is she?"

"Gone," Ellie explained as she collapsed into a chair and fished the ice bag from the floor before pressing it against Lola's head again.

"That's cold, Ellie."

"What do you mean?" Nathan asked.

"She ran off," Mia said with a sharp inhale as Rick wiped the blood from her hand and assessed the wound.

Nathan and Rick exchanged a glance.

"She got really agitated when we told her you wanted her statement. She took off and pulled down the crystal bowl when I chased her. I slipped and fell and sliced my hand open. She took off out the front door."

Ellie shifted the ice bag on the dog's head. "Then Lola barreled down the steps, smacked into the table, and knocked over the vase. It smashed on her head."

Rick offered the dog a consoling glance. "She needs to go to the vet?"

"I don't think so. Unless she has trouble walking, she should be okay," Ellie answered. "How about Mia? Does she need to go to the hospital?"

"No," Mia said with a shake of her head.

"I think she'll be okay. Doesn't look like this needs stitches. But we should dress it. Do you have a first aid kit?" He focused his gaze on Mia. "Did you hit your head?"

She answered with a headshake as Ellie rose. "Yeah, I've got one in here."

Jake waved her back down. "Just let me know where it is, and I'll grab it."

"Right in the pantry," Ellie said, poking a finger at the partially open door. "Hanging inside the door on the left."

Jake nodded before he disappeared through the door. Rick flicked his gaze to Nathan. "We need to find Lana."

"I'm on it."

"Call for backup. She's dangerous."

Nathan nodded as he reached for his radio and hurried toward the front door.

Ellie crinkled her brows. "Dangerous?"

"She's a killer."

"What?" Ellie asked, her voice breathless. "But she said…"

"I know what she said," Rick answered, "but that's what all guilty people say."

Ellie shifted the ice into her opposite hand, shaking her cold digits as she released her grip. "She seemed pretty upset about her husband's death."

"I'm not saying she's not. But we have an unknown set of prints that very well could belong to her. We have witnesses who say she and her husband were having problems. And we have her disappearing not once, but twice when she knew we wanted to talk to her. It all points to guilt."

Ellie sucked in a breath as she parsed through the laundry list of reasons. It certainly added up, but something niggled at her.

"Who said they were having problems?" Mia asked as Jake emerged from the pantry and handed off the red box with the cross.

Rick pulled it open and retrieved the supplies he needed to treat and dress the wound. "Two of Zane's family members."

"Kylie and Gloria?" Ellie asked.

"Yep. Both of them said they've been fighting, and he's been talking to a divorce attorney. Said they were having money problems, mostly caused by Lana's shopping habit. If Zane left her, she'd have nothing because he can prove she was cheating."

Ellie lowered her eyes to the floor as she considered it. Lana had seemed so genuine. Had she been snowed by a master liar? The story Kylie had told about Lana had some similarities to the story Lana had told about Kylie. Which one of them was lying?

"Did you check Kylie's prints?" Ellie asked.

"No match," Rick answered.

Ellie's stomach turned over. Lana was the killer. She had means, motive, and opportunity. If her husband died, she'd get everything. No worries about the divorce leaving her destitute. They'd spoken to the murderer less than an hour ago, and now she was on the loose again.

She let her head fall into her hands. "Oh, wow."

"I'm just thankful this is the only injury we have to take care of," Rick answered as he carefully cleaned Mia's wound.

She winced, instinctively pulling her hand away. "Ouch, watch it, Rick. I can't believe we sat there and listened to a murderer lie to us for hours."

Ellie stared down at Lola, shifting the makeshift icepack. Lola's tail slowly wagged back and forth. "How you feeling, old girl?"

Lola tried to bite the edge of the bag Ellie held. "I don't like that cold on me."

Jake squatted down and called to the dog. "Come here, Lola."

Lola's tail wagged more, and she wandered toward him.

"Seems like she's walking okay," Ellie said as she followed the pup with her eyes.

"Yeah. I think she's okay. Not even a bump," Jake said.

"I'm okay. I feel fine," Lola said as Jake rubbed her ears. "I feel better now with you scratching my ears."

Ellie heaved a sigh as Rick wrapped gauze around Mia's hand. "I still can't believe Lana is the killer."

Jake rose as Lola sprawled on the floor with a sigh, her eyelids heavy. "Sounds like she's got motive."

"Yeah, but…" Ellie began, another sigh escaping her as she struggle to pinpoint the argument niggling at her.

"And I thought we said she was missing from the group when the murder occurred," Mia added.

Ellie chewed her lower lip, staring over at the shiny white surface of the refrigerator across the space. "It doesn't make any sense."

"Why not?" Jake asked.

"Why did Lana come here? Why would she sneak into my bedroom and ask for my help? She was home free."

"Could be any reason," Rick said, securing Mia's bandage with tape. "Maybe she came back to retrieve something."

"But why not just sneak in and get it? I was asleep, and she woke me up. Why would you wake me up?"

"What if she was snooping around in your room looking for some clue to the treasure and was afraid you'd wake up so she woke you? You know, a good offense is defense."

Jake cocked his head and rubbed his chin. "Isn't it the other way around?"

"It's the best defense is a good offense, Cookie," Rick said.

"Whatever, you knew what I meant. Maybe you moved or something, and she figured it was best to control the situation."

Ellie narrowed her eyes as her mind considered it. She opened her mouth to speak when a commotion sounded outside. A scream ripped through the night air followed by a scuffle, then another shriek.

"What the heck is that?"

Lola leapt to her feet, a shrill bark escaping her. Jake grabbed the dog before she could race out into the messy floor.

"Get your mitts off me. Let go! I didn't do anything wrong! It was all Kylie."

"Oh, wow," Mia said, her eyebrows shooting high and the

corners of her lips turning up as Rick raced past Jake and the dog.

The others followed her, with Jake carrying Lola. Ellie's feet crunched over the broken crystal on the floor as a red-faced Nathan struggled to hold a flailing Lana.

"Let go of me."

Rick tugged handcuffs from his belt. "Did you read her her rights?"

"I did. I'm not sure she heard any of it. She's been screaming the entire time."

"I didn't do anything. Let me go!"

"If you didn't do anything, we'll figure that all out at the station. Just calm down, ma'am."

"Oh, don't you call me ma'am, Georgia. You're dying to pin this on me."

Rick reached for her hand, handcuffs at the ready. "I'm dying to pin this on the guilty party. And right now, you're acting awfully guilty."

She wriggled in Nathan's grasp again. "I'm fighting for my life."

"Hardly," Rick said with a huff, holding a hand out in front of him. "Ma'am, Lana, calm down. If you're innocent, we'll find the proof."

"You won't!" she shouted, her cheeks blazing. "You won't even look at anyone else. You're determined to close this with the wife as the guilty party."

Rick pressed his lips together and shook his head. "Now, that's not true. We just need your prints to rule you out."

She wagged her head back and forth. "No."

"Can I ask why?" Ellie interjected.

"Ellie, please, let us handle this?" Rick whispered.

"I'm sorry, but I'm serious. If you're innocent, why wouldn't you want to prove that?"

Lana stopped her flailing, her chest still rising and falling with heavy breaths. "I…I may have touched the knife and didn't know."

"When?" Ellie pressed. "You passed out at the table when we told you, so you didn't touch the body after the murder. You could only have touched it before."

Mia's jaw dropped before she recovered and added to Ellie's statement. "Which means if your prints are on the knife, you either killed your husband or you knew he was dead and said nothing."

"I didn't know. I don't remember what happened after the murder. I remember nothing. When I woke up, I was in a hospital."

"You passed out and hit your head on the table," Ellie said.

"Ladies!" Rick hissed.

"There are four sets of prints on the knife. Val, Toby, Anna, and the killer. If you didn't kill him, there's no way your prints could be on it. All you need to do is agree to be printed and you can prove your innocence."

Lana's shoulders slid down her back, and she licked her lips. Her eyes searched Ellie's, then Mia's, then Jake's. "You believe me?"

Ellie crossed her arms and bobbed her head up and down. "I do. I don't think you did it."

Lana lifted her chin. "All right. I'll go to the station, but only if you take Kylie, too."

Rick shook his head. "No."

"She's the killer!" Lana shouted.

"She's not," Ellie answered. "Her prints checked out. She didn't do it."

Confusion scrunched Lana's features, and her shoulders sagged as she ceased her struggle against Nathan. "But…if she didn't kill my Zane, who did?"

"That's what we aim to find out," Rick said, stowing the

handcuffs on his belt. "Now, if you'll oblige us with a finger-print sample, we can move on to other suspects."

Tears formed in Lana's eyes. She raised her glassy gaze to Ellie, her forehead scrunched.

Ellie forced a weak smile onto her face and nodded. "Go with them. Get it over with and then we'll find the killer. I promise they won't railroad you."

Lana stared down at the mess on the hardwood at her feet before she thrust out her wrists. "Okay, go ahead and cuff me."

"No need," Rick said. "If you're coming willingly, we don't have to get into all that. But you do need to take a ride in the back of the cruiser."

Lana bobbed her head up and down as a tear fell to her cheek. "Let's get this over with."

Rick motioned for her to follow him from the house as Nathan released his iron grip on her arms. The trio exited into the cool fall air. Ellie followed them to the door and swung it shut behind them before collapsing against it.

"Whew," she said as she scrubbed her face, "what a night."

"Yeah, really. Who did it? If it's not Lana and it's not Kylie…" Color drained from Mia's face as she shot Ellie a panicked glance. "Toby's prints are on that knife, El."

"I know. But so are someone else's. Someone they haven't identified yet. That fourth set of prints must belong to the killer."

"But who would it be?" Mia asked as her feet crunched on the broken crystal when she shifted her weight. "Unless it is Lana, and she's just a really good liar."

"I don't know, but I'd better clean this up before Jake's arms fall off from holding the tank."

Lola's furry face wrinkled. "I'm not a tank, Ellie, I'm a dog."

"It's okay, I've got her. I'll put her out on the porch and come back to help."

"I've got it," Ellie said with a wave. "Keep an eye on the patient and make sure she doesn't need to go to the vet."

"Vet?" Cleo screeched from a stair above them. "Again?"

"Don't come down here, Cleo. Or you'll be going to the vet, too."

A hiss emerged from the small cat before she darted up two stairs and settled on the landing with her tail curled around her feet.

Ellie followed Jake as he headed for the porch, stopping off to grab a broom and dustpan and returning to the foyer for the clean-up.

Mia perched on a low step, scratching Cleo's head. "Who do you think is the killer, kitty?"

"How am I supposed to know that? I barely got to investigate. I was trapped in the car the whole time."

Ellie swept the remnants of her crystal bowl into a neat pile. "What do your spidey senses say, Cleo?"

"Huh? I'm a cat, not a spider."

"Kitty knows something, and she won't tell. What do you know, kitty?"

"I don't know anything. And for the hundredth time, my name is Cleo, not Kitty. I know a few Kittys. They are not the type of cat you want to hang around, if you know what I mean."

Ellie held back a chuckle at the cat's words as she swept the pieces into the dustbin before moving on to the shards of the vase. She emptied them into a bag and stuffed the flowers inside. "Looks like I'll need to do some shopping to replace these."

"I'll buy you a new bowl. It's my fault Lana broke that one."

"It's not. And it's fine. I never liked that bowl anyway."

She tugged the drawstrings on the trash bag tight and tied it. "I'm going to put this in the dumpster. I don't need it spilled across the floor if one of the animals gets into the trash can...again."

She shot a pointed glance at Cleo.

"I admit to nothing."

"I'll meet you on the porch, and we can see if Jake has any updates from Scarlett. Come on, kitty." Mia wrapped her hands around the slim cat and lifted her.

"Get off me! Get off!" Cleo shouted as she wriggled around in a desperate attempt to free herself.

Ellie headed toward the kitchen, chuckling. If only Mia could hear Cleo's protestations whenever she came near the animal. Too bad only she could hear it.

She pushed through the back door, shivering as the air hit her. She hurried across the patio to the dumpster tucked neatly under the trees and flung the floppy lid open.

A cloud of flies escaped from inside, sending Ellie stumbling back a step as she swished her hand in the air to keep them away from her face.

"What the heck?" She stepped forward and lifted the bag to sling it into the bin when a glint of metal caught her eye.

She peered over the edge of the tall dumpster, her fingers wrapping around the edge as she rose to her tiptoes. A scream rose from her lungs, becoming stuck in her throat as her eyes widened instinctively at the sight.

In the dim light from the house's floodlights, she spotted the heavily shadowed face of a woman. Kylie, with open but unseeing eyes, lay sprawled on the black trash bags littering the bottom of the bin dead.

CHAPTER 27

"*O*h, my word!" Ellie gasped out. The trash bag slipped from her hand, thudding to the ground near her feet as she spun around, searching the area as though the killer remained there.

She twisted back to the dumpster and peered inside again. Maybe her eyes had deceived her. *Nope.* Kylie's dead body was still inside. A trickle of dried blood painted her face.

"Ohhhh," Ellie moaned as she stared at it. What should she do? *Call the police.* But should she leave the body? Should she shout for help?

No, shouting for help may attract attention she didn't want. She chewed her lower lip as she curled and uncurled her hands into fists.

She needed help. She took a step when the object in her pocket banged into her thigh. *Duh.* "My phone."

With shaky fingers, she grabbed the device, bobbling it as she tried to toggle it on. She cursed under her breath before righting the phone and swiping it open. She scrolled past

Mia's name and cursed again as she reversed direction with her thumb, then pressed the call icon.

The line trilled as she pressed it to her ear. "Come on, answer it."

She smacked a palm against her forehead when Mia's recorded voice rambled on about leaving a message. "Are you kidding?"

She stared at the device for a moment before she shook her head and tried another number. The line rang on the other end twice before Jake's voice sounded. "Ellie?"

"What are you guys doing in there? I called Mia, and she didn't answer."

"Oh, uh…"

Mia's garbled voice sounded in the background. "Okay, you're on speaker," Jake said a moment later.

"Get out here now!" Ellie hissed.

"What's going on? Why are you calling us?" Mia asked. "Did you fall and break your ankle or something?"

"No," Ellie whispered, her eyes darting around in search of any danger as she clenched her teeth, "there's a body out here."

"What? Say again," Mia answered. "You're really quiet. Stop whispering."

"Just come out here!"

Ellie pulled the phone away from her ear and jabbed the end-call button. She shifted her weight as she wrapped her arms around her midriff. The cool night air seemed especially frigid. Her eyes drifted back to Kylie's expressionless face.

She squeezed her eyes shut and shuddered. The door burst open across the patio and Mia and Jake spilled from inside.

"What's going on?" Mia called.

"Shh, quiet!"

"Why?" Mia asked in a hushed tone as they closed the distance.

"In case the killer is still here."

"Killer?"

Ellie pressed her lips together and bobbed her head up and down before she poked a finger at the dumpster.

A second later, a bloodcurdling scream ripped through the night air. Mia clapped her hands against her cheeks. "There's a body in there!"

Jake winced as he glanced at it before closing the lid.

"I told you that. That's why I called. I didn't want to leave her alone."

"I don't think she would have minded, to be honest, El," Mia answered.

"Very funny. I meant in case the killer tries to move the body, and we lose track of it."

"Oh, right. OMG." Mia gasped, clamping a hand around Ellie's arm with wide eyes. "Do you think the killer is still lurking around here?"

Ellie winced, her gaze darting around at the dark trees again. "I don't know. We have no idea how long the body's been here."

"Wait," Jake said with a scratch of his head, "Jim said Kylie was asleep earlier."

A cold tingle raced through Ellie, and she swallowed hard. "What if Jim killed her and dumped her body hours ago?"

"We need to see how long she's been dead."

"I'm calling Rick," Ellie said, pulling her phone from her pocket.

Mia swung the lid open again and stared at the body. "Okay. But we need to figure out if there's a killer in there or not before he gets here."

"How are we going to know that?" Jake asked.

"We've got to see if her body is cold. If it's warm, she hasn't been dead too long. If it's cold...well..."

"Ewww," Ellie said, "don't touch the dead body." She pulled the phone away from her ear with a huff. "No answer."

"We have to! Why aren't you talking to Rick?" Mia asked.

"No answer. I tried his phone, Nathan's, the station."

"Call 9-1-1," Jake said.

"Yeah," Ellie said with a nod as she keyed in the three emergency digits. "Oddly, that's the longest response time, so I used it last."

"Okay, I'm going for it," Mia said as she reached toward Kylie's wrist.

Ellie waited for the emergency dispatcher to finish her spiel before she explained the situation.

"Wait!" Jake hissed. "Don't touch it. It's a crime scene."

Mia puckered her lips into a pout as she eyed the dead woman. "There's something in her hand."

"Well, don't touch it," Jake said.

Mia drummed her fingers on her forearm before she shook her head as Ellie ended her call. "I'm touching it. I can't wait that long. It could be the clue we're looking for."

"No!" Ellie shouted a moment too late. Mia wiggled the paper from the dead woman's fingers before she shuddered. "Ew. She was sort of cold."

"I told you not to touch her."

"I didn't. But I did get this." Mia waved the crinkled paper in the air before she unfurled it.

"What does it say?" Ellie asked.

Mia shrugged. "I don't know. I can't read it. It's too dark."

Ellie toggled on her flashlight and shined it on the scrap of paper. A crude drawing showed what appeared to be a grandfather clock. The weights were drawn in various locations above the pendulum.

"Why does she have a drawing of a clock?" Mia asked.

Ellie flicked her gaze into space. "Use the clock to find the pendant. The clock."

"There aren't any weights or a pendulum on the clock in Town Square."

Ellie shook her head. "No. Because that's not the clock we need to use. We need to use the grandfather clock in the foyer."

"OMG," Mia hissed, "why didn't I think of that? Of course, that's the clock we're supposed to use."

"Come on. Let's go," Ellie answered, dragging Mia behind her and motioning for Jake to follow.

They crossed the patio and pushed into the kitchen, finding a quiet house. Ellie skirted past the table and headed down the hall to the massive clock on the entryway wall.

She stared down at the swinging pendulum before she glanced behind the clock. With her fingers wrapped around the edges, she tugged at it. "Won't budge."

Jake poked a finger at the note still clutched in Mia's hand. "I think we have to do something with the weights."

"Move them to these positions?" Mia asked.

"Maybe," Jake said.

Ellie stared down at the swinging pendulum. "Won't that mess up the clock?"

"Who cares! You can have it fixed with all the money you collect from finding the treasure." Mia tugged at the round knob to open the clock. "Locked. Where's the key?"

"Ummm, I don't actually know," Ellie answered. "There were some spare keys on a ring in the pantry. I'll grab them."

"If they don't work, we'll just pry it open," Mia called after her.

"Don't ruin my clock," Ellie answered over her shoulder as she hurried to the kitchen. She found Lola standing near the treat bin, wagging her tail. "How are you feeling, Lola?"

"I'm hungry."

"That's nothing new. Maybe you should go up and lay down with Cleo while we follow up on this clue." Ellie ducked into the pantry and retrieved the keyring.

"What clue?"

Ellie glanced at the dog as she jangled the keys in her hand. She'd rather not explain. "Never mind. Just go upstairs so you don't get hurt anymore."

"Okay," Lola said, shuffling her way from the kitchen down the hall with Ellie following her.

"That's it," Ellie said as the dog rounded the railing. "Up you go. Go to sleep with Cleo."

"Cleo is not asleep," the black cat said, peering through the spindles from her perch near the top of the stairs.

"Take Cleo to the bedroom," Ellie said as Mia snatched the keys from her hand and began rifling through them.

"Why? So we can listen to the banging again?" Cleo asked.

Ellie shooed the dog up the stairs, trailing behind her until they reached the bedroom. Lola leapt onto the bed as Cleo stalked across the room. Ellie swung the door shut and arched an eyebrow at the cat.

"What?" she asked, her green eyes reflecting in the room's dim light.

"What banging are you talking about?"

"The banging I was trying to tell you about earlier. While you were out walking goofy–"

"Cleo," Ellie said, setting a hand on her hip.

"Lola, I meant. While you were walking Lola, someone was banging downstairs. Every couple of seconds. Bang! Bang! Bang!"

Ellie crinkled her brow. "Who? Where?"

"How am I supposed to know? I didn't look. It was rattling my brain, though. I couldn't get any sleep."

"Where did it sound like it was coming from?"

"Downstairs."

"Where downstairs? Back of the house, front of the house?

"Right underneath me. It was so loud, it shook the bed, I swear."

Ellie pressed her lips together as she considered it before a bang sent her leaping into the air.

"There it is again." Cleo stalked to the bed and jumped onto it with a yawn. She curled into a ball, her eyes closing to slits. "I hope they knock that nonsense off soon."

Ellie wrinkled her forehead as she pulled the door open and stepped into the hall. Another bang echoed through the space. She secured the door behind her to ensure the animals would be safe before she peered over the balcony.

"What is going on down there?"

"We're trying to set these weights," Mia called up to her.

Ellie hurried down the stairs to join them. "By breaking it?"

"No, of course not." Mia clicked her tongue at her friend.

"They're hard to move," Jake said with a grunt as he tugged on one. "See?"

The weight shifted down a bit while another rose in the air. A loud bang split the silence between them.

If Cleo had heard banging earlier, had someone already toyed with the grandfather clock? "You must be doing something wrong."

"How can you do it wrong?"

"Let me see the paper." Ellie grabbed the note and held it away from her face, squinting at it. "Should have brought my glasses."

"We can't get these into the positions they are supposed to be in. Every time we move this one, that one changes. Then we set that one and the middle one moves. Set the middle one, then the first one is off again." Mia pressed the palm of her hand to her forehead.

"This is like one of those puzzles in a computer game," Ellie said. "Let me see."

She pushed between the two of them, studied the paper for a moment, then eyed the golden cylinders hanging in the clock's cabinet. She grabbed hold of the leftmost weight and pulled it. Banging echoed off the walls as it dragged the rightmost weight up.

With narrowed eyes, she yanked the center weight, finding it controlled the first.

"See what I mean?" Mia asked. "This is useless."

"It's not useless," Ellie said as she moved the rightmost weight and found it also lowered the center. "Just give me a minute to think."

Ellie straightened, her eyebrows pinched together, as she stared at the paper. "Right needs to come up. Left needs to go down, and center needs to go down."

She wrapped her fingers around the leftmost weight and adjusted it to the correct position. "Okay, now, if I'm right, these two should go into the correct position if I pull the rightmost one."

With a deep breath, she reached for the cylinder and slid it into position. The center one lowered simultaneously until a click resounded.

"There," she said. "This looks like the paper."

Mia studied the clock for a moment before she wrapped her hands around the edge and tugged. It slid easily away from the wall.

A gaping hole yawned behind it. The trio exchanged glances, and Mia wrinkled her nose. "Yeah, that's not creepy at all."

"What do you think is in there?" Jake asked.

Ellie pulled her phone from her pocket and toggled on the flashlight. "There's only one way to find out."

With her heart pounding, she lifted a foot and stuck it into the blackness.

CHAPTER 28

"*E*llie, wait!" Mia latched onto her friend's arm. "You can't go in there."

"Why not? Wasn't the whole point of this to find the treasure?"

"Yeah but…"

"But what?" Ellie asked. "We used the clock to find the treasure. We could be steps away from all that loot, and you don't want to check it out?"

"There could be bugs in there. Or worse."

Ellie rolled her eyes and continued into the passage. "Go get Cleo. Maybe she'll keep them away."

Mia ducked to stare into the hole, her lips tugged into a grimace. "Doubt it. That cat's lazier than I don't know what."

"You're right. You'll just have to brave it, I guess. Or let me find the treasure."

Mia wrinkled her nose but toggled on her cell phone's flashlight and stepped into the dark corridor behind the walls.

"Wait for me," Jake said as he hurried to follow them.

Ellie shuffled a few steps forward in the narrow passage,

sweeping her beam around. Cobwebs stretched along the unfinished walls. Mia blew a raspberry as one tickled her cheek, and she swatted it away.

"Where's the treasure?"

"This passage continues around a corner up there." Ellie poked a finger ahead of them toward the kitchen.

"This is going to run straight into the pantry," Mia said.

Jake ducked past a hanging web. "Or back into the hall with the turn."

Ellie inched forward and peered around the corner. "Or not."

Mia waved her hands in the air at another string of spiderwebs. "What is it? A dead end?"

"No. It goes down a really old, really creepy set of stairs."

"Old creepy set of stairs?" Mia asked. She offered Ellie a glance before she took a gander at what lay in front of them. Her lips tugged back into a grimace. "Eww."

"Told you," Ellie answered as her light bounced off a crumbling set of stone steps leading into darkness.

"Maybe I should go first," Jake suggested.

"Why?" Mia asked, shining the light on his face.

He squinted against it and held up a hand. "I'm less likely to fall or get hurt if it collapses."

"I can't let you do that," Ellie said with a shake of her head. "It's my property. If anyone's falling and getting hurt, it's me. You have your entire life ahead of you. You don't want to break a hip."

"I mean, I doubt I would but–"

"But nothing," Ellie said as she stepped onto the first step. A few pebbles skittered from it, bouncing down the remaining stairs. "You're not falling on my watch."

Ellie pressed a hand against the rough wall next to her as she stepped down to the next step. "So far so good."

"You've only done two," Mia said.

"But they're the two highest. Any steps after this will result in a shorter fall." She took another step down, planting both feet before she tackled the next lower step.

"I made it," she called as she stepped onto the concrete floor at the bottom. "Come on down!"

"What do you see?" Mia's voice echoed.

Ellie wandered a few steps forward in the narrow underground hall. "I see a big safe!"

"A safe?" Mia asked as she spilled onto the floor behind Ellie.

"Yeah, look." Ellie aimed her light forward, illuminating a black floor-to-ceiling door with a dial and handle.

"Oh, wow. I bet the treasure's behind it."

"Yeah, but how do we open it?" Ellie asked. "We don't know the combination. And Charles didn't leave a clue for that."

"Maybe we can crack it," Jake said as he joined them.

"Oh, yeah, okay, kid."

"We'll yeet it," he said with a grin. "Is there any clue about the combination on the safe?"

Ellie swept her beam across the matte black surface. "I don't see anything."

Mia fiddled with the dial. "I don't think he scratched the combination into the door. Maybe it's important dates or his date of death or something?"

"Did it say anything on the clock drawing?" Jake asked.

Mia pulled the crinkled paper from her pocket and studied it. "Nothing about a combination."

"Wait," Jake said as she let it drop to her side. "Let me see that."

Mia handed him the paper as she spun the dial again, trying a few numbers before jiggling the handle.

"There are numbers on the weights. Really tiny numbers," Jake said, squinting at the page.

"Let me see." Ellie glanced at the paper, then shoved it back in his direction. "I can't see that. You'll have to read them to us."

"Umm, okay, from left to right, it's seventy-seven, thirty-four, thirteen."

Mia spun the dial, landing on each before she tried the handle. "Nothing."

"Try the other way. Counterclockwise first instead of clockwise," Ellie suggested.

Mia nodded and input the combination in the opposite direction, but the handle didn't budge. "Nope."

"Maybe it's the opposite order," Jake said. "Thirteen, thirty-four, seventy-seven."

"I'll try it both clockwise and counterclockwise." Mia dialed in the combination twice but to no avail. "Shoot."

"What are we missing?"

"Should we try all the combinations of the three numbers?" Mia asked.

Jake tapped around on his phone. "Just a second. I'm searching for this safe. It's taking forever, I barely have a signal down here."

"How are you searching for it?" Mia asked.

Jake pointed to the gold letters at the top of the safe as his blank white screen lit his face. "I searched Falls Safe and Lock and the year."

"Do you think it'll help us?"

"Can't hurt," Ellie answered.

A few results populated the screen, and Jake scanned the list. He pressed one with his thumb, returning the phone to a blank page. With a sigh, he tapped his finger against the side of the phone. "Come on, come on."

"Easy, kid. You're going to have high blood pressure."

"Sorry, I don't have the patience of the 'be kind, rewind' generation."

"Here we go. It's coming up." Images and words slowly snapped onto the screen. Jake skimmed them before he grasped the phone tighter. "Here."

"Got something?" Ellie peered over his shoulder, squinting at the too-small text on his screen.

"It says these safes usually had the characteristic of needing to be spun five times counterclockwise before landing on the first number. Then pass the second number four times before landing on it. Finally, pass the last number three times before landing on it. The safe will then unlock once the dial is returned to zero while depressing the handle."

"Seriously?" Mia crinkled her nose. "Okay, walk me through this again."

"Spin five times counterclockwise, then land on the first number," Jake said, raising his chin to study Mia's movements.

She twisted the dial before she landed on the first number on the paper.

"Okay, now, go the other way and pass thirty-four four times before you land on it," Jake instructed.

Mia counted under her breath as she slid the dial in the opposite direction, passing the number four times before she slowed and stopped on it. She wiped a bead of sweat from her brow. "Okay, got it. This is hard."

"Now, three times counterclockwise past thirteen, then land on it."

Mia turned the dial in the opposite direction. "One, two, three, okay."

"Okay, now, spin the dial back to zero while you push down on the handle."

Mia nodded, pressing against the lever as she spun the dial. Her features pinched as it approached zero. "Oh, it's super hard to turn."

With a resounding clang, the dial finally hit the center and the handle swung down. A creak split the air as Mia pulled the massive door open.

Stale air wafted past Ellie's nostrils. "This hasn't been opened in a while."

She shined her light inside as she stepped into the walk-in vault. Thick pouches lay on shelves and tables stacked in the cavernous space.

"I'm almost afraid to open one of these," Mia said with a wrinkled nose as she followed behind Ellie.

"What would be in there that's scary?" Jake asked, running his hand over a dusty velvet pouch.

"Body parts."

"Ew, what? Why would that be inside a velvet pouch?"

"If someone was a serial killer, maybe they collected trophies and put them in this vault." Mia wrinkled her nose as her light caught the dust motes flying through the air.

"I'm going for it. Let's hope this isn't a brain or something." Jake grabbed hold of a navy-blue bag and wiggled open the top. The drawstring holding it shut disintegrated, dropping in pieces to the floor below.

He glanced at the two women in the safe with him and arched an eyebrow before he turned the pouch over and spilled the contents into his hand. A large sapphire necklace smacked into his palm, its gems sparkling in the bright lights of their cell phones.

"Wow," he whispered.

Ellie stared down at the ostentatious jewelry piece before she looped a finger around it and pulled it up to dangle in the air. "Do you think it's real?"

"Heck yes, it's real," Mia said with a slap against her thigh. "And I bet these pouches are filled with tons more valuable stuff from all those robberies."

"Like Pizzaro's pendant," Jake murmured, dumping the

pouch on the shelf where he'd found it and waving his beam over the other packages. "These are all too small."

Mia spun to scan the shelf across the room. "Maybe over here."

"Uh, guys," Ellie said, aiming her beam at a specific item. "Could this be it?"

Jake followed the direction of her light, finding a large cloth draped over a bumpy object propped on the table in the center of the room.

Mia sidled to Ellie's other side and arched an eyebrow. She slid her eyes sideways at the other two. "Who wants to do the honors?"

Jake ran a hand through his hair and shrugged. "I mean, I could do it, but it feels like maybe Ellie should. It's her place."

Mia nudged her friend with her elbow. "You do it, El. You deserve it."

Ellie swallowed hard, setting her gaze on the dusty cloth. With a deep breath, she lifted the corner and pulled it away. A massive, bejeweled gold cross sparkled in their flashlight beams.

"Wow," she whispered.

"That's it. Pizzaro's pendant!" Jake exclaimed.

"We did it!" Mia shouted with a fist pump. "We found the treasure!"

"Yeah, and not a moment too soon," a voice answered from behind them.

Ellie's heart skipped a beat, and she spun to face the new arrival. He shielded his eyes from the glare of her light. "Jim?"

"Oh, I *knew* it," Mia said, one hand closing into a fist. "You killed Zane and then offed your wife. That's why you said she was sleeping earlier. You lied. You killed her!"

Jim shoved his hands into his pockets and shook his head. "I didn't."

"You did!" Mia shouted, jabbing a finger at him. "And for what? Treasure? Was it worth two people's lives?"

Jim craned his neck to stare at the massive hunk of cross-shaped gold on the table. "It looks like it's worth a good bit, yeah. But I didn't have to kill anybody to get it."

"Oh, right. Like we believe you." Mia crossed her arms, a scoff escaping her lips.

"Were you the one making the banging noise earlier?" Ellie asked.

"Yeah, I was trying to open that stupid clock but I couldn't figure it out." He shook his head as his features pinched.

"So, now what? You'll kill us too?" Mia asked.

"I told you. I didn't kill anyone."

"But your wife is dead. And you said she was asleep. Asleep with the fishes, maybe," Mia retorted. "How could you kill your own wife?"

"I didn't!" Jim shouted, balling his hands into fists. "Stop saying that!"

Ellie narrowed her eyes at him as her heart pounded. They'd notified the police. Rick should be here any minute. If they could keep Jim talking, maybe they stood a chance of escaping alive. "Then who did?"

"That would have been me," a new voice said. A hand with blood-red fingernails snaked around Jim's shoulder and patted his chest. "And I was happy to do it."

Ellie's jaw dropped open as the woman stepped around Jim to enter the safe. "Gloria?"

"In living color," the woman answered with a flick of her eyebrows. "You know, this is your fault, really."

"Mine?" Ellie said, her features pinching. "How are these two murders that you just admitted to committing my fault?"

"If you would have just given your idiot ex-husband the

list back, maybe he would have found the treasure, and we wouldn't have had to kill two people to get it," she snapped.

"My idiot…" Ellie clamped her jaw closed as her nostrils flared. "You were so into my idiot ex-husband that you stole him from me. And now he's an idiot?"

She shrugged. "I thought he had some use after you inherited this place, but turns out he was as useless as I thought two months ago."

"I can't believe this," Ellie answered, massaging her temples. "Does he know?"

"Nah," Gloria said. "He doesn't know Jim and I have been together the entire time I've been with him either. What he doesn't know, right?"

"Wait, you were having an affair with your cousin's husband, and *then* you also had an affair with mine?"

"Ewww," Mia said. "That's skanky."

"Stop judging me, *Cookie*," Gloria said as she shoved her hand into her pocket. "Who moves to a new town and hops into the sheriff's bed five seconds after their husband left them?"

"That's low. At least I–"

"Enough with the commentary," Gloria said, whipping a stubby gun from within her pocket. "Time for you three to bite the dust and us to abscond with the treasure. This time I won't miss."

"So, you're the one who shot at me?"

Gloria feigned shock. "You're smarter than you look." She nudged the gun forward.

"Wait, wait, wait," Ellie said, "let the kid go. He's too young to die."

"I guess he should have thought of that before he joined the party. Tell you what, though, I'll kill you first so you don't have to watch him die."

"How kind of you," Ellie said with a disgusted sigh.

"Of course. It's the least I can do given what I put you through over the last year." Gloria raised the weapon and aimed it at Ellie.

"Wait!" Ellie shouted. "Just a second. Before I die…I have to know…did you ever love Toby?"

Gloria shrugged a shoulder and arched an eyebrow. "Maybe a little."

"Why did you do it?" Ellie asked, her voice breaking.

"He was there. He was cute. It happened."

"Unbelievable," Ellie murmured as Mia slipped an arm around her shoulders.

"No more interruptions. Time for us to end this." The gun shoved forward again, and Gloria slid her finger around the trigger.

A crack resounded but the gun didn't fire. Instead, Gloria's eyes rolled back in her head, and she slumped to the ground. Next to her, Jim pitched forward, his chin smacking hard into the floor a moment later.

Ellie leapt back a step, her hip hitting the table and her hand pressed against her chest. "Oh, wow," she murmured as she stared at Rick's dark form, holstering his weapon before reaching for his handcuffs. "I thought we were goners."

"Nope," he said as he wrangled the weapon from the unconscious woman and tugged her limp wrists into handcuffs. "Got your call about Kylie. When Lana heard, she immediately accused Jim."

"I didn't do it!" the man yelled, still pinned down by Nathan's muscular arm.

"Yeah, I didn't think so. You were at the table when Zane died according to the other diners. Why would you suddenly kill your wife?" Rick asked.

Ellie wrinkled her brow as her heart began to slow. "So you knew it was Gloria?"

"It was her or Toby, and I doubted it was Toby from the

time I arrested him. With the diner as busy as it was, he'd never have had time to kill Zane. And he definitely couldn't have killed Kylie."

Ellie blew out a sigh. "Well, at least I wasn't married to a murderer."

"Nope. He just left you for one," Rick said as he hauled a now-conscious and confused Gloria to her feet.

"I didn't do anything," she claimed. "It was all Jim. He did it. He was the mastermind."

"Yeah, yeah, yeah," Rick murmured as he strong-armed her from the room.

"I did not!" Jim yelled after her with Nathan pushing him to follow behind them.

Ellie collapsed against the table when they disappeared. "Whew, that was a close one."

"Yeah," Mia said. "I can't believe Gloria was behind this whole thing."

"Me either. She never would have been in our lives had it not been for Toby."

"I wonder if she knew," Mia said.

"How? She couldn't possibly have been that calculating to know my aunt owned this and it may be willed to me. Right?"

Jake held the flashlight under his chin, an evil grin on his face. "But that's what Scarlett will say happened."

"I'm sure. I can't wait to read the headlines on this one," Ellie said with a groan.

Mia swung her flashlight beam around the room. "I can't wait to see what all of this is worth!"

"Maybe you can work on that instead of becoming a PI." Ellie pulled herself off the table and dusted off her pants.

"I'll do both," Mia answered. "Salem Falls needs a new PI."

Ellie shook her head. "I really hope not. What else can possibly happen in a small town like this?"

The End
To be continued…

Want to Read More About Ellie?
Click here!

And look for Ellie's next full length novel in December 2024!

ABOUT THE AUTHOR

Award-winning author Nellie H. Steele writes in as many genres as she reads, ranging from mystery to fantasy and allowing readers to escape reality and enter enchanting worlds filled with unique, lovable characters.

Addicted to books since she could read, Nellie escaped to fictional worlds like the ones created by Carolyn Keene or Victoria Holt long before she decided to put pen to paper and create her own realities.

When she's not spinning a cozy mystery tale, building a new realm in a contemporary fantasy, or writing another action-adventure car chase, you can find her shuffling through her Noah's Ark of rescue animals or enjoying a hot cuppa (that's tea for most Americans.)

Join her Facebook Readers' Group here!

OTHER SERIES BY NELLIE H. STEELE

Cozy Mystery Series

Cate Kensie Mysteries
Lily & Cassie by the Sea Mysteries
Pearl Party Mysteries
Middle Age is Murder Cozy Mysteries

Supernatural Suspense/Urban Fantasy

Shadow Slayers Stories
Duchess of Blackmoore Mysteries
Shelving Magic

Adventure

Maggie Edwards Adventures
Clif & Ri on the Sea

Printed in Dunstable, United Kingdom